The Minoan Psychopath

By

W. Sheppard Baird

The Minoan Psychopath

Published by W. Sheppard Baird Publishing

www.minoanatlantis.com

First edition printed 2007

ISBN: 978-0-6151-4344-6

Printed in the United States of America

Dedicated to my loving mother, Joan

and

compassionate family

Table of Contents

Chapter 1

The Killing

It was very late into a cool, crisp, windless night lit by a strong crescent moon amid the shimmering stars in the night sky. Winter was fading away with the coming of spring. The many-colored wild flowers were just beginning to blossom on the lush green fields in all their beauty. The utter quiet among the tall cypress trees on Knossos' west hill suddenly ended.

A young, nine or ten year old, girl ran frantically from the southwest toward a large three-story villa repeatedly screaming out, "Samra! Samra! …"

Her small arms and legs were a blur of motion. Reaching the front of the villa, she breathlessly extended her arms to grab the end of its stairway's balustrade with both hands whirling her body to the left to scramble swiftly up the steps. Just before she came to the second floor landing, its door slammed open with a bang framing a naked woman standing at the ready with a large dagger in her hand. The child was instantly stunned silent in surprise and fear. Her body momentarily froze in mid-flight. But she, immediately, with unwavering commitment regained control and again grabbed the balustrade to hurl her body left up the second flight of stairs to the third floor in a flurry of quickness. Reaching the door, she began hysterically kicking and pounding on it with her little fists screeching, "Samra! Samra! ..."

Realizing on fully waking the assumed threat was only a small child the woman lowered her dagger and calmly walked out onto the landing. Looking down to her left, she saw a large armed man looking up the stairway at the crazed child. The man glanced up at her quizzically before they both reset their focus up on the frantic little girl.

In his dreams he could hear someone faintly crying out his name over and over. The frenetic voice grew louder as it came closer and closer. Instantly, his dreams vanished and reality gripped him with a jolt. Using his entire body, he bounded from the bed landing on his feet like a big graceful cat. He swiftly reached for his large razor-sharp bronze dagger by the bed table in the dark. The pounding and screaming at his chamber door was no dream. With amazing agility, he readied himself to kill anything that came near when he realized the cacophony of yelling and pounding at his door was from a child.

Making his way to the door, he carefully cracked it open to verify the presence of a young girl. Seeing the door move, the child became even more agitated and frenzied. He abruptly opened it in a rush and took a step back as he saw her falling forward toward his legs. With lightning quickness, he firmly seized her shoulder and straightened her to help her regain her footing. Pulling her to his left, he quickly took a step forward to scan the landing and stairs for any real threats. He saw only the woman on the second floor landing and the man standing at the foot of the stairs with relaxed postures.

He returned his attention to the little girl heavily sucking in air from her run. Still holding her by the shoulder, he crouched down and asked, "Why do you come here like this? What's happened?"

He recognized her as one of the many children in the neighborhood but couldn't quite place her name. Heaving and gulping air, she put her face in her hands and began to sob pitifully. Suddenly, she looked up into his eyes and loudly wailed, "My sister Ponaji, they killed her!"

He stood and lifted her in his arms to comfort her grief. As she sobbed and rained tears on his shoulder, she haltingly said, "You must come, Samra."

"What's your name?"

"Lokeniji." she sputtered.

He set her down on the floor and said, "Stay here."

He hurriedly wrapped his loincloth about him and strapped on his shoes. After buckling on his weapons belt, he secured his glittering dagger in its leather sheath and tied on a shoulder cape for the cool night air.

"How could it be that a young child is the first to reach me?" he wondered.

Returning to Lokeniji standing by the door, he picked her up in his arms and firmly said, "Show me."

While rushing down the stairs he passed the woman, now warmly dressed, on the landing and told her, "I'll be gone for a while, Jena."

He didn't notice as she began to follow just behind them. Reaching ground level, he quickly stopped to set the girl on her feet. Addressing the man, he said, "Thalion, stay here." just as the man's very young son rushed to him, grabbed his father's thigh, and started nervously looking around to see what was happening.

He knew he would make much better time if he put the girl on his back to guide him. Motioning for her to mount him, he turned and stooped down to let her wrap her arms about his neck. On standing, she tightly grasped his waist with her legs. Feeling she was firmly attached to him, he asked, "Ready?"

She shook her head affirmatively on his shoulder and pointing her finger toward the southwest said, "There!"

Jena was standing just behind them when Samra took off at a very fast pace. She started racing after them trying to keep up as best she could. She couldn't sustain his pace even with the child on his back. But she was a fast runner and was able to keep them well in sight as they maneuvered through the homes and trees up the gentle hill.

The girl was desperately trying to cling to him while Samra ran at a fast pace. She was struggling to lift her body up by forcing her arms down on his shoulders with her hands as far in front of him as she could get them. Even in her grief-stricken state, she was mindful of impeding the full swing of his arms or wrapping her arms around his throat to restrict his breathing. He realized what she was trying to do and bent his body forward slightly to let gravity help her. Her whole face was wet from the constant tears and mucous flowing from her nose. Her wetness dripped into his hair and flowed onto his neck and shoulder. In her sorrow, she occasionally wept the name of her sister softly into his ear, "Ponaji ..."

Rounding a cluster of cypress trees and moving up onto the paved stone road, someone with a torch came into view. He recognized him as a deputy he had met in the administration building the day he took over the assignment. He shouted ahead, "Turn around! Lead me fast, but look for evidence!"

The deputy was startled and briefly frightened with the sight of Samra running at him so fast. Pumped with adrenalin, he spun around and began to run as quickly as he ever had. But he slowed to look on the ground for anything he could see when the word "evidence" registered in his mind. Samra was constantly scanning the ground ahead of him for anything he could see.

Turning left on the road, torches could be seen moving in the dense cypress trees off to the right near one of the rest areas. Lokeniji was very tired, but she could feel they were getting close. Lifting her face from his shoulder when the torch lights came into view, she weakly pointed to them in silence before returning her trembling head back to the comfort of his warm wet shoulder. He ignored her attempt to direct him and continued following the deputy.

Samra's purpose for rushing to the murder scene was to minimize any disruption of the evidence by a growing crowd of curious onlookers. He felt this had obscured and degraded the evidence from the prior three murders. He had never been asked to lead a domestic criminal investigation before, being primarily concerned with foreign assignments, and had assumed control only a few days before.

The outraged community clambered riotously at the palace for new leadership on the investigation as one child after the other was brutally maimed and killed with no perceivable progress made.   The people were ecstatic that such a highly regarded "Master" was to assume the lead.   They were filled with relief and high expectations for an end to the horrors.

After interviewing the investigators and deputies assigned to the case and reviewing the collection of evidence, he determined, early on, the methods used to secure and manage the previous murder sites were lax, imprecise, and sorely in need of improvement.   One of the first directives he issued was that any future crime scene was to be left as pristine as possible.   When the first deputies arrived, the people in the immediate area were to be much more rigidly controlled and restrained from the scene to preserve what its evidence could tell them.

He had already intensely instructed them on how it should be done.   As soon as the first deputy arrived, he was to order those already there to stand fast and look on the ground around them for anything they could see; no matter how small.   After surveying the site, the deputy was to have the witnesses carefully move to an evidence-free area nearby for later questioning.   He was then to carefully stake off the area to restrain any new arrivals and await the assistance of additional deputies.

Samra came on the scene and bent down to let Lokeniji slide to her feet from his back as Jena arrived to stand beside them. They were both winded and breathing hard.   He looked down at the child with a muted smile and pulled her to him.   He hugged her softly for a moment and began to affectionately stroke her face and hair.   After a few silent moments attempting to sooth her pain, he gently pushed her from him and said, "Lokeniji, go rest over there with the other people and stay nearby, so I can talk to you later.   Okay?"

She looked up and softly said, "Yes, Samra."

She hung her head sadly and turned to go where he had indicated. Turning to face Jena, Samra curtly said, "You shouldn't have come." before abruptly moving off to take command of the deputies.

More deputies were arriving at the scene amazed to see the new head of the investigation standing ready to give them their assignments. They were not used to this, to say the least. All of them were filled with admiration and respect for him and felt his leadership grip them with purpose. He sent one of the deputies to guard the witnesses and posted another by the murder victim. He directed other deputies to secure each approach from the roadway in order to better secure the area from anyone not authorized. As he had instructed them at the administration building, each deputy carried several small stakes painted white, as evidence markers, in their pouch. They also carried a bundle of longer painted stakes and a coil of rope to mark out the crime scene. Once it was secured, Samra organized the remaining deputies to begin a careful systematic search of the immediate area. It was only then that he reluctantly compelled himself, as the lead investigator, to observe the victim's body.

He walked slowly with great trepidation toward the dark form lying on the ground under the guard's torch. The torch's orange and yellow light flickered and danced on the sheen of sweat of his reddened face and chest as he looked down on the victim. He had heard the grizzly stories of the past three murders and it hardened and prepared him. But he was still aghast, awestruck, and astonished at the wrecked young life beneath him. At that instant, he felt a piece of his soul being torn from him, never to be reclaimed or mended. But look he did in horror as it was his duty. He marveled as he gazed on the small torn and mutilated body that it was possible for a human being to do such an incredible thing. No demon from the hills or animal had done this!

She was lying naked, as if posed, on her back with her arms spread out to her sides and the palms of her hands facing up. Her abdomen had been deeply split open with a blade from her pubis to her ribcage. She had been cut again across it in the form of a cross. The flesh had been opened up, and her internal organs were lying in the dirt at her sides. Her feet were spread open about a meter, and her head was turned to the right with her eyes and mouth open. There was a mass of wounds on the left side of her neck. Smeared and splattered blood covered her entire body. It was as if someone had crudely painted her in her own blood!

The wounds of a sharp bronze blade riddled the young girl's chest and thighs in what looked like a studied pattern. It appeared she may have been sexually attacked, as the first three victims were, but she would need to be examined before it could be confirmed. Besides her abdomen, her neck seemed to be the main focus of the killer. She had two severe gapping knife wounds on the left side of her neck with deep multiple teeth marks about them. It looked as if some of the flesh had been chewed and possibly bitten off. There was a much smaller shallow, more or less, vertical cut into the front of her throat. Samra observed the victim's wounds were very similar to what had been described to him from the previous killings.

He thought the non-lethal stab wound to the front of her throat was probably deliberately done to silence her while she was unconscious. Once this was done, there was almost nothing the young child could do to interfere with the killer. It appeared as if he, or she, had deeply cut into the side of her neck to start the blood gushing and began biting the open wound in some crazed frenzy. From the look of the neck wounds and the pattern of the splattered blood around them, he could only assume the murderer was deliberately trying to eat the flesh and drink the victim's blood. Some of the blood evidence indicated it was dripping down onto her heavily from above. Her neck wound must have spurted copiously onto the killer's face and torso with some of it falling back onto her as he painted her body with his bloody hands.

"I hope she wasn't conscious when he opened her neck. She wouldn't have lasted long." he thought.

Samra's mental engine continued hypothesizing about the evidence before him. He imagined that when the killer was satisfied with his blood feast he must have, while hovering over her dripping in blood, opened her abdomen and spilled out her insides before repeatedly stabbing her as if to mark her with his personal seal. While analytically gazing down on the victim, he suddenly felt an intense wave of loathing and disgust wash over him.

"Only animals do things like this, but animals can't use a sharp bronze blade! How could any human being do something like this? It must look human but is really an animal." he thought.

He immediately considered his father's theory of the "Others". He knew what his father would be thinking at the sight before him. He had begun developing a theory during Samra's childhood that stated there were people among us that were not human. He called them "Others". They appeared to be human but were really something quite different. The evidence showed the stalking and killing of a predator like a lion in a cold and calculated fury. Tears began to uncontrollably well up in his eyes.

Suddenly, the night was pierced by a woman's gut-wrenching screams from behind him, "Ponaji!!! Ponaji!!! ..."

Lokeniji's mother arrived hysterically trying to make her way to her daughter's body on the ground. The deputies had to forcibly restrain her and slowly pushed her back toward the group of witnesses trying to comfort her as best they could. Lokeniji ran to her screaming panic-stricken mother and fiercely grabbed her in their joining.

Tearfully, she looked up into her mother's face and said, "Its true, mama! She's dead! It... It's terrible!"

Their grief was indescribable. Her mother lifted her face to the night sky groaning in terrible agony and fell to her knees sobbing; shaken to her core. They held each other tightly spilling their tears on each other in their overwhelming sorrow. Samra instructed the deputies, "Stand by and care for them with whatever they need. But they can't see her yet."

He sadly thought, "It would be far better if they didn't see Ponaji. In time, she will understand the evidence is paramount and must be preserved above all else if this maniac is to be caught."

By this time, over thirty deputies had arrived on the scene as well as many other people from the surrounding area. After reinforcing the posts of some of the guards to control the growing crowd, Samra assigned the rest to join the others to expand the search for evidence as he had instructed them. The torches of the searchers lit up the whole area of dense cypress trees around the murder site on both sides of the roadway.

Samra had five scribes from the civil authorities assigned to the investigation to record relevant information from any future murder scenes with diagrams, drawings, and the syllabic script. Two of them were art scribes known for their precise drawing skills. The recording scribes were already busy questioning and writing down the identities of the group of witnesses with Lokeniji.   One of the art scribes was assigned to draw a diagram of the layout of the site using the victim's body and roadway for reference.   This diagram was to be used to identify the location of any evidence they found in relation to the body. The other art scribe was initially assigned the task of making detailed drawings of the condition of the body including the immediate area around it.

Once anything was found, it was to be left untouched and marked with a stake.   Samra had the deputies describe to him the evidence they found, so he could determine if it warranted a personal examination.   Its location would then be marked on the layout diagram by the scribe.

The killer was literally dripping in blood as he left the dark crime scene.   There was an easily identifiable blood trail leading away from the body to the east through the forest.   The killer's shoes left clear fresh footprints in the blood soaked earth by the body.   A full hand print could clearly be made out next to the victim's head.   The size of the prints led Samra to believe the killer was most likely a large man.   All of this and much more was very precisely drawn and recorded by the scribes.

Samra was gently questioning Lokeniji and her mother about what they knew of the crime and Ponaji's movements earlier in the day.   They knew nothing about the crime itself, but young Lokeniji was unlucky enough to discover her sister's mutilated body.   Several worried family members, friends, and neighbors began frantically searching the area when Ponaji didn't return home after sunset.   All of the people living in the hills around the palace complex were intensely on edge since the killings started many months ago.   The horrendous image of her sister's ravaged lifeless body scarred young Lokeniji badly and would never leave her.   As he continued to comfort and talk to the young girl and her mother, a deputy ran up to them and anxiously stated, "We've found something, sir."

Samra kissed Lokeniji's forehead, put a comforting hand on the mother's shoulder, and quickly stood to leave with the deputy. A short distance away from the witnesses, the deputy said, "There's a pool of dark bloody matter to the east in the forest, sir."

As they carefully walked away from the body through the trees, the deputy pointed out the splatter and drips of blood marking their path. It appeared the killer briefly halted his escape to violently vomit. The spray of blood and the remains of his meal must have occurred while he was still standing. The area of the spray was quite wide and could be seen well up the side of a tree. He assumed the killer must have become extremely nauseated from drinking Ponaji's blood. Shoeprints, identical to the ones at the murder scene, could be clearly made out in the soil near the bloody splatter on the ground. The deputy told him one of the art scribes would be coming soon to record the scene. He then took Samra further along the blood trail away from the vomit site.

About ten meters further on, the trail turned left to cross the roadway into another dense stand of cypress trees with patches of evergreen shrubs at its edge. The killer was heading north toward the villas, homes, and apartment complexes that lined the inside of the roadway. The blood trail abruptly ended behind a group of tall shrubs near the tree line. A jumble of the same shoeprints could be seen on the ground in the torch light. Samra surmised he probably used the hidden spot to wipe off the blood and put on clean clothing before emerging from the trees to make his way into the passageways of the buildings.

The shoeprints continued until they reached a stone road leading into the district with homes tightly on either side of it. The tracks completely disappeared on the stone. Samra and the deputy searched the immediate area under torch light for some time. They found nothing, but Samra felt the killer, at that moment, was probably very close to them sleeping in one of the nearby villas or apartments. After continuing their search for a time and finding nothing, they began walking back to the murder scene.

Jena had been standing tensely by her self near the witnesses while Samra was managing the murder scene. The deputies assumed she was someone important having arrived with Samraleos, so they left her alone and let her move about as she wished. When he left with the deputy and everything had quieted down, she slowly began walking toward the body. There was a big part of her that didn't want to see. But, as if in a trance, she moved forward with a mixture of foreboding and curiosity. The guards let her come close unimpeded. She had just come around the back of one of the guards when, in a blazing flash under the torch light, she clearly saw the whole of the horror lying on the ground in front of her.

She had seen many terrible things in her life, but this made her sharply recoil her head away and gasp with an emotional response that took her breath away. She brought her hands to her face and tried not to scream but still let out a short uncontrolled yelp before going mute in obvious physical and deep emotional distress. Many people heard this and turned to look at her. Jena was a naturally compassionate empathetic person. The sight of the young girl's hideously mutilated body shook her beyond what she ever imagined possible. Unconsciously, she began walking slowly away from the body with a nauseating revulsion she had never felt before. It sickened her to imagine the fright and terror the young child must have felt.

"There can't be a greater horror for a child than that, even in their worst nightmares of monsters." she thought.

Looking up, she noticed she had moved several meters away from the body without realizing it. Then, very shaken, she slowly made her way to sit on the ground and began to weep into her hands. A guard walked up to her and asked, "Are you alright? Do you need anything?"

Silently, without raising her head, she nodded negatively as the tears flowed into her hands. He felt her anguish and left her in peace to return to his post. He was restrained by the demands of his duties but felt the same horror when he first saw the body. Besides the grizzly sight, the first thing that shot through his mind was the victim could easily have been his own daughter who he loved beyond all things. He felt a deepening welling of rage building in him toward the killing beast, as he imagined Jena might feel later. He would do anything to help their new leader Samraleos catch this monster as he repeatedly squeezed his dagger handle in angry agitation.

Samra told his deputy to run ahead and get several other men for a more thorough search of the neighborhood the killer had entered. Walking back alone, he thought the murderer must be getting bolder, or sloppier, having left so much evidence. But he must have coldly and methodically planned the killing in detail for some time. The killer seemed to be a patient and cautious stalker but left much more, especially blood, evidence this time compared with anything the authorities had described to him from the first three killings.

When he returned to the murder scene, the art scribe assigned to the body walked up to tell him the killer might have been scratched by the girl's sharp finger nails. All of her finger nails were bloodied but a few of them seemed to have skin matter in them. As he continued speaking, Samra noticed something was wrong with Jena. She was still sitting on the ground with her head in her hands. Concerned, he abruptly excused himself and swiftly walked to her.

"Jena, what's wrong?"

She looked up at him with a tearful face, shook her head, and then lowered it back into her hands. He put a comforting hand on her shoulder saying, "I'll be back soon, and we'll go home."

Without lifting her head she nodded affirmatively. Samra rose, knowing she must have seen the horrible mutilation, and went to talk to the head of the deputies nearby.

"I've seen all I need here tonight. Everything's well in hand and working smoothly. I'm going home and leave it in your hands."

"Yes sir."

"Tell the investigation team to send a messenger when they've had time to complete their initial report. Good night."

"Yes sir. Good night."

Returning to Jena, he softly said, "Lets go home now, Jena. Okay."

She slowly raised her head to look into his eyes and gave him her hand to help lift her. Regaining her feet, Samra took her in his arms to comfort her. She cried deeply against him for several moments before they separated to begin silently walking back toward the villa. He put his arm around her shoulder in support. They both felt drained and badly needed some sleep with the dawn approaching. After a time, Jena stopped and looking up at him sadly said, "Samra, I saw her and I wish I hadn't!"

He opened his arms to embrace her saying, "I wish I hadn't either. It was incredible. It could have been my daughter."

At that instant, his eyes suddenly and uncontrollably filled with tears.   He dropped his head and began deeply sobbing and groaning as she held him.   His tears rained down on her.   For a moment, she was startled and surprised having never seen him react like this before.   But she was very touched by his compassion for the young girl and tightened her hold on his chest as if to mother him through his grief.   This then brought back her tears again and they stood there for a time crying in each others arms.   When they had quieted somewhat, Jena stood up on her toes and in a soothing voice whispered in his ear, "Samra, we need to go home and rest."

Dropping back on her heels, she put her arm around his waist and turned him back in the direction of the villa.   After a few steps, he stopped with his face soaked in tears and looked into her eyes to say, "Thanks."

She felt they had truly shared a terrible pain in a way she could have never anticipated.   As she looked up at him, she gently said, "Come home, Samra."

She led him slowly back to the villa as he continued to wipe the tears from his face.   He realized, at that moment, he felt much more than just friendship and fondness for Jena and would never again think of her as only his assistant.   Further on, his mind began to calm and work more normally.

"There's a limit to my ability to deal emotionally with such horrors.   In time, I would lose far too much of myself." he thought.

As they walked on and his tears dried, he felt an unexpected perplexing outrage grow within him at the inexplicable thing he had just witnessed. He would use these feelings to motivate him to be especially ruthless and cunning in the hunt for the child killer. Perplexed he asked himself, "Why?"

"I must use all my training and power as a "Master" to rid the people of this diseased evil." he thought.

He wished his father was here to assist him in catching and killing this aberration. He hoped it would be a very long time before anything like this ever happened again. But he knew his father's theory of the "Others" said it eventually would. He hoped his father's theory was wrong.

Chapter 2

Samraleos

Samra was usually the last to awaken in the household, and he slept till early in the afternoon. For a moment, as he rolled his head on his pillow, he dreamily thought last night had been just some terrible nightmare, but then the stark images of mutilation filled his vision to thoroughly wake him. He quickly sat up on the edge of his large bed, put his head in his hands, and brushed his hair back. The young girl's torn body kept flashing in his mind's eye. He had to use his power to consciously wipe the pictures away and began readying himself for the day ahead. He had only quickly washed before finally going to sleep just before dawn. At that moment, he wanted, more than anything, to have a good hot refreshing bath to feel fully cleansed. He walked over to the window shutter by the door and opened it to call down for Thalion to prepare his bath water.

Samra's villa was a three-story structure made of stone and masonry with a large covered water cistern built beside it. Rain water flowed into the cistern, mainly in winter, from a terracotta drain pipe connected to the roof. The roof and floors of the villa were supported by thick beams of oak with slabs of stone laid at right angles over the beams. The slabs were overlaid with hay, packed level with earth, and smoothly finished with waterproof clay before being sealed with paint.

The villa had a south-facing stairway that led up to the landings of the upper floors. The second and third floors were used exclusively as living quarters composed of multiple partitioned rooms. The first floor was the largest by far. It included a household kitchen with ample food storage and a large workshop equipped with, among many other things, a pottery kiln and a furnace used mainly for casting bronze.

There were three steam distilleries. One was quite large. They extracted the oils from aged iris roots and many other plants used in making perfumes and consumer items for sale in the palace and local markets as well as for their own use. Samra's perfumes were quite popular and in great demand. The workshop was capable of producing many other things as well. This included the making of fine household pottery, and the weaving of wool and hemp into cloth. Typically the pottery and textiles were for their own use. Samra's employee Thalion and his young son Antoneos had their own spacious apartment. He managed the workshop's operations as well as doing most of the labor.

The workshop was a business for household self-sufficiency and profit that produced a significant part of Samra's wealth. Even without his income from the palace, which was considerable, the workshop produced more than enough income to provide for all of their needs with a considerable amount of excess. Jena and Thalion were paid a monthly sum of gold and a share of the profits they produced. The workshop's secondary operations were Jena's occasional cloth weaving and Thalion's casting of bronze mainly for tools and, to a lesser degree, weapons.   Thalion was equipped with all the tools needed to keep the workshop running – bronze saws, axes, chisels, knives, awls, punches, nails, hammers and grinding querns among others.

By far the most important and profitable operation of the workshop was the production of Iris oil perfume, Chamomile shampoo, and Lavender soap bars derived from the plant oils produced by the distilleries.   The steam separation process was essential to more delicately process the temperature sensitive plant oils that would be destroyed if they were exposed to the heat of the fire.   The process allowed the oils to evaporate at the much lower temperature of the steam.

The distillery consisted mainly of two pottery vases with one used to boil water to produce steam and a second vase that contained the plant materials to be processed.   The steam was fed into the bottom of the vase with the plants in it using a terra cotta pipe.   The injected steam more gently broke down the plant's oils that evaporated to the top of the vase into a long down sloping cooling pipe.   The pipe allowed the heavier oils to drip into a collection vase as the steam vented off into the air. Thalion and Jena worked together to keep the distilleries running as much as possible.

The yellow flowering iris plant was the primary ingredient used in Samra's perfumes.   This was his most profitable product. The roots of the plant were harvested, aged for up to five years, and put into the steam distillery to produce a thick wonderfully smelling oil.   Some of the other distilled oils used in making the perfumes were from the flowers of the Carnation and Saffron plants and the leaves of the Mrytle plant.   Saffron, with its beautiful purple flowers, had many uses especially as a culinary spice, a cloth dye, and a healing tea.   The Carnation plant, with its fluffy pinkish hued flowers, was an essential ingredient in Samra's scented body oils and was added to the soap, and several other products, for its scent.

The people processed a wide variety of herbs and plants for medicinal, cosmetic, and culinary uses. The most valuable plant known to them for the treatment of injury and wounds was the opium plant with its incredible ability to dramatically alleviate pain, no matter how severe the injury, and induce sleep. The people viewed it as a miracle cure for many ailments and a gift to ease their suffering from the gods. But there were a large number of addicts in the city and throughout the region.

Other plants the people found beneficial were the flowering herbs like Chamomile that was used as an effective insect repellant. Chamomile looked very much like a daisy with its greenish yellow bulb-like centers ringed with white florets. It was one of their most valuable herbs. It had many internal and external medicinal uses. Its flowers could be brewed as a tea for its mild sedative effects that helped people deal with fever, anxiety, and insomnia. But it was mainly used to treat stomach problems as well as many other internal ailments such as intestinal worms. The tea was believed to promote the healing of wounds, sores, and inflammation. It helped regulate women's monthly periods, and it was used as an eye wash to sooth sore eyes. Chamomile oil was distilled in Samra's workshop to make shampoo because of the luster it added to the hair.

Lavender with its fragrant pale purple flowers and buds was another herb widely used to make the peoples lives more comfortable. The scent seemed to have a calming effect that reduced anxiety. When the flowers were brewed as a hot tea, it was consumed at night for relaxation and to induce sleep. It was also believed to help to relieve tension headaches when breathed in as a vapor or diluted and rubbed on the temples.

Lavender oil was very important as an insect repellant and was added to many of the perfumes, body oils, creams, lotions, shampoos, and soap bars for that purpose. It was also known to soothe and heal insect bites.

Thalion made their soap bars by adding lye to olive oil with a mixture of lavender and carnation oil along with other ingredients added for fragrance, color, and texture. Anise was used to make their toothpaste, among other things, and could be mixed with wine to make an effective cough syrup. Beeswax was a vital ingredient used as a thickener and emulsifier in the making of ointments, creams, lotions, and lipstick. Beeswax had a honey-like fragrance and naturally locked in the moisture of the skin leaving it fresh and hydrated. Honey was used to beautify the skin and as a universal antiseptic to heal cuts and wounds. It was added to many of the products made in the workshop especially the body oils and skin creams.

Thalion knew Samra well and had his bath water ready far in advance of his expected call. He soon came through the door carrying two large pitchers by their handles. Thalion was a very big man and easily dealt with the weight. He had done this many times over the years. He walked up three stone steps leading up onto a one meter high ledge adjacent to the bathing basin on the south wall. The ledge allowed him to pour the hot water into the wide shower vase without having to lift the heavy vase with his hands. He could just tilt it on his shoulder to pour the water. The shower vase was tied by strong hemp ropes to bronze hooks embedded in the beams of the ceiling. The large bowl-like vase was made in the workshop and had a top lip that turned inward to reduce any spillage when being filled.

As Thalion poured hot water into the shower vase, it immediately started falling through the many small holes in its bottom. Samra stepped over a short raised wall, about a third of a meter high and fifteen centimeters wide, into the shallow basin of the bath. The basin wall kept water from splashing out onto the floor. The waterproof clay floor of the bath basin was slightly sloped to direct water into a drain in its southwest corner. Terracotta drain pipes were built into the walls of the villa and emptied into the district's sewage and water runoff system. Samra loved the feeling of the cascading water warming his skin as it showered onto his head and body.

Thalion took the empty vases and put them just outside the door on the landing. Grabbing another large vase he replenished the raised wash basin on the west wall near the flush toilet, the toilet vase, and the smaller vases used to give Samra's hair a final rinse. The side wash basin had a smaller diameter drain that used a cork plug to retain water. The wash basin had all the normal toiletries – a fine bone comb, bronze razor, shaving cream, toothbrush, toothpaste, etc. An additional bar of soap, a small vessel of shampoo, and an extra vase of water sat nearby on the sink top. Most noticeably, it had a standing polished bronze mirror placed between the basin and the wall that was used for shaving and hair preparation. Once Thalion completed filling everything, he set the empty vase outside the door and removed the brazier from the room for cleaning.

Jena walked in as Thalion was leaving. She carried a new bar of lavender soap, a small vase of Chamomile shampoo, and several fresh soft towels made of hemp. She wrapped a towel around her head to keep her hair from getting wet. Approaching the basin, Jena removed her loincloth and stepped into the bath with him. Samra moved from beneath the shower, and Jena began lathering his body with the lavender soap bar starting with his feet and working her way up his body. Once his body was fully soaped, he stooped down to let her pour shampoo into his hair, and she began working it in to create a thick lather. She handed him the lavender soap bar so he could rub the soap into his face and neck. When he was completely lathered, Samra moved back under the flow of hot water and let it rinse his hair, face, and body thoroughly. When he was ready for his final rinse, he stepped from beneath the shower and squatted down to let Jena pour one of the smaller vases of water onto his head. She worked the water into his hair to thoroughly clean it and poured a second vase of water on his hair and body to complete his rinse.

Jena handed him a towel and stepped forward to wrap another one around his head. He dried his face and body while she rubbed the towel into his hair. Taking another dry towel from her, he wrapped it around his waist and walked over to sit in the oak chair in front of the wash basin for his shave. Jena stepped behind the chair and put a towel around his neck draping it over his chest. Moving over to the basin, she added water to a small bowl of shaving cream and began swirling a brush made of coarse boar's hair into the mixture. When she judged it was ready, she began applying the cream to his stubble. She didn't need to prepare Samra's razor. Thalion always kept it as sharp as bronze could be with the fine-gritted sharpening stones and straps in the workshop.

With Samra observing his reflection in the mirror, Jena began shaving away his beard's daily growth. Unusually, neither of them had said a word to each other since she entered the room. Recently, bath time had become a much more talkative and happy, even flirtatious, time. But both of them were reticent to speak after the trauma of last night's killing. When she finished shaving him, he rinsed his face in the basin feeling the smoothness of his skin in his hands. He marveled at how good of a shave Jena always gave him with the razor. Smiling, she handed him another towel. When he finished drying his face, he dipped his toothbrush into a small jar of toothpaste by the basin and began to clean his teeth.

After rinsing his mouth clean, it was time for his body to be oiled. He joined Jena back in the shower basin, and she began rubbing the scented oils into his skin. After applying a light coat that covered his entire body, she toweled off any excess. This left a pleasant smelling, very light, and comfortable sheen on his skin. The mixture of oils covered his entire body in antiseptic, insect repellent, and skin moisturizer. The final touch was putting a small quantity of Iris oil perfume under his ears, and he was ready to have Jena prepare his hair. He dressed in his normal way for the palace with one of his fine tasseled kilts belted to his waist with his large dagger attached and a shoulder cape tied below his neck to warm him in the cool air. He strapped on his best pair of shoes. Looking at his reflection in the mirror from a distance, he judged he was presentable for the palace.

Jena had worked for Samra for almost a year now. But it was only within the last several weeks that she had come to fully realize just how truly good and strong of a person he was. In the beginning, it was all business with very little small talk. He was away much of the time on foreign missions, so they never really had a chance to get to know one another for several months. From the start, she felt he was somewhat cold, aloof, and even intimidating but certainly not now especially after their experience together last night.

Jena was a lovely twenty nine year old woman who had lost her husband and young son in the plague that swept through Knossos two years earlier. Samra lost his wife of many years in the same plague. It was a terrible year with many thousands of people dying throughout the city. Life could be very precarious. Like Samra, Jena was alone without any family left in the area, and in time she was forced to seek employment for her livelihood. She had been recommended to Samra by friends of his. He found her very intelligent and quite beautiful, but he told her that if she couldn't do the work to his requirements she would have to go elsewhere. He made this perfectly clear to her from the beginning.

Jena's job was to be his personal assistant in all things. This included bathing, feeding, and dressing him as well as many other tasks. The more tedious and time-consuming chores like much of the food preparation, clothes washing, and house cleaning were done by local service people. She was there to save him as much time as possible, so he could concentrate on his palace assignments. She was very well paid for this. She lived for free in the spacious beautifully decorated and furnished second floor apartment of the villa.

If she desired, when Samra was away on assignment or when she wasn't needed, she could assist Thalion in the workshop and share in any profits from the products she helped make. She had learned from the time she was a little girl how to spin and weave cloth on the loom and was as good of a wheel potter as Thalion except for the very largest pieces. She became fascinated with the plant oil distillery operation and had taken to it vigorously with great interest. It seemed like an instrument of magic to her that the invisible inner oils could be extracted from the raw plant parts with such purity.

She felt the same way about the metal furnace that could turn rocks into pure shiny metals hard enough to cut and shape anything in nature. The casting of the molten metals that hardened into any form desired always amazed her. She didn't like working around the furnace because of the heat and fumes, but she sometimes helped Thalion make the molds for casting. The furnace wasn't used very often. Thalion used it mostly to recycle old worn out bronze tools and recast them into new ones with useful sharp edges. He sometimes produced daggers, swords, and other items for sale in the market and for their own use. She considered the workshop to be a place where magic was regularly performed.

Her job could be very challenging, but the most fascinating aspect of it was Samraleos himself. She knew he was just a man, but he was a big, strong, athletic, and, in her opinion, very handsome man. He was quite well known throughout Knossos and far beyond to be a great warrior trained from early childhood by his father in hand-to-hand combat and a master's use of all the bronze weapons and the composite bow.

She had noticed on one occasion that Thalion, a giant originally from Thrace and much bigger than Samra, had actually shown her his fear of him. They were in the market observing their competitors products when a man became belligerent with Samra over something very petty. The man was looking for trouble. He was a big man and he motioned his intentions to strike Samra while Thalion stood quite close. When Samra readied his body to defend himself, Thalion almost gasped and backed away very quickly. It was as if he feared being so close to what he knew was going to happen. The man noticed both their reactions and reconsidered his intentions. He immediately backed off and quickly exited the scene. Jena was amused with the man's foolish behavior, but she was startled at how Thalion had reacted. She didn't think he was afraid of anything including Samra.

But the most interesting and amazing thing about him was that he was a recognized "Master of the Way" like his dead father, Karasos. She had first heard of the "Masters" from her parents as a small child. She was told they were potent constructive forces of good in the world and were reputed to have almost magical mental abilities and powers over people and nature. They were held in the highest esteem by all especially those in the palace and administration.

As time passed, Samra found Jena to be extremely intelligent and resourceful in managing the business of the household. She was producing an excellent profit for all of them. She had a wonderful sense of planning and organization.   Her hands were marvels of nimble dexterity as Thalion's were of raw power and strength.   Samra felt that Jena and Thalion complemented each other's talents and skills and had coalesced over time into a potent team for profit.   He treated them both with great respect and compassion.

Recently, after Jena swore an oath of secrecy, he began to confide in her his inner thoughts regarding his palace and now criminal assignments to get her perspective on them just as he would with his father when he was still alive.   He found that she helped him refine his thoughts to a greater clarity and made many of her own valuable contributions as well.

One night she cautiously asked him if he would consider instructing her in the "Way of Nature".   He was surprised, slightly amused, and agreed to it immediately.   By that time, he knew she was far more than just capable of it.   Jenaloi could easily be a "Master of the Way", but she had much to learn.   He told her he would be delighted to teach her, and if she wanted they could start tomorrow.   This pleased her very much and she excitedly rose to give him a kiss on the cheek.   Samra started her lessons by telling her the story his father had told him about the beginning and the basics of the "Way of Nature".   He followed that with a brief, but thorough, introduction to the 'Method of Nature".

Chapter 3

The Way of Nature

Perhaps tens of thousands of years ago a tribal genius crystallized the thought that since nature seemed perfectly consistent in its workings it must be governed by a set of unchanging laws. The light of day was always followed by the dark of night in succession, and the sun, moon, and stars moved in the sky predictably from season to season. If this was true, it was asked, "Could these laws be understood by humans?" Boldly assuming the affirmative he, or she, may have thought, "If we could learn the language of nature's laws everything could be understood in time."

These beliefs probably involved the intellectual contributions of many people over a long period of time. But it is possible that a single individual in an explosion of Paleolithic intellect conceived and began communicating them to others. The torch had been lit. Human intelligence and curiosity would drive it into the future.

The impetus for these ideas was the desire to lift humanity out of the filth, drudgery, chaos, and brutality of their daily existence. The idea developed that people could begin to remove themselves from the vermin and danger of the natural world by increasing their understanding and knowledge in it.

As they achieved greater insight, they could manipulate and transform nature to suit their needs, safety, and happiness.

Communicating these concepts at that time must have been quite a challenge with no writing and inadequate language tools. New words must have been invented to encompass these new ideas. The philosophy of "Nature's Way" became a part of tribal discussion and inexorably spread. Wherever it went, it offered "stone age" people the hope of progress. It became a vital part of the oral traditions passed down from generation to generation.

As more of the tribal thinkers began to take seriously these ideas, people began to intensify their examination of the materials around them. Everything (plants, soils, rocks, etc.) was thrown into the fire or in their pots and transformed by the heat to observe the results. Plants were much more systematically examined for their useful properties. They began to replant and spread the plants they found beneficial to make them more plentiful. As the results of their investigations were exchanged from tribe to tribe and generation to generation, their knowledge persistently grew.

Sometimes great leaps of discovery were made with simple observations. Someone noticed that certain rocks (probably lead bearing ores) left a pool of odd-looking slag in their fire pits. Lead melts at about three hundred and thirty degrees centigrade, and their camp fires could easily reach well over five hundred degrees centigrade. Their curiosity was ignited.

They reasoned that if reality was governed by perpetual laws, the next question became - how can we 'best' gain greater knowledge in them? These new ideas must have consumed a great deal of time in conversations around the fire among the early believers as they began to ask themselves abstract questions like: What is a fact? What is the truth? How do we know what is true?   Is there a best way to investigate nature to better gain knowledge?

Eventually, the collective discussions of the philosophers concluded that a fact is simply the way something actually is in nature, and knowledge is what is known to be true about some aspect of nature.   Why are things the way they are?   Using these fundamental questions, they realized the need for a powerful mental technique to proactively attain knowledge by searching for the 'causes' of things in nature.

It was decided that it was critical that nature's truths be free of the influences of human religious, political, and psychological considerations.   The search for knowledge makes no moral judgments.   Spirituality, opinions, biases, intuitions, and feelings are strewn with emotional and instinctual components and are simply statements of belief.   The philosophers were learning what nature had always been telling them by carefully examining the validity of their facts.

As nature's truths accumulated in their collective memories and reached new heights, people were better able to invent new technologies that improved their lives and those of their children.   The philosophers concluded that the search for nature's 'causes' was the only practical and effective way of achieving and sustaining human progress.   Nature's method is what their combined mentalities created, over time, to help humanity to this end.

The goal of the method was to create a conceptual construct that accurately explained some aspect of nature.   After much effort and irregardless of their culture or language, their rational intellects were able to coalesce, clarify, and refine the mental tools they needed to find the causes of things:

Empirical Observation – all valid facts are dependent on what is attainable by the human senses and verifiable measurements with the understanding that they have limitations.

Objective Logic – is the study of the relationships between facts for binding them together to reach a conclusion. The conceptual tools used in applying logic to factual relationships are:

Premise – is a set of ideas that support a valid conclusion based on the logical connections of the facts.

Argument – is an effort to discover the validity of a conclusion based on its premises.

Inference - is deriving a conclusion based on what is already known.

Conclusion – is a testable idea derived from the premises of an argument.

Deduction / Deductive Reasoning – is concluding that something is true because it is a particular case of a valid general theory. The theory is the premise. If the premise is true, the conclusion is true. It moves from the general to the particular and is logically valid.

Induction / Inductive Reasoning – is concluding that a general idea is true because the particular cases observed are true. The particular cases are the premises. Induction constructs a general principle from particular cases. The premises may predict a certain likelihood of a conclusion but do not ensure its validity. It moves from the particular to the general and is not logically valid.

Causality (Cause & Effect) – is the dependent relationship between causes and their effects. Causes always produce effects. Causes are beginnings and their effects the result. Causes always precede their effects in time. The search for causality is, when given a set of valid facts as effects, an attempt is made to discover their causes and the reasons for them. When causes are revealed, new knowledge is born. Causality is the essence of nature and gives the human intellect the ability to understand its workings.

Hypotheses – is a working assumption developed after objective logic has been applied to a set of observed facts to discover their relationships and causes. Experimentation is required to test its validity. If its validity is upheld, it becomes a theory.

Theory – is a conceptual construct that explains all known observations and predicts new ones from it. If a theory cannot explain new observations, the search will begin to replace it with one that does. A single fact can invalidate a theory.

With observation and logic as their basis, they constructed the best method for extracting truth from falsehoods and delusion ever discovered. Samra and the other believers called it the "Method of Nature" or simply the "Method".

The "Method" is a thought process that has the following steps:

Observe – apply empirical observation to some aspect of nature.

Hypothesize - invent a hypothesis that is consistent with the observations.

Predict – use the hypothesis to develop and implement predictions for testing.

Test - the validity of the predictions through experimentation and modify the hypothesis in the light of new observations.

Repeat – the 'Predict' and 'Test' steps until there is consistency between the predictions and observations.

When the hypothesis' predictions are consistent with what is observed through experimentation, it becomes a theory. The theory provides a testable coherent set of propositions that explains some aspect of reality. A theory's acceptance is based on the reliability of the results obtained through its experimental observations that any doubter can reproduce. A theory assumes an invitation to others to overturn it, if they can. Therefore, it is devoid of bias and is entirely unprejudiced.

Samra continued with Jena's lesson by saying, "The "Way of Nature" is a way of thinking. It's a philosophy of constantly learning to build true knowledge for your own benefit and the greater good of all through the sharing of it. It changes the way you look at everything around you."

He told her that by the time he was twelve his father had him commit the "Method" to memory in the form of a narrative poem like some of the other children in the course of their studies. Early on, he realized the true power of "Nature's Way" and by the time he was seventeen his subconscious mind had incorporated it as a powerful engine in the search for truth. He used it without thinking. It was simply a part of him.

This is how his father Karasos had lovingly willed it by beginning his son's training in the "Way" very early. He consistently and patiently imparted the intricacies of his knowledge and techniques as Samra grew in his ability to digest them.

Chapter 4

Conspiracies

Samra was in his thirty eighth year and felt he was at the height of his physical powers, but he considered this secondary to his efforts to improve his mental techniques in the "Way". He felt quite fortunate to have a father like Karasos. He was a compassionate and loving man whose tremendous physical prowess was more than matched by his brilliant intelligence. He would always miss his father's presence dearly.

Karasos died mysteriously over four years ago on a mission against a group of pirates that raided and captured two of the King's grain ships in the northern Aegean; off the southern coast of the island of Tenedos about forty kilometers southwest of Troy. The ships were heading north into the head winds of September to trade with the Thracians for their vast stores of grain at harvest time. The King's ships carried gold, silver, large quantities of cloth, and many other luxury items for trade. The voyage was to take the fleet well past Troy into the straits to the east to enter the great northern inland sea. They would then follow the western coastline north to the delta of a huge river.   The Thracians had an immense grain storage facility located up river about fifty kilometers.   This was the land and people of Thalion's birthplace.

According to witnesses from the lone surviving ship, a pirate fleet of seven thirty-oared ships attacked a group of three of the King's ships that became separated from the grain fleet in rough seas.   The ships rowed to the east for the protection of the southern coast of the island to wait out the strong north winds. They reached the western cape of the island and were nearing the coast when they were attacked.   The pirates appeared suddenly from behind a small neck of land rowing hard at them in a line with their sail booms down to conceal their numbers. The oarsmen of the King's ships were tired from their long row in the wind and white capped waves.   They were slow to respond to the threat.   As the pirates quickly closed in on them, they, in panic, tried to raise their sails to catch the wind to escape as they prepared for a fight.

Two of the grain ships were soon boarded and captured after a brief fight.   The third ship was trailing the other two and was in a better position to escape, but two of the pirate ships raised their sails and were furiously rowing after them with fresh arms. With the distance closing, the ship master ordered the crew to begin throwing crates of cargo overboard.   He did this, not only, to lighten the ship to make better headway, but he was hoping the pirates would stop to gather the crates before they sank into the sea allowing them to escape.   The tactic worked, and the King's ship quickly sailed far away to the south.   The pirates let them go for crates filled with woolen cloth and linen which they valued greatly.

The ship master decided his best course of action, as a single ship filled with valuables with no protection, was to sail south to the port city of Thera to notify the authorities of the attack and obtain further instructions. On entering the huge ringed harbor of Thera's volcanic caldera, the master took his ship directly to the military dockyards. He noticed there were only a few ships moored to the docks. He was told most of the vessels were already dispersed on missions throughout the Aegean. It would be quite some time before they were able to mount a serious effort against the new pirate menace. After some discussion, they decided it would be best if he returned without delay to Amnisos and notify the authorities there. Given the current situation, they would be far more capable of swiftly assembling a fleet to respond to the threat. A ship of warriors was hastily readied to escort the cargo vessel back to Amnisos.

When the ship returned to Crete, the authorities were quickly alerted and rushed to assemble and provision a military fleet to hunt down the Tenedos pirates. The fleet, with the cargo ship's master accompanying them as a witness, was assigned to first search the area around the island for any evidence they could find in an effort to determine the identity of the pirates. When this was complete, they were ordered to sail to Troy for consultations. They wanted to obtain information on the passage of the remainder of the grain fleet and request the Trojans to add some of their own ships to the operation. When negotiations were complete and the joint fleet was ready, they were to fan out into the northern Aegean to scour the islands and coastlines in a search and destroy mission.

While the ships were being assembled in Amnisos, the head of the intelligence committee in the palace at Knossos, a man named Kalpoulis, unexpectedly asked Samra's father Karasos to be the new fleet's leader and "Master of the Way". At the time, Karasos was an adviser to the King's committee and looking forward to retiring in another year or two to his western estates in Khania. When Kalpoulis approached him about the assignment, he portrayed it as a simple courtesy call on the

Trojans and a search of the northern islands to destroy a small pirate fleet. Karasos hadn't been on a military mission in two years, but he missed the action of his youth and decided one last operation would do him no harm. At the time, Samra was far away to the north in Kolonna on the island of Aegina resolving a series of trade conflicts there with the Myceneans.

On his return to Knossos, a few days after the departure of the warrior fleet, he was very surprised to hear that his father had decided to take the rushed assignment. He knew his father loved the action of leadership in conflict, but he had said many times that he dreamed of finally leaving the palace to retire to a peaceful life on his large estate in the west. It angered him that Kalpoulis requested his father to be the leader for an offensive combat mission when there were other less senior "Masters" ready and eager for battle available. His father had been a leader of many foreign negotiations and conflicts during his life, and he should have already been retired.

Samra wasn't really concerned and even pitied the foolhardy pirates when the warriors lead by his father descended on them. But when word came to him on the return of the fleet to Amnisos that his father was missing overboard in a storm and assumed dead, he was shocked and filled with disbelief, grief, and sorrow. He took a temporary leave from his duties and stayed at home for several days with his wife and children dealing with an unrelenting sorrow. His father wouldn't have wanted him to dwell for long on the sadness of his loss, and he returned to his duties with a new personal mission of discovering the truth behind his death.

Information he gathered from those who returned from the mission told him that after a fierce battle with a group of pirates, a ship-eating north gale began to blow upon them. Several of the King's warriors were killed and wounded in the fight, but his father had survived unscathed. Somehow Karasos had fallen overboard in the storm with no one being a witness to it. He was one of only three men lost in the storm.   Samra knew his father, even at his age, was stronger than most of the warriors in the fleet.   His mind was never able to digest this story as factual.   His suspicions of assassination were roused especially after hearing the ship master's final mission report to the King's committee.   There were many others that felt the same way.   He suspected the mission was a ploy used by someone in the palace to murder his father for political purposes.

Over a period of weeks, he personally interviewed each of Karasos' personal guards and all of the surviving warriors that were on the ship with him.   He learned very little, but he suspected that only someone his father trusted and was close to could have killed him.   He hypothesized that the assassin was most likely one of his father's personal guards.   During his interviews, he used all of his techniques for determining the truth but was left with only feelings and suspicions of who might be responsible.   He narrowed his list of most probable suspects to two of the personal guards and one possible suspect among the warriors, but with no evidence to prove it he could do nothing more without putting a blade to their throats.   He needed more evidence and believed it could be found somewhere in the palace.

Over the intervening years, he narrowed his list of suspects to a small group of people active in their work with the intelligence committee.   Near the top of the list was his boss Kalpoulis. Another one of his prime suspects was Kalpoulis's niece, Synboliki.   She was relentless in her involvement with matters of state under the tutelage and cover of her uncle.   With a brilliant mind, she had the ear of not only her uncle but many others on the top committees.

He was friendly and cordial to her in their sporadic encounters in and around the complex, but he always felt there was something odd about her especially the way she responded to emotional things that would cause joy or tears in most people. She always seemed to just coldly stand there with a chilling stillness in her eyes at moments like those. She possessed many of the traits of one of the "Others" as described to him by his father. His belief in his father's theory was becoming stronger as confirmation of it continued to grow.

Many years before, Synboliki overtly displayed a virulent hatred toward him at the time of his unintentional humiliation of her childhood friend Danaloi in a boxing match during the spring festival. He never forgot the cold maniacally evil look in her eyes at that moment. She never outwardly displayed any further anger toward him over the years, but he couldn't help thinking she was just hiding her true feelings. It seemed to him that all she ever showed anyone was a mask. Her friend Danaloi was also on his list. Samra had a personal distaste for both of them. His network of informants and associates fed him a great deal of information on their predilections and idiosyncrasies which were many and lurid to say the least. They seemed to be meant for each other. As an authorized "Master of the Way" of the palace, Samra could detain, interrogate, and even kill anyone he pleased within reason. But he could only do the same with people so close to the committees if he had undeniable proof or his own life could be seriously in doubt.

Synboliki and Samra were born in the same year and grew up in adjacent neighborhoods in the palace district. They first met as five year olds playing games with the other children in the parks around the palace. They were never friends. Samra wouldn't have had any problem being friends with her or anybody else. He was a well balanced, confident child that was innately compassionate to all the people he came into contact with.

Because of this he was well liked and quite popular. He tried to be fair with everyone and treated them as his equal with their own unique talents. Any normal child would have felt secure, comfortable, and even joyful in his presence as they played.

Synboliki felt resentment toward him from the first. His mere presence irritated and annoyed her deeply. He was a beautiful, well-formed, athletic young child that was more agile, quick, and coordinated with his body than her. But the thing that really disturbed her was the way other people favorably reacted to him. He was a natural leader. The feelings of resentment that sprouted on the fields of play blossomed into envy and hatred from a very early time.

The first time she deceitfully did something to intentionally hurt Samra was when she subtlety instigated some of the slightly older, bigger boys to harass and threaten him physically. The boys began taunting him and, on one occasion, trapped him and started pushing him around inside a circle of them. One of the boys tried to hit him with his fist. Samra dodged the blow by quickly moving down to the ground and jumping from between the legs of two of them. The boys chased him for a short distance, but he easily outran them. He ran all the way home angry and crying straight to his father in the workshop.

Rushing up to him, he grabbed him about the waist crying, "Father! Father! They tried to beat me and hurt me father! Why? Why?"

Karasos picked him up into his arms and said, "Samra, what happened? What did they do?"

"They chased me and trapped me. They were trying to hit me, father."

"Did they hit you?"

"No, I jumped from between them and ran away."

"So you're not hurt?"

"No, I'm fine. But why would they do it, father? Why? I didn't do anything to them, and they wanted to hurt me <u>bad</u>!"

"Come Samra, we're going to have a talk with you're mother, and I want you to tell her just what you told me, okay."

"Yes, father."

They walked upstairs to meet with his mother, and a family discussion ensued about Samra beginning his warrior training. Up to then his mother had refused to have Karasos start his training. For now, she thought it was enough to begin teaching him about the "Way". He was still a very young playful child, and she saw no need for his physical training to begin. But she realized he must start his training now that he had come under the threat of these bullies. She was brutally taunted by hecklers and bullies when she was a young girl and knew there was only one way for her son to deal with them. She nodded her agreement to Karasos for Samra to begin his schooling.

His father immediately took him down into the workshop and began instructing him. Samra had no idea who was training him. He knew his father did something different from the other parents in the neighborhood but that was all. Karasos first began showing him how to defend himself using the motion of his body with his hands and feet. He had a lot of fun with his father pretending to hit him to observe he was learning his lessons. Once he was satisfied Samra was doing well, he began to show him how to defend himself by striking others to hurt them but not permanently. Those lessons would come later.

After he was pleased Samra was doing very well with his lessons, he said, "Son, this is what they call a tactic. When the bullies next approach you, fool them into thinking you are scared of them and strike hard when they least expect it."

Samra was still afraid and worried, but he learned what his father taught him very well and felt his confidence. He was overjoyed with his father's praise of his progress. He felt more powerful with his new knowledge and heartened by his father's recognition of it.

"Son, if you do this, as I know you can, you will never have to worry about bullies again."

"Yes, father."

The next day he stayed around the house not wanting to confront his tormentors just yet. He dealt with his feelings of fear while he practiced the movements his father had taught him. He did the same the next day. The morning of the third day, he gathered all his courage and set off for the park to play with his friends as he normally would. Inside his stomach was quacking, and his fear soared and receded as his courage wavered wildly. He knew a confrontation was inevitable when he noticed one of the bullies had seen him and was walking away to gather the others. He was playing happily with his friends for a while when a group of five of them came up to him.

They closed in tightly around him, so he couldn't escape like the last time. He was extremely frightened and let it show. They expected his reaction and began to call him names and push him around. He limply let them push him for a few moments and suddenly struck the boy on his left in the face with his right fist. He hit the boy very hard on the nose and upper lip with his little fist. The boy fell back on the ground dazed and unable to move with blood pouring from his nose. Stunned, he slowly brought his hand to his face to touch the warm liquid he felt running from his nose. At the sight of the red blood on his fingertips, he began to cry. His head dropped back onto the ground in a faint, and he laid there in shock.

Immediately after hitting the first boy, Samra hit a second one in the head, and he fell to the ground unconscious like a falling tree. The other three boys were amazed, stunned, and terrified. They just had enough time to turn and run as fast as they could as Samra quickly moved to do the same to them. They would never bother Samra again. He smiled to himself as he surveyed the two boys lying peacefully on the ground and happily went to go play with friends. From that day on, the bullies never bothered his friends either. He never found out that it was Synboliki that had instigated the bullies on him in the first place.

Even at this early age, she realized and began to use the power of the 'plausible lie'. She told the bullies she had heard Samra was saying mocking things about them. The convincing lie incited the insecure envious boys in their belief in it. She deflected any responsibility from herself by saying she had heard it from someone else. She would refine her tactics of the 'plausible lie' to a very high level and would continue her vengeful plots against him throughout their childhood and beyond.

Some years later, Samra, like many of the other teenage boys in the area, entered the boxing competition at the spring festival. Synboliki's friend Danaloi was one of the entrants. He was a very powerful excellent boxer and let everyone know it. She was thrilled with the thought that Danaloi was going to fight Samra in the tournament and hopefully hurt him badly. She reveled in the hurting of others.

They both worked their way through their competitions and ended up matched against each other for the boy's championship. Danaloi had overpowered the other boys, but Samra was almost as big as he was. Just as the match began, Danaloi tried to surprise Samra by immediately lunging at him to strike his head. In a blur, Samra stepped to the side, blocked the strike with his right arm and, in a flash of cat-like movement, turned his body to swing a crushing blow with his left hand to Danaloi's temple. He crumpled hard onto the ground into a sprawled heap and didn't move. The match lasted for only about a second or two.

People rushed forward to see if he was badly hurt as Samra backed away. Danaloi lay there for a three or four minutes before beginning to regain consciousness. Everyone was very relieved when it appeared he was not hurt except Synboliki. She was infuriated at him for disappointing her vengeance. As he moved away from those trying to care for Danaloi, Samra momentarily made eye contact with Synboliki to see her unmasked and glimpsed her true inner-self. He thought her eyes were voids of evil. This was the time when her hatred for Samra blossomed into a maniacal rage to destroy him and everyone else that gave joy to his life.

Many years later, Synboliki arranged for and financed the murder of Samra's father, Karasos. She did this to secure her uncle Kalpoulis' position, as head of the intelligence committee, and therefore her political influence in the palace. It came to her that the King and Queen had offered Karasos her uncle's position beginning in the spring of the next year. She never received the information that, a few weeks later after considering the offer, Karasos told them he would like to stay active in the palace for another year or two but eventually wished to retire west to his estates. He declined the position.

By this time, she relentlessly wanted to hurt Samra and considered it just another step in destroying him in her psychotic vengeance.   He was on her list for destruction not only for the affronts she felt he had done to her, but she envied the attention the elites of the committees showed him and his burgeoning political clout.   The leadership considered him to be the equal of his father the great "Master" Karasos.   She saw him as a serious rival to her long-term influence in the palace as she saw Karasos as a threat to her uncle.   She hoped the death of his father would be enough to tear Samra down into remorse, erode his competency, and, over time, credibility with the committees.   He instead resiliently arose to be even stronger and more brilliant in their eyes.

Synboliki worked very hard to convince certain members of the committees, which held great influence with her uncle Kalpoulis, that Samra was the best man for a highly probable upcoming mission to Avaris in Egypt.   In the background she subtly created political pressure on her uncle to have Samra assigned to the mission as its leader and "Master of the Way".   In her uncle's presence, she agreed that he was the only choice if they really wanted the mission to succeed.   Indeed, Kalpoulis and many others in the committees would have begged Samra to take the mission even without Synboliki's encouragement or political manipulations.

Chapter 5

The Assignment

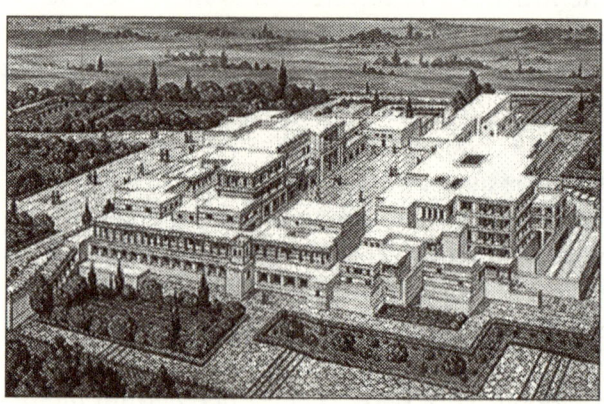

Before beginning his walk to the administration building to speak with the civil authorities regarding the child killings, a messenger from Kalpoulis appeared to request a meeting regarding something important as soon as possible. This was very unusual and he wondered why he would call a meeting on such short notice. He had heard talk of a mission being considered for Avaris for a few months now. But surely Kalpoulis wouldn't send him on a foreign mission when he had just taken over the child murder investigation. He assumed it must have something to do with last night's killing.

"He probably has something of relevance to aid the criminal investigation." he hoped.

It was a beautiful bright sunny day as Jena watched Samra leave on his way to Kalpoulis' office. The immense palace complex's white gypsum walls were brilliantly lit up by the sun. It was far more than just the official residence of the King and Queen. It was a huge structure of nearly twenty thousand square meters and was five stories high in some sections. It hosted many political and religious functions throughout the year but was primarily the seat of the central government for the entire kingdom. The strategic and day-to-day operations of the kingdom were administered by several committees with varying power, but they always conducted their affairs in the name of the King. The King and Queen were very influential but not omnipotent.

The key to the treasury's wealth was the government's exclusive control over foreign trade. Only ships authorized by the King were allowed to conduct international commerce. Whenever products were placed on these ships a share owed to the King was accounted for. Another way the treasury nourished itself was by the large scale production of finished products for export. The palace complex was the nucleus for the mass production of textiles, fine pottery, oils, jewelry, and finished bronze goods in the greater area around it. There was an insatiable demand for these goods throughout the entire region.

Samra lived on the hillside to the west of the complex. It was only a short walk away. As he entered the great building and approached Kalpoulis' office, he found him standing in the hallway just outside his office door talking to small group of people. One of them was his niece, Synboliki. When he saw Samra coming, he abruptly ended his conversation and bid them farewell.

"Ah, Samra, please come into the office. I have some good news for you."

Leading him through the doorway with a broad smile, he said, "There is much gold in your future."

"It must be the mission to Avaris." Samra thought as they took their seats at his desk.

"I want you to take the assignment as leader and "Master of the Way" for a new fleet of long ships in Kommos to recover the King's treasury gold in Avaris.   Your reward will be great if you are successful and we both know you will be as you always are."

"But sir, I've just assumed the lead and am deeply involved in the child murder investigation.   Many of the people are saying the killer isn't human.   They say it's a demon spirit with bronze teeth and claws that sweeps in from the dark forest to prey on the children like some cunning, crazed lion.   How can I possibly leave Knossos now?   Please, I beg you Kalpoulis don't ask me to take this mission and have me abandon my assignment here.   It means a great deal to me to rid the people of this beast, and I don't really need the gold.   I already have a great deal.   Besides there are others just as qualified for the task." he stated emphatically.

Kalpoulis smiled at this saying, "But Samra, we don't know of anyone other than you that gives us the needed confidence this critical undertaking will succeed.   You are the very finest "Master" we have.   This is the most important operation I have ever been involved with on the intelligence committee, and the King and Queen agree you are the best man for the task.   I beg you Samra in the name of the King and Queen.   Please reconsider for the greater good of the people.   I vow I will have three times the deputies assigned to the murder investigation while you are gone."

Samra sat quietly for several moments looking at him and began to respond, but Kalpoulis interrupted him saying, "The top committee members all agree they want you and only you to lead this mission.   They are ready to put their seal to your orders if you accept, but if you don't I'm sure the King will command you to go because of the overwhelming need for success.   Besides you will be working for the first time with an old friend of your fathers; the great Admiral Cronymartis himself. If he is going on this operation, you must realize how truly important it is."

"I know how you feel about the murders. I've heard how horrible last night's killing was. I would feel the same way if I was you, and I respect you even more for it. But the Avaris mission is for the greater good of all the people. Please, Samra!"

He realized the die was cast. He must take the assignment and interrupt his investigation.

"Very well, sir. What is my assignment?"

Kalpoulis smiled in relief saying, "I'm sure everyone will be pleased to hear of your acceptance. Let's begin."

He commenced by explaining the top committees had been considering the mission for several months; ever since word came to them the Egyptians under Ahmose had defeated the Canaanites at Heliopolis. The city was despoiled of its wealth and its people enslaved. Heliopolis was only eighty kilometers south by river from the King's commercial district in Canaanite Avaris. The Egyptians, with the winter harvest approaching, had recently mounted raids on the city and set the fields of grain ablaze all around it.

The King felt it was essential the commercial district should be stripped of its gold, valuables, and many of its people before the Egyptians took them for themselves by force. The wealth was very considerable judging by the reports. It would be the largest single shipment of gold, silver, and valuables ever to enter the King's treasury. There was also a long list of officials, administrators, and bureaucrats to be evacuated to safety.

"This is a big one, Samra!"

If the Egyptians realized we were removing the King's treasure from Avaris, there would certainly be military consequences from them.   The latest reports indicated they were massing their forces south of the city for an overwhelming military assault from the land and the river with their huge barges of warriors.   As far as they knew, the great city might already be under attack or taken.   News from Avaris had just come from Amnisos with the arrival of a fast diplomatic ship and was, at least, eight days old.   The situation was not good, and time was of the essence.

The twelve ships assigned to the Kommos fleet were all sturdy fifty-oared long ships especially suited to deal with the well-known Egyptian tactic of massed torch arrow attacks.   Besides the ship master and his small team of skilled specialists, each ship would have a crew of one hundred and twenty of the best warriors available.   A number of official passengers were also assigned to the mission.

The ships would carry no cargo for trade as they usually did. Instead, they were to take on additional military equipment and extra provisions for the expected evacuees.   The ships would appear to be carrying a normal load of trade goods when they were first spotted from the walls of Avaris.   The smallest deception could aid the mission's success.   If the Canaanites knew the true nature of the mission, they might seize the King's treasure for themselves or even the ships for that matter. Nothing was certain.

Weeks earlier, secret correspondence was delivered to a few of the King's top officials in the district instructing them to quietly prepare for an evacuation if the Egyptians moved north toward the city.   They feared the reaction of the Canaanites if their plans became known. Both the Egyptians and Canaanites were well-known to have intelligence agents in Knossos. The recent arrival of the diplomatic ship from Egypt forced their decision to launch the mission now. Preparations were being conducted in extreme secrecy both here in Knossos and in Avaris to allay any suspicions from either of the warring parties.

The King took no sides in the conflict. His only interest was the continued acquisition of wealth through economic trade that grew and enhanced his kingdom. He saw this as a quarrel between two of his trading partners. It was merely an inconvenient disruption to his lucrative business dealings in Egypt. For a time, it looked as if the Canaanites were unstoppable and would take the whole of Egypt, but now the tables had turned. The King wished to play both sides to his advantage in this tumultuous time. He was saddened the profit from trade had fallen off since the start of the latest Egyptian uprising. But he was determined to remain neutral and maintain friendly links with both parties, if possible, no matter what its conclusion.

Samra's assignment in Avaris was to arrange the acquisition and loading of the gold and valuables of the treasury into the holds of the fleet, alert the many people on a list for evacuation, and contact intelligence operatives to measure the intentions of the Canaanites and Egyptians in that order. He was to assess their capabilities and the current and future potential threats to the King's commercial district. Also, it was critical for the committees to be advised if any additional ships were needed for future evacuations or the transport of valuables.

Kalpoulis told him Telecaneos had been temporarily assigned, subject to his approval, as the interim military commander to oversee the initial selection and gathering of the warriors. Samra would have all of the normal powers of a "Master of the Way" on the mission. The military powers of a "Master" were considerable, and, in extreme cases, he could even assume unquestioned command of the entire fleet.   But the ultimate responsibility for the fleet was the domain of Admiral Cronymartis whereas the responsibility for the mission as a whole was Samra's.

"Sir, I realize the critical nature of the mission.   I'll select the commander of the warriors and men for my personal guard soon. Is there anything else I should know?"

Kalpoulis nodded affirmatively and continued with a description of the quantity and value of the gold, silver, jewelry, and other objects of wealth to be returned to Knossos.   Samra was amazed by what he heard.   When he was told of what his share of the spoils would be, it was hard for him to remain unimpressed in Kalpoulis' presence.   He would be a person of great wealth and need never concern himself with attaining profit ever again.

The fleet was scheduled to sail to Avaris from Kommos in three days.   Three hundred and sixty of the finest warriors in Knossos were being selected and assembled for the march south to fully man three of the ships of the fleet.   The rest of the warriors were already being gathered in Phaistos and would be waiting for them in Kommos on the southern coast.   Three newly constructed ships were being readied to sail in the dockyards.

The Knossos warriors would be assembled in the palace courtyard at dawn on the second morning from today.   They were to march south to Phaistos with a midday stop in Kalathiana.   After arriving in Phaistos from their long march, the warriors would stay there to feast and sleep.   With the next dawn, they would march the last six kilometers to Kommos on the coast to begin boarding the ships.   Messages from the shipwrights assured them all twelve ships of the fleet would be fully equipped and ready for the voyage.

"What are the provisions for the ships to deal with the Egyptian fire attacks on the river?" Samra asked.

Kalpoulis explained what he knew, but the details of such things often eluded him.   Samra realized the fleet would be vulnerable to torch arrow attacks from the city, the river banks, and the river itself sitting in the narrow four hundred meter wide river at the docks in Avaris.   They would be vulnerable to attack from all sides.   The ability of the fleet to maneuver in the highly restricted space on the river would give them few options for escape.   If the ships weren't supremely capable of defending themselves against fire attack all could be lost.

"The best defense against fire is an offense of fire. We must be able to quickly respond to any attack with a mass of torch arrows against whomever our enemy is." he thought.

"I'm going to compose a letter to Cronymartis with my thoughts for defending the ships in the river.   I will need it delivered as soon as possible to help them prepare, if they haven't already done so." he said.

Samra wanted the warriors to carry, at least, triple their normal complement of bronze arrows and torch wadding.   He also wanted the ships to carry several additional fire pots to quickly feed the warrior's empty bows while they were under attack.

"I have great confidence the planning and arrangements in Avaris will be carried out well by the authorities, but I have little confidence in their ability to keep secrets for long."

Kalpoulis nodded his agreement saying, "An express runner will be available to go south within the half hour awaiting the completion of your letter.   Also, the temporary commander in Knossos will be notified of the warrior's additional arrow and wadding requirements as soon as possible."

"I need to return home to compose my thoughts, so could you have the runner sent to my villa to pick up the letter."

"I'll have him on his way as soon as he can be summoned, Samra.   About a half hour I would think perhaps sooner."

Just as the meeting seemed to be ending, Samra asked, "Do I have your word the authorities assigned to the murder investigation are authorized to triple their resources?"

"The authorization letter will be sent within the hour."

"I'll meet the authorities later with your letter and instructions for their utilization.   Could you have a sealed copy of it sent to my home also?"

Smiling broadly, Kalpoulis said, "Anything you wish.   It will be in your possession within the hour.   Is there anything else I can do for you, sir?"

Acknowledging the humor of the situation, Samra said with a smile, "No sir."

Samra wanted to proceed in no uncertain way in the matter of the killings and would do his best to help ensure the safety of the children while he was away.   He wanted surveillance teams stationed at specific locations in the palace district in anticipation of any future attacks by the murderer.

He sincerely thanked Kalpoulis for his authorization and standing from his chair said, "I must leave now and prepare myself.   Have a good day, sir."

Kalpoulis rose from his chair, walked around his desk, and hugged him as if he were a son saying, "Thank you very much, Samra."

As he turned to leave, Kalpoulis smiled and felt buoyed with confidence for the mission. He thought if anyone could make the extremely dangerous, if not suicidal, Avaris mission a success it was the son of Karasos. No one knew what the current conditions in Avaris were, but their latest reports indicated the Egyptians were massing very close to the south.

As Samra walked home from the palace, he was drenched in trepidation. The gold reward for success was bountiful, but he wondered how probable the mission's success was. If the Egyptians were already in Avaris when they arrived, they could easily fall into a trap with no escape. Their route back to the open sea could be cut off by the sudden appearance of barges filled with thousands of warriors in their path. The Nile would become a river of death with waves of torch arrows being thrown at them from all sides.

If the Egyptians had not already taken the city, they might still have to deal with hostile attacks from the Canaanites. It was possible they could be faced with simultaneous attacks from both of them. Success was more than possible, but they would need all the luck they could get. It just depended on the conditions in Avaris when they arrived. Doubtlessly, the sooner they arrived the better their chance the city had not already come under attack. If that was true, their probability of success would be much higher.

Another reason for his trepidation was that he thought it was very probable he was being setup for assassination by someone in the palace just as he suspected his father was on the pirate mission in the northern sea. He believed he would have to just assume this possibility was, in fact, a reality in order to ensure his survival to lead the mission. He also thought that having him removed from the murder investigation, just after the last killing, was the best thing that could possibly happen to the child killer.

As his eyes viewed the beauty of the scenes around him, he put his mental engine into its highest state of creative readiness and analytical alertness. He began scanning every scenario and situation he could think of that facilitated his enemy's ability to assassinate him. He had a day and a half to plan and prepare. He wouldn't waste any of it.

On his return to the villa, he walked into the workshop to inform Thalion he would be leaving on a mission. Thalion was busy maintaining the fires of the steam distilleries processing a batch of iris roots. The wonderful smell of the iris oil filled the air. After greetings, Samra said, "I'll be off on a new mission to Egypt in two days and will probably be gone for three or four weeks. Let me know if you need anything while I'm away."

"No, I sure I'll be able to keep the workshop running if you aren't gone any longer than that. Do you have any special instructions for me?"

"I have many things to think about now, but there may be some danger to the household. I'm not sure. I'll talk with you later once I've considered my thoughts. But if there is danger, I know there is no one better than you to deal with it."

Acknowledging the compliment, Thalion bowed in respect saying, "Thank you sir. You can rely on me I assure you."

Samra knew full well he could rely on him. Thalion had worked for him for several years now, and he had seen him handle extremely difficult situations with the certainty of the giant he was. As he turned to leave, Thalion thought Samra was being very humble in his compliment to him. He had seen Samra deal with extreme situations also and was amazed and actually frightened by the agility and quickness of his great physical power. He would never want to deal with that himself and pitied anyone who did. Thalion had never been afraid of anyone in his life until he met Samraleos.

Samra walked up the stairs to the second floor landing and knocked on Jena's door. She answered with a smile and invited him in. He noticed she had been busy redecorating the apartment and had purchased some new oak furniture and curtains.

Surveying the chambers, he said, "It looks beautiful in here, Jena. You must have spent a good deal of gold."

"Yes, I love nice things around me, and I had the gold to spend. It makes life much more pleasant and bright. Don't you think? I'd like to have a new fresco done on the west wall if that's all right with you."

"Yes, that's fine. But please use my gold."

After a short pause, he said, "Jena, I'm leaving in two days on a mission to Egypt, and I'll be gone for three or four weeks, so we won't be able to continue your lessons until I return. I have a great deal to consider before I go, so I'll need to be alone to concentrate."

"Very well, is there anything I can help you with to prepare?"

"Just bring me some wine for now and feed me later whenever it's convenient. Maybe I'll be able to tell you more then."

She could tell much of his mind was somewhere else, and it concerned her something very serious was happening.

"I'll get your wine, Samra." she said as she walked from the room beginning to worry.

Early that evening, Jena brought in a tray of meats, flatbread, vegetables, and fruits that he loved and set it down on the large oak table by the brazier.   Samra was sitting in a chair looking out the large north window toward the great city below.   He stood and as he walked to the table asked, "Have you eaten already, Jena?

"No."

"If you'd like, why don't we share our meal this evening? There's much I'd like to talk to you about."

"I'd love to dine with you.   I'll be back with my tray in a minute."

Savoring their meal, they enjoyed some light conversation about her ideas for redecorating the apartment and how well the perfumes were selling.   When they were done, Jena placed the trays outside on the landing.   Samra was already pouring wine in their cups as she retook her seat.

"Jena, what I'm about to tell you is as secret as it gets, so I want to give you the choice of whether you want to know it or not. If you don't, I completely understand."

"Samra, that's silly.   You know there's no way I'm not going to want to hear it whatever it is.   I've already sworn my secrecy to you, so tell me."

"I'm going to Avaris in Egypt.   The King has a large commercial district there.   I'm to lead a mission to remove the gold and valuables from its treasury and evacuate the King's officials.   The Egyptians and Canaanites have been fighting for some time now.   It looks like the Egyptians are going to win and take Avaris by force soon, if they haven't already.   The mission itself is dangerous, but I believe I'm being setup to be murdered by someone in the palace.   Very much like what happened to my father."

Jena was shocked, stunned into amazement, and sat there speechless with worry and concern taking a strong hold.   She could feel her body tensing up.

"I don't want you to worry about what might happen, if I don't return.   I've made arrangements by letter with my son in Khania.   I have his letter of confirmation with his personal seal on it stating he agrees to my wishes.   If anything happens to me, he will take control of the property and offer it for lease or contract with you and Thalion having the first and most favorable choice of any offers made."

She interrupted, "Samra, you don't have to do anything special for me.   I've already earned more gold than I've ever had since I've been in your employment.   You don't have to worry for me."

"No, Jena.   You and Thalion are very special to me, and I want it to be this way.   Please hear me out."

After a short pause with each of them looking into the other's eyes, Samra said, "My son would be happy to be an absentee landlord if you and Thalion don't wish to purchase the household outright.   He will let you run it as if it was yours as long as he realized a fair profit from the arrangement.   Jena you will be the head of the household not Thalion.   He is a wonderful and talented man, but he doesn't have your natural sense for business and profit."

Jena was speechless, and, in the midst of her growing worry for Samra's safety, she was overjoyed and deeply thankful that he would be so concerned with her security. At that moment, she reflexively rose up from her chair and lifted her arms toward him wanting to rush forward and hug him in appreciation. But she quickly stopped and sat back down fully in her chair.

Samra noticed this and, a few moments later, lowered his head and began to softly laugh. Smiling, he returned his gaze on her and stood from his chair. He walked around the table to stand in front of her with his arms open saying, "Come hug me if you want."

She rose from her chair saying, "Yes, Samra.   Thank you.   Thank you." and rushed into his arms.

She hugged him briefly like a brother and pushing away from him slightly to look into his eyes, she said, "Samra, I want to kiss you. I want to kiss you like a woman kisses a man."

He looked down at her and slowly lowered his lips to meet hers in a soft touching kiss. They explored each other with their lips.   Soon, they began to return their kisses more intensely with their tongues in a growing passion. A great flame was beginning to light in both of them.

Samra tenderly, but firmly, pushed away from her saying, "Jena, I would dearly love to continue this, but I think our kiss would take a very long time to complete, and I must do my work tonight. I'm so sorry."

She looked up at him with a smile of disappointed understanding and said, "Yes, I know you have to work, and I want you to concentrate very, very hard, so you can come back and finish our kiss."

Laughing, he said, "I will I assure you. You've given me much more motivation."

She moved with a knowing smile toward the door and stopped to snicker when she observed the growing bulge in the front of his loincloth. He silently stood smiling at her; looking into her eyes. Looking him up and down, Jena smiled sultrily and said, "Is there anything else I can do for you, Samra?"

At that moment, he thought she looked especially radiant and beautiful and with a hearty laugh said, "No, just leave me the wine. I'll be fine."

Both of them started laughing, and they moved back into each others arms to caress each other for several more moments before finally kissing good night.

Before leaving she said, "Let me bring you some snacks and light your brazier. Would you like some cannabis for the fire?"

"Yes, thank you, Jena."

She returned with a fresh vase of wine and a tray of fruit and snacks with a small quantity of cannabis for the fire. Looking at him with a beaming smile, she said, "Good night, Samra."

"I don't want you to worry for me. All will be well. It wouldn't be the first time those who would do me harm became my prey. Good dreams, Jena."

After she closed the door, he had to use much of his mental power to calm his sexual energy and begin to focus on the many tasks at hand. A series of plans had already coalesced in his mind for the Avaris mission, so he thought he would start by concentrating on thwarting any possible assassination schemes. He had already decided he was going to simply assume the plot was real and work from there. He began by making lists of candidates for his military commander and personal guards. He compared them to what he thought many in the palace would assume to be his most probable choices.

He already had someone in mind for the commander of the warriors that Kalpoulis would never suspect to be chosen. The guards on his last mission were all excellent warriors, but he thought he couldn't risk selecting any of them. He would sooth any ruffled feathers on his return unless he found any of them were involved in the plot. There would be many surprises for those in the palace. He would do almost nothing normally on this mission.

After he made his final selections, he turned to how he could rid the large troop of three hundred and sixty warriors gathering at the palace of any possible assassins. He knew he wouldn't be able to purge the formation of all of the plotters, but he could, at least, reduce their numbers and weaken them. He spent quite a bit of time on this. Once he was satisfied he had a workable plan, he began imagining every stage of the mission. He started working his way through every possible scenario, contingency, and their alternatives attempting to step into the minds of those working to destroy him. He focused on analyzing the opportunities he would have to protect himself, disrupt the plot, and force the truth to be revealed. Finding out who was behind the plot was the most importance thing to him. He would plot against the plotters with this goal in mind. It was quite late by the time he decided to find his bed, but he soon calmly drifted into the deep restful sleep of a well prepared, confident lion.

Chapter 6

Palace Preparations

The next morning was a blur of hectic activity in the palace courtyard with the gathering and provisioning of the many incoming warriors.   Temporary facilities were being erected, and food was being prepared.   People were scurrying in every direction.   More and more men were arriving in the courtyard every hour and given their assignments.   When Samra came on the scene, he turned to the task of notifying the six men he had chosen to be members of his personal guard.   Messengers were sent out with orders for them to report to the palace as soon as possible.

He arranged to meet the temporary military commander assigned by the King's committee.   He was the least senior of the commanders available to him for the assignment.   His name was Telecaneos.   He was well known to him as highly competent and courageous; having worked with him on two other missions in the past.   Even though the assignments were much smaller than the Avaris one, they were still very dangerous, and he performed extremely well. When Samra picked him for the post, he knew everyone, including Telecaneos, would be very surprised.

Kalpoulis, and everyone else in the palace, was certain he would choose one of the two more senior, qualified, and politically connected men sitting in their luxury palace apartments awaiting their imminent selection. Samra knew there would be a sigh of relief by the leaders of the committees and probably the King and Queen if he did the expected thing. But he would choose no one Kalpoulis or anyone one else expected to be assigned to the post. Besides, Samra truly believed Telecaneos to be the most talented and capable of all his choices and would probably have selected him regardless of the situation.

They greeted with a warrior's hug.

"Telecaneos, I haven't seen you since you left for Pylos a few weeks ago. How was your trip?"

"All went very well, indeed. It's so beautiful there. I think I will make it my home when I retire."

"You must know someone very special there."

"Yes, I do. She is very special!"

Moving closer, Telecaneos whispered in his ear, "What do you know of the Avaris mission, Samra? I just overheard some of the committee members discussing how suicidal it was with the Egyptians attacking so quickly. I heard one of them say the only reason the mission was approved was because they all agreed it must, at least, be attempted before the city was sacked."

Samra laughed and said, "Yes, it is a perilous mission, and luck will be at a premium, but I certainly don't think it's suicidal. Besides you are the first to hear I have selected you for the mission's military commander, if you want it."

Telecaneos stepped back from him in surprise with his mouth open momentarily unable to respond. Samra stood there calmly observing his reaction with a smile. The commander regained his ability to speak by saying, "But, yes sir, I would love to be the warrior's commander for this mission especially with you as its leader!"

He briefly laughed and, after a pause, he stammered, "You don't know how much I appreciate this, sir."

"You will only appreciate it if we succeed."

"Yes sir. They say the reward in gold for success is very high. If I survive, I'll be able to return to Pylos and live quite well with my love. What are the obstacles we need to overcome?"

"There are many I assure you, but I have a plan with many contingencies I think could work quite well."

Telecaneos relaxed in the realization Samra was serious about his selection and began to talk to him like they normally did, as friends.

"I've never known you not have a plan with many contingencies on a mission, Samra. I'm sure now the great "Master of the Way" Samraleos himself will save my life and help me live in wealthy retirement in Pylos." he jokingly said with a grin.

Telecaneos laughed and continued with, "Seriously, sir, I thank the gods you are leading us.   If you weren't, I probably would have rejected the offer for command.   What are your instructions, sir?"

"Above all else, the military operation in Avaris requires shock and surprise to our potential adversaries combined with a severe reduction in their ability to aggressively respond.   It would be advisable to begin choosing men for an elite force of shock troops.   I know all of the warriors selected for this mission are elite, but we will need the very best of them to strike fiercely with awesome power and seize control so make your considerations on this theme."

"Yes sir.   I will consult with my captains here in Knossos and when we arrive in Kommos with the captains of the other warriors there."

"I want all of the warriors to gather in formation in the courtyard tomorrow morning with the troops assigned to each captain and sergeant forming up together as cohesive units. Each warrior will be individually inspected by me, my personal guards, or others assigned to the task.   No warrior not passing the process will be allowed to go on the mission, and the march will not begin until the entire process is complete.   So prepare them, but tell them nothing about an inspection.   The process, absolutely, must be a surprise, and it might save many of our lives.   This is an official King's secret."

"Yes sir, I will inform my captains immediately and order them to meet with their sergeants discreetly as soon as possible. They will be ready for you."

"As soon as you can arrange it, I want to begin personally interviewing your captains and sergeants to approve them for the mission.   Bring me your captains first and once that's complete we'll begin with the sergeants.   Tell them nothing."

"I'll notify you when they are gathered and ready.   Is there anything else, sir?"

"Not for now.   I have much to do.   But it was nice seeing you again.   I'm very happy you have decided to join us on the mission."

Telecaneos respectfully bowed saying, "Thank you, very much, sir.   It is my honor, and it's great to see you again, too."   Samra nodded to him with a smile in leaving as he turned and hurriedly walked off.

Telecaneos returned about a third of an hour later with his three captains for their interviews.   He walked over to Samra and stood at his side, slightly behind him, demonstrating his respect and deference to the captains.   They noticed this and, at a nod from the commander, quickly straightened standing at attention in front of him.   All of them had heard of Samraleos' reputation and knew he was a "Master of the Way", but none of them had ever met him before.

"Gentlemen, this is our leader, Samraleos." announced Telecaneos.

Samra looked at each of them squarely in the eyes and appraised the quality of their presence.   After many long moments, he began to slowly pace in front of them saying, "You have been called here for a personal interview to be conducted by me.   This is simply for me to get to know better those that will be commanding my warriors that are treasured far beyond gold by me and the King.   There will be times on this mission when the lives of those warriors will rest on the clarity of your thoughts and the wisdom of your judgments under great pressure."

Samra could see in their eyes that they were sometimes glancing in Telecaneos' direction.   He knew the commander was giving them slight visual cues to show the highest respect and obedience.   Samra wanted them to be keenly aware the lives of the warriors were to be protected and risked as little as possible.   In a more forceful voice of command, he said, "Is this clear to you?"

They all immediately nodded affirmatively and spoke up loudly in a jagged collection of "Yes sir" as the wide-eyed Telecaneos was exhorting them.

"Now, I will escort the first of you to the interview room to begin.   Come."

The nearest of them stepped forward and followed Samra out the door to an office down the hall; far beyond the others ability to overhear them.   The captains were all somewhat surprised by what Samra proposed to do.   None of them had ever been interviewed at the start of a mission before especially by a "Master of the Way".   But all of them were left in absolutely no doubt about who was firmly in command of the mission.   The remaining captains looked at Telecaneos with expressions of questioning concern on their faces.   Gazing at them silently, he said, "Take your seats and stay quiet.   We may be here for some time."

They took their seats and all of them sat in silence until they were each summoned by a messenger, one at a time.

Samra decided the previous evening that initially the interviews were to be general assessments of each man's mental composure and balance.   He would then begin to perform his standard probing for weaknesses that he usually did informally. But, this time, he would put a much greater emphasis on detecting the "Others". He would be looking for the characteristic behaviors first described to him long ago by his father. He would do this by presenting them with a set of questions and statements intended to provoke heightened emotional responses. He thought that removing any "Others" from the warriors would strengthen them, as a whole, even if they weren't involved with the plot. According to his father's theory, the "Others" would only create chaos at the very moment you needed them the most.

The interviews lasted about a half hour each with Samra first querying them about the members of their families and who they cared for the most. He was looking for someone the man was closest to in order to personalize his later "Other" inquiries. After completing this, he asked them where they lived, what their normal activities were, and especially if they knew anyone in the palace. Samra wanted to know everything about the people they associated with there and how often they frequented the complex.

Knowing their words would probably tell him very little if they were attempting to deceive him, he focused on observing the slightest of their verbal and physical responses. He arranged to be seated about three meters away from each subject. This gave him a clear full view of their entire body. He was looking for any body movements especially with their face and hands. More importantly, he observed how they formed their words during their verbal responses to his statements. If they hesitated, he tried to determine if it was due to having to work hard searching for the right words or if it was the normal reaction of someone under stress. If they continued to hesitate, he would observe their hand movements to see if they became more agitated as they tried to find the words. If they repeatedly responded with short, muted, dull, unemotional responses to his inciting comments, he would suspect they might be one of the "Others" and reject them from the mission.

He wore a mask of deception and carefully picked the best moments to incite them. He did his utmost to maximize their surprise from his position of credibility. He would say things like;

"It has come to my attention your sister is to be arrested for stealing from her employer." or

"I'm sorry to inform you that your mother has been found beaten and raped?"

He would swiftly carry through with each scenario to further incite them. When his subjects finally realized his lies were untrue, it angered them. They thought it was a ludicrous waste of time and were insulted with his outrageous statements. But after Samra completed each interview and determined the person had passed the process, he said, "I must apologize for my audacious comments. I was attempting to determine your mental acuity using a theory on the workings of the mind I've been studying."

When their interview was complete, Samra gave each of them a brief introduction into the theory of the "Others" and how to use its techniques for the well being of their warriors and their own personal use. As he expected, Samra did not detect any problems with the captains. When the last captain's interview ended, he sent him into the adjacent office with the others while Samra performed the same procedure on Telecaneos.

Samra called all the captains back into his office to rejoin Telecaneos and said, "You need to study these interrogation techniques very closely. You will be interviewing your sergeants looking for the same things I was looking for in you.

Also, you will be instructing your sergeants, if they pass their interviews, in the uses of these same techniques, so they will be able to conduct their own examinations. Are there any questions?"

Silence and dismayed confusion reigned.

"Very well, I will now begin to instruct you in much greater detail on these techniques. I will then perform two more interviews in your presence with your sergeants to insure your grasp of how it is done. Feel free, at any time, to ask any questions you may have."

Once the second sergeant passed his interview and left to join the first in isolation in a nearby office, Samra asked them again if they had any questions. There was still no response.

"Excellent, you will now complete the interviews of the remaining sergeants, and then I'll give you your final instructions. There are enough of you. It shouldn't take much longer. Let me know if you detect anything or come across any suspicious information, and I'll take over the interview to instruct you further. When the interviews are complete, send a messenger for me. Everyone is to remain secluded in the office until I return."

Some time later, Samra was summoned from his office. He was informed nothing unusual had been heard or detected, and all the sergeants had passed. He brought all of them together and told them, "This procedure and anybody's knowledge in it is an official King's secret."

"You captains need to thoroughly complete the education of your sergeants in these mental techniques. All of you and those you recruit and train must be meticulously prepared to interview the entire troop at first light tomorrow morning."

The warriors must be processed rapidly, so you need to select a group of interviewers that can best wear a mask of deception and believably incite their subjects for the initial interviews. These should be as brief as possible by immediately subjecting each man to an intense emotional attack after subtly soliciting information on their loved ones. Only those responding inappropriately will then be sent on for further scrutiny and examination.

We need thirty bowmen to secure the formation in the morning, and we need many more interviewers, so I suggest you combine your efforts there. We can't delay the march any more than necessary. There will be offices available throughout the palace for each interviewer. Train them well. I leave any further details to you.

Some of you may think this is silly or a pointless waste of time, but I assure you it is not! Remember, the ones we are looking for are few, so don't get discouraged if we don't immediately detect anything. Your secrecy and diligence in this matter could save many of our lives. I leave it in your hands. Telecaneos must see to his command now. Be ready and be sharp! Remember to send for me if you detect anything."

A strong chorus of "Yes Sir" preceded Samra and Telecaneos leaving the office. About two hours later, a messenger arrived requesting his presence. When he arrived, he was escorted to another office further down the hall. Telecaneos was standing outside the door waiting for him. The commander quietly told him, "Samra, I think we've detected one of your "Others". They're still interviewing him and awaiting your arrival."

Telecaneos calmly opened the door, and they quietly walked in. One of the captains was talking to the suspected "Other" and ignored their entrance. After listening to the man's answer to his previous question, the captain looked over to Samra and asked, "Is there anything you wish of us, sir?"

"No, carry on."

The captain continued with another follow-on question. The man expressed very muted and dulled emotions when most people would have been highly agitated. Once he was satisfied he could seamlessly continue the interrogation, he waited for a silent moment and called to the captain saying, "Let me sit in for a time."

Taking his seat Samra began to definitively demonstrate to Telecaneos and the others the characteristics he was looking for. When he finished, they were all convinced Samra's "Others" were something quite real.

Word swiftly spread to the other captains and sergeants about the first "Other" discovered. Satisfied his demonstration was insightful Samra rose from his chair to say, "This interview is complete. Detain this man for further interrogation. Continue with those that remain and be as effective and efficient as you can."

He waved for Telecaneos to follow him, and they walked from the room into the hallway.

"Have all the "Others" and any other suspicious individuals detained separately in isolation in the palace indefinitely. Use this first "Other" for the training of all the new interviewers. I think the process should move more quickly now."

"Yes sir."

Telecaneos lowered and shook his head chuckling softly and said, "I hope you don't mind if I say this, Samra."

"No, go ahead. Anything you wish."

"I have always been amazed at some of the things you do to make a mission successful, and I have learned much from you. But, today, you showed me something I would have never, ever imagined being true. It puts light on some things in my own life I have always found curious. Thank you very much, sir."

"You can thank my father, Karasos. He was the first to theorize the "Others". I didn't believe it was true for a very long time, but it's becoming more and more undeniable as confirmation keeps building."

"Tell me, Samra. Are these "Others" really as dire as you think them to be?"

"Apparently, yes. I'm beginning to believe they are the bosom and cradle of all the evil in humanity. They look the part but don't seem to be humans like you and me at all. The difference between men and women is nothing compared to the difference between them and us. They're something else altogether."

There was a long pause between them as Telecaneos pondered Samra's words.

"As many of the people as possible should be informed of this new knowledge." the commander said.

"I've been thinking about that, and there are some big questions that need to be studied. It will have to wait until after our return. I will need to demonstrate the truth of it to the committees and the King and Queen. Perhaps, then, something can be done to protect the people."

"I hope this interlude hasn't delayed your preparations, commander.   Make sure everything is ready for the morning. We need it to run smoothly.   I must see to other matters now."

Telecaneos straightened himself and said, "Yes sir.   All will be ready."

They nodded in leaving and went to attend to their duties.   As Telecaneos walked to his command, he broke out in a broad grin and joyfully thought, "There's no doubt I will survive this mission now.   Pylos is assured!   I wonder what other marvels Samraleos has in store for us."

By this time, two of Samra's personal guards had arrived and reported to his office.   They were waiting fully equipped outside his office door when he returned.   He knew them well, and they greeted him very warmly; vociferously expressing their gratitude for being selected for the mission.   They knew their reward in gold would be great, but the prestige of being selected was considerable.   He waved to one of the palace guards in the hall he had instructed earlier and escorted the two of them into his office.   He told them he was going to interview each of them, one at a time, before giving them their orders.

"Whoever wants to start first take the chair in front of me?   The interview is confidential, so the other one will have to leave and be escorted down the hall to a room to wait his turn.   Please close the door behind you."

As they arrived, the palace guards directed each of Samra's remaining four guards into the designated waiting room to await their interview.   Samra performed his, now, almost standard interview with each of them in turn.   As he suspected from his previous knowledge of them, they all passed their examination. Not long after he completed the last interview, the midday feast was just beginning to be served.   He gathered all of them together saying, "Men, I have a private table reserved for us. It's in the garden nearest the northwest corner of the palace. We can be served and eat in peace well away from any prying ears while I tell you of our mission."

After their meal and drinks were served, Samra directed several of the palace guards to secure the area well around the table. They were to be left undisturbed while they feasted. He told them that after their meal, they were to report to Telecaneos for interrogation training. When they completed their training, they were to return to him for further instructions. He then began to tell them everything about the Avaris mission and its opportunities and risks. This took quite a while with him only occasionally stopping to enjoy his food and wine.

"There is something else for you. I have reason to believe there will be an attempt to murder me on this mission. You will all have to be keenly alert to this threat. This is one of the reasons I subjected you to your interviews earlier, and why you will be receiving more training on how to administer these interviews to others when we are done here. Telecaneos will give you complete instructions on what I'm looking for. Now, let's enjoy our feast and this wonderful day among the greenery and flowers."

As they were finishing, Samra called one of the palace guards over and informed him his guards were to be directed to the commander Telecaneos when they were ready. The guard acknowledged his instructions and stepped away to wait.

"Men, I need you to be at your most diligent for your interrogation training."

He lifted his vessel of wine into the air and toasted loudly, "Here's to our success and wealth." with loud cheers shouted by all.

Later, after his guards returned from their training, they were all quietly talking among themselves about what they had just learned. After entering his office, he directed them to sit in front of his desk. He could see the questions in their eyes and invited them to ask. They proceeded to have a lengthy, detailed discussion on the "Others".

"Men, I want you to secure your equipment and mingle with the other warriors as if you were one of them in search of anything you can find."

Samra felt his presence was no longer needed at the palace. It was time to meet with the civil authorities to give them his instructions for the child murder case while he was gone. He instructed them to position small surveillance teams at specific strategic locations in the district especially in the vicinity of the outer roadway to monitor any unusual activity and to aggressively continue their efforts in detecting and capturing the killer. They told him they were already discreetly deploying more people into the areas he had previously designated and would station their best teams in the new locations he indicated. After their wishes of luck and farewells, Samra left to attend to his household.

He walked into the workshop to find Thalion sitting near the furnace. He was preparing to pour a few new tool castings using recycled bronze. He told him what he had discussed with Jena the evening before; she would be in charge of the household and what was to be done with the household if anything happened to him. Thalion was profusely thankful and very happy about everything. Almost dancing, he took him into a joyful hug. Jena and Thalion had become good friends over the last year, and he knew very well Jena was much more suited to the business and management end of the household.

He was ecstatic she was the one to be doing it; much to his profit.

"Thalion, I think there will be an attempt on my life during this mission. I don't think there is danger for you or Jena here, but I'm not certain. It would be best if you prepared yourself for anything that might happen. Someone wants me dead, and they could try to interfere with you here. Always keep your weapons nearby, and protect Jena as you would your son. If you decide to shutdown the shop while I'm gone, it means nothing to me."

"Samra, you know how I feel. I will make sure everything is well here. Don't concern yourself at all about us while you are gone."

"Thanks, Thalion. I know you'll do your very best. Now, I'll let you return to your castings."

"Samra, I've arranged for there to be a stout donkey ready to be packed at first light in the morning."

He nodded his thanks and said, "I'll talk with you later."

He walked up to his apartment to find Jena sitting on her knees on a floor mat packing the last of the items for his travel kit. She looked up and smiled at him as he entered.

"Samra, is there anything special you need for your trip?"

"No, Jena, just my standard kit as usual."

She had worked throughout the day preparing and assembling everything he needed - clean bedding, body oil, antiseptics, opium, and all of his many weapons. She had done this four times before and his mission kit was almost ready to go. She rose to her feet and faced him with one of her striking smiles. At least, he thought they were striking.

He moved towards her and offered her his hands, and they fell into a warm embrace kissing passionately. He loved the softness of her skin and lips and indulged himself. Jena pushed slightly from him asking, "Do you have to work very hard this evening, Samra?"

"No not at all."

"Do you think we might be able to finish our kiss?"

"Oh, yes. I would love to finish our kiss."

His grin turned into a good laugh as they embraced.

"Why don't we have a wonderful dinner, and then perhaps we could have a bath together. Would you like that?" he said.

"Yes, I'd like that very much."

They tightened their embrace and kissed again briefly.

"I'll go get things ready for dinner and leave you, so you can get some work done until then. Okay, Samra?"

Happily, he said, "Yes, whatever you wish."

Samra went to rest on his large oak bed and soon fell asleep. Later, Jena's knock at the door woke him, and he called for her to come in. She entered with a large tray filled with food. After she set it down on the table, she went back to the door to retrieve a second tray with a vase of wine and cups. After they had been eating for a time, Samra informed her of telling

Thalion about the household arrangements and the possible threat to the villa; warning her to be on her guard.

"Jena, please take Thalion with you for protection whenever you leave the villa just to be safe. I would worry greatly, if you didn't."

Caressing the side of his face with her hand, she said, "Don't worry, Samra, we'll take care of any problems here, and I promise to be extra safe, so you don't have to worry."

He took her hand and tenderly kissed it.

"That makes me feel much better."

They sat and enjoyed talking about things that ranged far and wide as they shared their wine when, out of the blue, she said, "Samra, I was hoping that sometime after your return you might teach me how to draw the sounds on parchment like you do to record your thoughts. Do you think it would be very difficult?"

"I don't see why. You have an excellent memory, and that's all you really need for it. The scribe's script is simply a collection of drawn symbols where each symbol represents a simple sound we all make with our voice. By grouping and arranging the symbols, you can form the sounds into the words that have meaning to all of us. You just need to memorize the symbols with their sounds."

"If you learned to draw the scribe's script, you could share your knowledge and thoughts with others much more widely as well as use it to your profit in business."

As she listened intently to his words, it always amazed her how he would speak so simply and clearly about things many people thought were far beyond their comprehension.

"He is an enemy of confusion." she thought.

"Yes, I think it would be very good for business. But if it's just a matter of memory, shouldn't all the people learn it from an early age in some organized way?   Wouldn't it be a great benefit for everyone and help spread the word of the "Way of Nature"?"

He laughed softly saying, "I agree.   They've debated it for as long as I can remember in the committees.   Almost everyone in the palace thinks it would be a wonderful thing, but they argue about how it could be done without a great cost in gold.   Many say the cost would be far too great and the benefits small and well into the future.   Some in the committees don't think the people are even capable of learning anything so abstract and complex.   They think it would be a waste of the treasury's gold. The religious leaders don't want the responsibility of continually teaching the people something that has nothing to do with their conception of the gods."

"I realize many would argue the children are needed for their labor, but couldn't they be taught these things when the crops don't require them?   If they were given the opportunity, the "Way of Nature" could become knowledge for all of the people."

"We need more people like you on the committees."

She chuckled and said, "I think I'll stick with learning to draw the sounds for now."

After a pause, she said, "Let me clean up here, and I'll get Thalion to bring the bath water whenever you're ready."

He sat quietly drinking from his cup of wine as he watched Jena move out the door and leave with the last tray from the table. He thought, "She is such a great beauty, but it's matched by her keen and powerful intellect. Her innate compassion for all is completely the opposite of the "Others"."

Alone his thoughts drifted and remerged. He wondered if the "Others" had always been a part of the people and what could be done to neutralize their insidious evil. The solution to the "Others" would be complicated and difficult, but the people must be informed of their presence and how to deal with them. He nodded silently agreeing with himself that he must work to accomplish this in the future.

He regained his focus on the present and considered the coming events at the palace tomorrow morning. He tried to think of anything he may have missed, but he soon concluded that everything was complete and set into motion. All he could do now was to wait for first light and see how well his team had accomplished their assignments. Freed of any concerns for the moment, his thoughts returned to his coming bath with Jena, and he smiled in anticipation of her coming embrace.

Soon, she returned to tell him his bath water was ready whenever he was. "Yes, Jena, tell him to bring it up. I'll get ready."

He stood and walked toward the dresser, near his hanging garments, and started to remove his shoulder wrap and kilt. He attached them to wooden hangers and sat down on the chair by the dresser to remove his shoes. He stood naked ready for his bath as Thalion entered with the vases of hot bath water. Samra stood watching his progress as he waited for Jena. When the water began to flow from the shower vase, he immediately stepped under it and began spreading it onto his skin. When Thalion was done, Jena entered the room as she normally would for any other bath she had ever given him. She was carrying a soap bar and towels with another one of her glowing smiles. Smiling warmly, he watched her intently as he stood before her with the water cascading down his body.

He noticed she didn't have a towel wrapped around her hair as she normally did but had her hair tied back on her head as she prepared to enter the bath. There was a quiet tension in the air as she slowly removed her loincloth, and he gazed on her stunning physical beauty. She walked toward him with the soap bar in her hand and stooped down to begin washing his feet as she normally did. He lifted his right foot to assist her. When she was finished with both of his feet, she began to soap up and down his calves and thighs. He thought how wonderful it was to be bathed by her. She gestured for him to turn around, so she could apply the soap to his buttocks and worked up a thick lather in cleaning him.

She tapped on his buttocks for him to turn around and was startled to see his erection waving in her face. She quickly stood and gleefully looked up into his eyes as if she had just received a joyful surprise. She looked down at his erection and chuckled lightly. Looking back up at him, she smiled and joked, "Well, you're human after all."

He started to respond, but she stopped him by putting her fingers to his lips. She hugged him lightly pushing her body into his erection and kissed him on the chest. She slowly pushed away from him to look into his eyes. He was smiling and put his arms around her; kissing her softly on the lips. It was a kiss of love. The flame grew quickly and they were soon fiercely embracing each other; their mutual pent-up passions unleashed and igniting. Still wet, they made their way to his bed and made love like an ecstatic roaring fire long into the evening. Thalion could faintly hear them as he lay in his workshop bed. With amusement, he wondered, "What took them so long?"

Later, in a light moment as they rested, Samra laughingly told her, "It was one of my greatest mental achievements controlling my erection while you bathed me."

She took a sip of wine and giggled, "I thought you found me unattractive or repulsive in some way all this time."

"No. No, you're much too powerful for me." he said as he put his arm around her and pulled her to him.

He kissed her and she returned it with passion and love. Finally, he said, "Jena, I must sleep. The sun's first light will be coming soon, and tomorrow will be a very long day."

He lay back on his pillow and she put her head on his chest with a smile. She thought, "Well, these "Master of the Way" guys are just men after all, but they are very special men, indeed."

That evening was their first night as lovers. Both of them hoped it would not be their last.

They blinked open their eyes just before dawn and briefly exchanged cuddles and kisses on waking. Quickly they were up and began preparing. Thalion was standing near the bottom of the stairs with the donkey waiting to be packed. Jena began carrying the weapons and different items of his kit downstairs for Thalion to securely pack onto the animal as Samra dressed. Within a few minutes, he was ready and hugged Thalion in farewell. He gave Jena a passionate, loving kiss goodbye and was off to the palace. The sunrise's light glowed above the high eastern hill as he made his way. As Jena and Thalion waved to him with their goodbyes, they both worried he might not return and they would never see him again. Thalion was much more confident than Jena, but he couldn't help feeling the thought.

There was a part of Thalion that wished he could go with Samra, but Jena and Antoneos needed him here. When he was out of sight, Thalion walked into the workshop to practice with his weapons which were many. He wanted to try out the new lead weights he had cast that were shaped like oblong river stones with his sling shot.

Jena walked up the stairs to her apartment and latched shut her door and window shutters. It was dark and cool inside as she lit one of her oil lamps on the table and moved to lie down on her large bed. At that moment, she felt empty with a sadness building as she acutely felt the loss of him just when their love was blossoming. Tears began to well up in her eyes as she quietly prayed for his safe return. She then rose to fluff her pillows and turned on her side to soon fall into a deep sleep.

Chapter 7

Fleet of Warriors

Arriving at the palace, Samra sat to have the morning meal with his personal guards and was joined by Telecaneos and his captains.

"What's the status, commander?"

"All of your orders have been carried out, and we are well prepared, sir. Everything for the succession of interviews is in readiness. We arranged for all of those already processed to take lodging well separate from the rest of the warriors. They are all sworn to secrecy. The warriors should be completely unsuspecting and unaware when they are interviewed. Their surprise will be at a maximum."

"Good. What of the other arrangements?"

"The bowmen are ready, and we informed the palace guards to evacuate the ground level areas all around the courtyard for the safety of the people from stray bow fire.   People will be allowed to observe the formation from the second and higher floors only. Sir, we stand ready awaiting your further orders."

"You always were a master of management, Telecaneos.   I commend you and all of you for your diligence. This should be a very interesting day."

After the meal, the commander's captains ordered their sergeants to assemble the warriors into a tight column of fifteen men abreast in the middle of the courtyard to ready themselves for inspection.   A large temporary wooden speaking platform had been erected in front of them.

The gathering warriors were dressed in full battle gear with a back pack and extra quivers of arrows.   Their light, tightly-woven wicker and oxhide shield was shaped like a big figure eight.   It's weight hung by a leather strap from their shoulder. The large shield was held and moved in front of them with their forearm fitted into a leather casing on the inside of it.   This allowed their whole arm and hand to move freely.   They could fight with both hands.   For close-in fighting, they carried a sword and dagger sheathed on their weapons belt.   Their two meter long throwing javelin with its long sharp bronze blade was intended to kill at distances of up to fifty or sixty meters. Beyond the range of their javelins, they used their sling shots armed with smooth river stones or oblong lead weights which were highly lethal.

The principle weapon they used for fighting at a distance was their two meter long composite bow made of wood, the bone of wild goats, and sinew with an outer veneer of bark bonded together with fish or hide glue.   Unstrung, the bow was shaped like a slightly curved flat arc.   The bow string was made of water resistant strips of treated animal hide.   The large, highly tensioned bow was designed for maximum range at sea when it was pulled by the tremendous arm strength of the warriors. Some of the warriors had practically grown up rowing the heavy oak oars in the rough open sea, and their muscles bulged well beyond normal especially their arms.

They used a relatively heavy arrow with a large piercing bronze tip that maintained its speed in the air; extending its range at sea. It was essentially a mini-javelin that was devastating when it fell with full force on the enemy. Many of the warriors could hit targets at four hundred meters or more. Their bronze arrowheads were treated with scorpion poison. If an intended victim wasn't killed outright by the sharp bronze, the poison would give them a particularly gruesome, painful, and contorted death from paralysis and asphyxiation within a half an hour. Straw wadding could be tied to the arrowheads, dipped in a combustible pine tar mixture, and lit as torches. The warriors carried two extra quivers of arrows strapped to the sides of their back packs.

They wore a helmet of woven strips of leather, to double its thickness, covered with flat, slightly curved boar's tusks tied tightly together and attached to the underlying leather using two small holes drilled into each end of the tusks. Some of the warriors wore a fitted woolen liner on the inside of their helmets. Boar's tusk side-flaps were attached to the helmets to provide some protection for the side of the head. The flaps had straps that were tied under the chin to secure the helmet to the head. The warrior's uniform comprised a woolen loincloth and fitted shirt with sturdy leather shoes. The torso was protected by body armor made of many layers of dense white linen glued and hot pressed to both sides of an inner oxhide core. It was very light and extremely effective against arrow strikes.

As the first sergeant in the formation moved his men into position near the platform, he sharply commanded his squad of thirty men to assemble into two tight rows of fifteen about five meters from and centered on the speaker's podium.   The sergeant formed the first row by setting the first warrior into position with the others assembling in a line to his left.   After he walked along and straightened the row, he had them move back and to the right into what he judged to be the correct position.   The squad's remaining fifteen men then began arranging themselves at arm's length behind those in front of them.   Once the sergeant gave a signal his men were properly in place, the process continued with the next sergeant's squad until all of the warriors, not withheld for other duties, were assembled and the formation was complete.   Each squad's sergeant stood to the right of their position in the formation.   There appeared to be twenty one rows of men bringing the assembly to three hundred and fifteen warriors.

It was a stirring, rousing sight to all those looking on it from above on the crowded balconies.   The King and Queen and most, if not all, of the top committee members were present for the spectacle.   All of the balconies were lined with throngs of people, but no one could be seen at ground level.   One of Telecaneos' captains stepped up onto the podium where he could be clearly seen by all and piercingly commanded, "Attention!"

To this they all deafeningly banged there spears on their shields and set themselves straight at attention.   The thunderous sound echoed in the courtyard.   As the people marveled at the grand sight, and the captain stood silently at the podium, two separate lines of fifteen warriors with their bows in hand suddenly streamed at a full run into the courtyard on each side of the formation swiftly taking up positions around its perimeter.   As each warrior reached their pre-assigned positions, they turned toward the formation and menacingly put their loaded bows at the ready.   There was a wave of astonishment among the spectators, and the formation wavered at attention in surprise and concern.

The captain waited for all thirty of the warriors to be fully set in position before commanding the formation back to attention with a sharp, blaring yell. Once he was satisfied with their compliance, he promptly turned and stepped down from the platform. Then Samra calmly stepped up onto the podium to address them.

Speaking in a firm loud voice, he said, "Men, I am Samraleos your leader and "Master of the Way". You are about to go on a mission for the King where success must be absolutely insured. With this in mind, I want you all to come to rest."

He waited several moments for them to settle themselves and said, "I now call on each sergeant to thoroughly inspect their warriors for those that are unknown to them. Each of you must now attain your highest state of alertness. Look at the men around you for anyone that does not belong and report it to your sergeant immediately."

Most of the warriors had lived and trained together for some time and should have known each other well. As Samra started to instruct them on the disposition of any unknowns, a warrior abruptly bolted from near the back of the formation. Breaking free, he immediately began running fast toward the northwest exit of the courtyard. He swiftly threw his spear and his dagger on the run at the nearby bowmen to make his escape. A second later, the man stumbled face first onto the ground to his death with three arrows piercing his back, buttocks, and left thigh. A loud gasp of shock and screams rose from the crowds on the balconies. The man had not struck or injured any of the bowmen.

Everyone in the formation strained to see what was going on in a wave of noisy astonishment. Worry gripped them all as word quickly spread to those that hadn't seen the incident. The noise from the spectators rumbled and chattered filling the courtyard loudly. On seeing the man fall Samra instantly thought, "The plot is real."

He tried to quiet the warriors and spectators by raising his arms high above him and shouting, but he was drowned out badly. He looked to Telecaneos and indicated to have the horns sounded. The overpowering horns sounded twice in succession before order began to be restored. As the courtyard quieted, and the sergeants brought the warriors back to order, he shouted, "My warriors! My warriors! I say this to any other traitors among us. The same fate will be yours, if you don't surrender immediately! Men, I command you to resume your examination of those around you. This must be done with diligence!"

He could see a warrior moving from within the formation slowly making his way to its edge. Once he was clear, warriors immediately approached him. He quickly dropped his spear and shield and removed his weapons belt letting it fall on the ground as he raised his hands in surrender. The warriors knew something serious was in the air and were intensely searching each other. A few moments later, there was some erratic yelling and movement. Two other men were seized by those around them, stripped of their weapons, and removed from the formation. The sergeants had the three warriors thoroughly searched. Their hands were bound behind them, and they were handed over to guards ready to escort them to their interrogators.

The warriors had fallen into an utter quiet of disbelieving amazement. None of them including those observing from the balcony had ever witnessed anything like this before. He shouted, "Men, continue the diligent scrutiny of your fellows. This is not a time to relax your guard."

Samra turned to step down from the platform to observe the prisoners. He wanted to see if he could recognize any of them. As he stood before the bound men, he looked closely at each of their faces. He had never seen any of them before. He asked the guards if they could recognize them, and they all shook their heads negatively.

Returning to the podium, he said, "Sergeants, indicate to your captains when all your men are accounted for as legitimate and authorized."

When the captains signaled Telecaneos that every warrior had been identified and the search was complete, Samra told him to have the prisoners paraded through the formation to see if anyone could recognize them. When that was done, he was to start the interviewing process.

The three prisoners were slowly paraded, about two meters apart, past every man in the formation one row at a time. Once each row had completed witnessing the prisoners, it was released for the next step in Samra's process – the "Other" interview. Palace escorts took the men to their assigned interrogators. None of them knew anything of what was about to take place. A feeling of confused compliance sweep through the warriors, and a building murmur started among the spectators. Only one of the prisoners was recognized as a criminal recently released from forced labor in the stone quarries. The three of them were taken into separate offices for interrogation.

The "Other" interviews of the warriors went smoothly and took a little over an hour to complete. Once a warrior was approved, he was escorted outside the palace and assembled in the gardens to eliminate any contact with those that had not yet entered the process. There were eleven warriors who caught the attention of the interviewers and detained as suspects or "Others". Ten of those were designated "Others". Those that failed were brought to be interrogated by pairs of Samra's personal guards in the presence of the civil authorities for their study. They only called for Samra's presence if they observed anything new that might be of interest to him. Replacements were quickly found and processed like everyone else.

When all the warriors and replacements had been interviewed, they were marched back into the courtyard to reassemble in formation and called to attention. Samra took the podium and said, "Men, I want to apologize for our treatment of you. But we have taken some from among you that would have eaten at our insides and torn us all down, if they could. Only you are the true lions of the kingdom!"

A wild roar of approval from the warriors filled the courtyard, and the throngs of spectators cheered madly. Samra lifted his hands to quiet them and said, "Now, you can fight in confidence knowing you have only brothers at your back. I would fight in honor along side any one of you!"

The warriors again roared in wild raucous approval at Samra's words. Waiting for the boisterous yelling and screams to quiet enough for him to be heard, he said, "My final words to you before we march are that if you stay alert and do your duty success will be ours!"

Samra waved to them and calmly stepped from the platform amid a wildly cheering roar from everyone present. A long loud chorus of frenzied thunder erupted from the warriors with them shouting and banging their spears and shields. The warriors and many of the spectators started chanting, "Samra! Samra! Samra! ..."

The warrior's confidence and morale couldn't have been any higher than at that moment. The captains signaled to their sergeants to bring them to order. It took quite some time to get everyone under control and ready them for the march. Finally, they began to stride away from the palace in a column of three men abreast. They were heading west for the nearest flagstone roadway leading south to Kommos.

After observing the events of the morning, the Queen dryly commented to the King, "This Samraleos puts on quite a show." and began to chuckle.

The King laughed and said adamantly, "Yes, he does! I feel as if the Avaris gold is already safely in the treasury."

Kalpoulis was amused and buoyed that Samra's brilliant performance was making him look like a genius. Synboliki's mask appeared mirthful and approving, but inwardly she was shaken by what he had done. She realized he had probably eliminated some of her assassins' right in front of her eyes. Her hopes for the plot were dimmed, but she knew there would still be others among them. She thought, "There's still a good chance for success, and now I won't have to pay out as much gold."

Samra walked out into the gardens with his guards to watch the warriors marching out of the palace courtyard when four men were escorted to him claiming to have orders from Kalpoulis. As Samra looked them up and down, one of his guards passed him a scroll of parchment showing Kalpoulis' signet ring impression in its wax seal. Opening it, the orders declared the men were intelligence couriers with memorized instructions for certain officials in Avaris. They were to return information from those officials back to Knossos. There was no doubt the orders were authentic.

Without any hesitation, Samra said, "You'll need to report to the commander, Telecaneos, so he'll know of your presence for your ship assignments.   Welcome to the march.   Just fall in at the end of the line."

The apparent leader of the four took a step forward and bowed to Samra saying, "Yes sir.   Thank you, sir.   We should have been here sooner to introduce ourselves.   Please forgive us for our delay."

Samra simply nodded and waved him on.   As he watched them leave, his suspicions soared.   The timing of their entrance with the sealed orders from his superior Kalpoulis allowed them to join the march without any scrutiny.   They had the well-muscled look of warriors.   He called his guards close to him and asked them if they recognized any of the four.   None of his guards had ever seen any of them before.

"Have them watched very closely on the march and in Kommos.   When we're at the docks, I'll have them assigned to different ships in pairs and put under surveillance.   I want them to have somebody to talk to in case their words give them away."

If they were assassins, he thought he could use them to find the truth.   Working on that assumption, he began to plot against them.   As the couriers fell in at the end of the formation, Samra and his guards waited a few moments and joined the column about thirty meters to the rear.   Once the entire column was well on the main road south, Telecaneos ordered one of his captains to have the horn sounded to command the formation to march at a faster pace to help make up for their delay in starting out.

It was a gorgeous bright, sunny day at the cusp of spring, and the wild flowers were blooming in striking carpets of color across the lush green fields.   The column was treated like a grand parade as they passed through the towns and villages along the way. Marches like this were rare, especially at this time of the year, and were great theatre for the people. In Arkhanes, thousands lined the roadway cheering and tossing flowers on them. Many were handed refreshing drinks as they passed.

They arrived in Kalathiana only about a half of an hour late. Everything was prepared and ready for the warrior's expected arrival. Great quantities of food and drinks were placed on feasting tables near both sides of the roadway. There were many long wooden benches with seating arranged in the grassy fields for their comfort. The food and wine was excellent and everyone got their fill. There was much talk of what had happened that morning in the courtyard with rumors running rampart throughout their ranks. Samra, using his guards, deliberately planted a false rumor about Canaanite spies being taken into custody. Part of the rumor was that all of the spies had been caught at the palace. He did this in hopes of putting any remaining plotters off their guard and to alleviate any worries they may have that he was aware of their presence.

At the sound of the drum, the warriors were assembled and the march south to Phaistos began anew. Their marching pace brought them into the great city before sunset. There were many officials, escorts, and servants awaiting them. The warriors were first taken to their sleeping quarters near the palace to stow their gear before bringing them to the feasting area. Phaistos was a large city of over one hundred thousand people. It filled the plains below its beautiful palace complex on a hill. The palace wasn't quite as large as the one in Knossos, but it was still very impressive. The accommodations for the warriors were quite elaborate with everyone eating well and being entertained with music and dancing in the fire and torch light. The captains and sergeants made sure none of them overindulged and soon sent them to sleep comfortably in their beds after their long march.

It was another sunny morning, and their short march to Kommos took them about an hour. Once the open sea came into view and they marched closer, they saw the extraordinary sight of the twelve huge long ships moored at their piers. The dockyards were a scene of organized chaos with preparations for the voyage frantically under way. Many of the ships were being provisioned and inspected with hundreds of men hurriedly working on the rigging, loading cargo, supplies, etc. You could see several inspectors walking back and forth on the docks going through their lists, and waving their arms; correcting this or ordering that.

Each one of the long ships was a mastery of craftsmanship in wood using bronze tools especially with their large two-handled saws that were almost two meters long and a third of a meter wide. The Admiral's ship was the newest and biggest in the fleet, but all of them were nearly as large. It was thirty five meters long with a beam of six meters at its widest. There were twenty five oars on each side of the ship for a total of fifty. The ship's complement was one hundred and twenty fully provisioned men, not including the ship master and his team of specialists, with a cargo capacity of about twenty-five metric tons.

They were constructed by first chopping down a single tall, sturdy Cypress tree and stripping off its branches. The log was then dragged to the shipyard by a team of oxen. After being laid on a smooth flat working surface, it was stripped of its bark. When the log was clean, the shipwright marked where he wanted it cut along its length. A team of men carved it with their sharp bronze axes and saws; shaping it to nearly its final form. The upward sloping curves of the bow and stern were bent into shape using heat and steam. After the keel attained its final shape, a long cleanly sawn plank of Cypress was 'edge-joined' to each side of it. They chiseled out deep rectangular matching slots (mortises) along the length of the keel and the length of one of the edges of the plank. Flat rectangular pieces of wood (tenons or tongues) were cut to fit snugly into the matching slots. When the plank fit onto the tenons sticking out of the slots in the keel, the joins were filled with a mixture of resins.

Round holes were cut, using a bronze bow drill, through the plank and keel into the top and bottom of each tenon sitting inside the matching slots. After sealing resin was painted into the drill holes, round wooden pegs were hammered from the inside of the hull into the top and bottom holes of each tenon locking the plank to the keel. Very little caulking was needed with edge-joined planking. When the ship slid into the water from its dry dock, the sea water would swell the cypress and create a water tight seal on the seams.

With the first plank in place, they added the second plank by edge-joining it to the exposed edge of the first using the same process. The mortise slots were cut about every twenty five centimeters. They repeated this process adding plank after plank on both sides of the keel to build up the shell of the hull. Once the shell reached a desired height, the inner bracing frames were constructed, and later the decking and rowing benches were installed. When it was complete, the outside of the hull would be covered in tightly woven, treated linen and coated in fir or pine resin. The surface was then whitened with lime, painted white, and decorated with beautiful scenes of the sea with blue dolphins, sea birds, etc.

The sturdy oak mast was about sixteen meters tall and sat in a reinforced structure that allowed for its insertion and removal. It was secured into position with rigging made of strong hemp ropes. The mast had a single boom of about ten meters in length to hold the top of the sail. The center of the boom was held to the mast with a thick strong ring of rope loosely wrapped around the shaft of the mast. This allowed the boom to freely pivot about the mast in the wind and be easily raised or lowered with ropes running through a bronze fixture on the masthead. The orientation of the boom and sail in the wind could be controlled from the deck with ropes allowing the ship to tack (take a zigzag course) quite well into a head wind. The sail itself was made entirely of densely woven wool; treated with oils for waterproofing. The oars were carved from oak.

Telecaneos left the disposition of the warriors to his captains while he accompanied Samra and his guards to Kommos' palace to report their arrival and meet the Admiral of the fleet, Cronymartis. On the way, Samra told the commander, "There are four couriers with sealed orders from Kalpoulis that joined the march late. I have my guards keeping a close eye on them for now, but I want them to be split up in pairs for the voyage and placed under surveillance. Be mindful of this when their ship assignments are made."

"I'll inform the captains as soon as I'm through with our meeting."

They were expected by the authorities, and, once they made their presence known, they were escorted directly to the Admiral. Cronymartis was immersed in animated conversation with a small group of shipwrights and inspectors in the main hall. As Samra entered the hall, he was struck by the exquisite new frescos of nature on its walls. They all slowed their pace to admire them. The frescos were adorned with fresh beautifully done images of people, dolphins, fish, and sea birds painted in bright vivid colors.

As they approached, their escort called to Cronymartis who hadn't seen their entrance. Samra was looking forward to finally meeting the great Admiral after hearing a great deal from his father, beginning in early childhood, about his achievements and their adventures together. As he turned in the direction of the call, they saw an impressive stout man with flowing silvery hair in his fifties. Samra consumed his presence immediately and perceived his eyes sparkling with intellect.

"Sir, this is Samraleos and his party." the escort announced.

Cronymartis began to smile and calmly looked Samra up and down to take a measure of him.

"You look much like your father when he was your age, but I think you are even bigger. Your face has the look of your mother which serves you well, Samraleos."

As Samra stood silently amused, Cronymartis approached him and they shared a warm warrior's hug. The Admiral released him saying, "It's good to meet you at long last. I've heard many commendable things about you over the years. Your father must have prepared you very well."

"I hope so, sir. I have looked forward to meeting you for many years. My father's stories of you are fixed in my memory from his many retellings of them."

They all laughed. Samra then pointed to Telecaneos and introduced him as their military commander. He continued by introducing all of his personal guards to Cronymartis. The Admiral greeted each warmly and gave them all a welcoming hug.

"Please, come in to my office. We have little time and a great deal to discuss." Cronymartis said.

He motioned for the shipwrights and inspectors to leave and led Samra's party to his office.

"Be seated, gentlemen.   Please sit here in front of me, Samraleos."

"Sir, please call me Samra as my friends do."

Cronymartis nodded to him saying, "Very well, Samra."

Once everyone was comfortable, the Admiral said, "Would you like to start with a report on the status of the fleet?"

"Sir, I have many questions to ask you regarding the fleet, and it may take a considerable amount of time.   Telecaneos needs to return to his command to address his captains soon.   I think it would be better if he began by giving you a report on the status of the Knossos warriors first."

"Very well, as you wish."

Samra nodded to Telecaneos to stand.   He began by giving the Admiral a detailed report on the weaponry, equipment, and provisioning carried with the warriors.   He thoroughly described their physical qualities and the level of their fighting skills.   Cronymartis sat calmly in his chair listening attentively and appeared quite impressed.   Telecaneos moved to the status of their morale and began to tell the Admiral of the culling of the warriors at the palace in Knossos.

Cronymartis interrupted him, "Culling of the warriors?   What is this?"

"Sir, those that were unworthy or traitors were removed from among us and replaced before we marched."

This caught the Admiral's attention and keen interest.   He said, "Tell me much more about this, commander."

Telecaneos told the Admiral a summarized version of the affair deferring to Samra a few times to let him explain in greater detail. But he waved him on allowing him to continue, so he could finish and return to his men. Cronymartis and all of those in the office smiled and chuckled occasionally during the report. The Admiral was very intrigued at his description of the "Others" and was quite impressed with the story of Samra's speech to the men in the courtyard. He could wait to hear Samra's telling of it.

"Sir, it is my opinion that the warrior's motivation and morale is at the highest state of readiness I have ever witnessed."

"Well done, commander. Are you finished?"

"Yes sir."

"An escort will show you where the harbor master's office is. After they are released, you will find the ship assignments for your men there. That's all I have for you now."

Samra then motioned Telecaneos to return to his command. After he bid him farewell, the Admiral slowly turned to Samra and with a chuckle said, "Very impressive, Samra! I must hear more of these things in private. Did the King and Queen see this?"

"Yes sir."

Cronymartis began to laugh heartily and slapped his palm down loudly on the top of the large desk. Still laughing he said, "He's just as cunning and dangerous as his father! The Queen must have loved the theatre of it."

He laughed for several more moments and when he settled down a bit, he said, "Come, let's sit more comfortably in the courtyard garden and have the servants attend to us. The flowers are lovely at this time of the year."

As they moved out into the courtyard, Samra's guards scurried to take up strategic positions around its perimeter. Taking their seats under a large shade, Cronymartis said, "I knew you're father well. He was a great warrior, master, and friend. I would not be standing here in front of you if not for him. I'm sorry he is not still with us. I will miss the sound of his laughter."

"I will too, sir. I miss him very much."

Cronymartis slowly shook his head and said, "Yes."

After several silent moments, they began to focus their vision intensely into the eyes of the other to form a better mental connection.

"Please, let's not call each other sir any more and talk as friends. Your father would like that. Does everyone call you, Samra?"

"Yes, that's what most people call me, at least, the ones that are not my enemies."

"I don't think it would be very healthy for someone to be your enemy." stated Cronymartis with conviction.

Samra sat silently with a small smirk on his lips and gave no other response. After a few moments, the Admiral said, "Come, let us share our knowledge. It is much needed for success."

They talked for over an hour with the Admiral agreeing to Samra's general plan for the taking of the treasury in Avaris.

Cronymartis had been there many times and knew the layout of the dockyards and city as well as anyone. They complemented each other's minds as they shared their creativity and knowledge; filling in the contingencies and details of their plan. With this complete, Samra told him of the now confirmed assassination plot and a much more detailed version of what had happened at the palace. Cronymartis, repeatedly, heartily laughed at the story and said, "That must have been quite an entertainment. Karasos would have enjoyed that greatly."

Then the Admiral sat quietly for a few moments and turned his attention to the assassination plot inquiring with fascination about what was truly known and what was suspected. Samra identified the four couriers and how he wanted them dealt with as possible conspirators. The Admiral said he would inform his ship masters and arrange for their surveillance. Samra assured him that at no time would the removal of the Avaris gold and evacuees be jeopardized as he worked against them.

At the end of their meeting, Cronymartis stood up with Samra and they hugged each other warmly.

The Admiral said, "You're father once told me the two of us could act together as one great ferocious lion, much greater than the sum of us, when our minds were joined in knowledge. Let us act as one from this moment on."

Samra hugged him back and said with acknowledgement and fortitude, "From this moment on."

Cronymartis told him it would be a few hours before all the ships were certified to sail and invited Samra to join him and the ship masters at the midday feast.

"Samra, I hope you are planning for you and Telecaneos to sail with me on the lead ship to Avaris?"

"Absolutely, that would allow us to refine every detail of the Avaris operation using your naval expertise and knowledge of the city."

"I've made a simple drawing of the arrangement of the treasury, buildings, and walls of Avaris in relation to the river and docks on parchment. It should help us more easily visualize our tasks. The scribes have made enough copies so that each ship will have one for reference." said the Admiral.

"Wonderful, I'll need to get one of those copies and give it to Telecaneos, so we can begin to plan the details of the deployment of the warriors when we arrive."

Cronymartis reached into his desk, retrieved a copy, and handed it to him with a smile. On examining it, Samra smiled and looking back at the Admiral said, "Now I must leave with your beautiful map and return with Telecaneos when his duties aren't so pressing to discuss our plans for the taking of the treasury. We must maximize the surprise of our troops to its fullest, so their deployment must be planned precisely. I'll return as soon as I can."

"Yes, I can hear my duties calling me too. But it was wonderful to finally meet the son of the great Karasos."

Cronymartis was truly impressed with Samra and thought his father had trained him exceedingly well in the "Way". They would need all of their combined powers for this mission and a great deal of luck as well. He didn't mind facing the Egyptians as long as they hadn't already taken Avaris and were able to set a trap on the river; cutting off their escape route to the sea. The Canaanites were more than capable of seizing the fleet outright if they quickly massed an attack while it was tied to the docks. Another terrible scenario was if both the Egyptians and

Canaanites turned against them simultaneously. "Our escape route must remain open, or we are doomed."

This was the greatest concern for both of them and one of the things they had the least control over. Their best chance was to arrive in Avaris as fast as they possibly could in hopes the city wasn't already under attack or had been taken. As a master navigator, he began to consider his alternatives for the fastest, most secretive route to Egypt.

There were many ship masters that sailed the open sea routinely on busy, especially in summer, well established trade routes, but Cronymartis was considered the best and most precise of them in the King's navy especially on the fast direct diplomatic voyages to and from Egypt and Canaan. Twice in his career he had undertaken voyages far into the western seas to trade finished works of bronze, weapons, tools, jewelry, cloth, pottery, and oils for the barbarian's gold, copper, tin, and whatever else they found of value. There was a network of trading posts that dotted the coastlines of the great western sea and far beyond.

The Admiral used every available indicator in nature and compared it to a mental navigational map of the region stored in his mind to plot his course. Since the currents and tides were generally weak, he focused on the sun, stars, and the predictable seasonal winds to guide him.

On a clear day when the sun's position could be observed, he knew that the sun arcs in the sky, relative to the horizon, from the northeast at dawn to rise to its midday zenith and then arcs down toward the northwest to set in the evening. The north-south position of the arc changed with the seasons. With this in mind, he could dependably deduce directional information from its position in the sky at any time during the day.

To this he added the information he gathered from the direction of the seasonal winds. If the wind died down, he would look at the swells on the sea. The direction of the wind could be estimated from the swells long after the wind had ceased. If the winds died completely or were confused, he would look for birds, like the terns, that fed at sea during the day and flew back to land with the approaching sunset to indicate a nearby landfall.

On a clear night, the countless stars gave him many more points of reference to help him navigate more precisely. There were stars in all quadrants of the night sky moving in a predictable, orderly way from dusk to dawn and season to season throughout the year. He used two groups of stars that were always visible above the horizon and rotated about the bright unchanging North Star. He called them the Two Bears. The Bears rotated about the polar star and changed their orientation to it as the seasons changed. He could tell what season it was simply by looking at the orientation of the Bears relative to the North Star.

The North Star also gave him his north-south position by observing the angle it made with the horizon from his ship in any given season. The North Star was visibly higher in the night sky in the far northern Aegean and was lower in the sky if he was well south near the coast of Egypt on any given night.

Cronymartis used a simple tool to measure the angle of the North Star relative to the horizon. It was composed of two cleanly sawn, thin sticks of wood that were about a half meter long. The two sticks were joined together on one of their ends into a hinge that pivoted on a small peg. The free end of the top stick pointed to the North Star, and the bottom stick pointed to the horizon. A string with a lead bobbin hung from the top stick. By opening and closing the sticks, the length of the string from the top one to the bottom one could be measured. He could get a good measure of the angle of the North Star from his position with this simple instrument. With a good initial angle measurement as a reference, if he knew what the difference of the angles was between the angle of his starting point and the angle of his destination, he could deduce his destination's north-south position at any time of the year no matter where he was in the open sea.

Cronymartis took a measure of the ship's speed in the water using a large piece of cork with a light line of rope attached to it. A sailor at the stern of the ship would drop the floating cork into the sea and count the number of heart beats it took before the line tightened in his hand. Another instrument he found useful in coastal areas, especially in the perilous shallows near the mouth of the Nile, was the sounding lead. It was a weight of lead tied to a rope used to determine the depth of the water when thrown overboard. It could also be used to detect the composition of the seabed and give the Admiral an indication of how much anchoring would be required to hold the ships in position in the current.

Knowledge of the predictable seasonal winds aided him greatly in navigation. The predominant winds in the open sea were the north and northwest winds. The north winds of winter and the northwest winds of summer sometimes grew into strong gales that could easily blow a ship out of control downwind. The other important winds were the East wind that blew in summer and fall, the West wind of late spring and early summer, the stormy South winds of late summer and autumn, and the Southwest wind of spring and late fall. Cronymartis categorized each of the winds with its own set of attributes such as dry, wet, hot, cold, dusty, clear, strong, weak, etc.

The sun, stars, seasons, winds, and his instruments provided the Admiral with reliable information he could compare with his navigational mental map to dependably get a reasonable fix on his position and determine his ship's heading in the open sea far beyond the sight of land.

Chapter 8

Avaris

Cronymartis knew the only way to insure their quickest arrival in total secrecy was to sail directly over the open sea to a position just north of the far eastern tributary of the Nile that led to Avaris. It would be very difficult to judge, but he wasn't concerned. He thought once the fleet took a position near to what he assumed to be his initial holding position, or rendezvous point, he would send a single scout ship due south to the coast to determine their actual position and what heading to take to their final rendezvous point just north of the tributary's entrance. Once the scout ship returned, the Admiral would have the fleet move to their final holding position; well out to sea away from the coastal trading routes to wait for the right time to make a high speed run to Avaris powered by the warrior's oars.

Samra soon returned with the commander Telecaneos to discuss their thoughts with the Admiral for the best use of the warriors in Avaris. The Admiral told them of his idea for a fast surprise night approach and the way he wanted to deploy the ships in the river for defense while the others were being loaded.

"Very well, let us have two groups of six ships each deployed in the river. The first group will dock and take on the treasury goods and evacuees while the other group maintains a defensive watch upriver in anticipation of the Egyptians.   If the Canaanites come on us, the ships can quickly move in to defend the docks and help our escape." said Samra.

"We must have our very best shock troops on the first three ships of the initial group of six to dock.   When the holds of the first group of ships are full, the second group can take their place and complete the loading of evacuees if all goes well." said Telecaneos.

The Admiral interjected, "Gentlemen, we will be lucky if everything goes well, but I think this is our best chance for success.   The immediate deployment of the warriors must be coordinated exquisitely in order to allow us to complete the operation and leave Avaris before the sun rises the next morning.   Telecaneos, you must arrange the ship assignments of your men with great care and coordinate it with my ship masters before we leave.   If you stay for a short time further, I have called my ship masters to a meeting to discuss our plans and have them implemented."

Samra said, "After the meeting, Telecaneos and I will meet with his captains to begin the process of assigning each warrior to a specific task before we land in Avaris.   We are limited in time here in Kommos, but we will have a great deal of time to refine our plans during the voyage.   We will be able to communicate the warrior's final instructions to all the ships at the rendezvous point.   We should be sitting in the water for several hours, don't you think?"

"Yes, at least, for a few hours depending on when we arrive." the Admiral responded.

They all believed the plan was an excellent one given the mission at hand.   Surprise and shock were their greatest assets, and they wouldn't squander them.   There was a feel of success to it. The meeting with the ship masters commenced with the Admiral calling Telecaneos to address them on the military plan for the deployment of the warriors on the ships and in Avaris. The commander gave a brief, but thorough, presentation informing them of their intentions. Samra and Telecaneos then left to meet with his captains and further instruct them.

Cronymartis immediately began to give the ship masters their instructions before starting the voyage. Each ship was assigned a position relative to the Admiral's lead one when they formed up in the open sea. He told them of his route and the details of their approach to Avaris. He distributed identical North Star measurement instruments to all of them. Once they were out to sea far enough so the true horizon wasn't obscured and the night sky had descended on them, the fleet would halt briefly so each of them could take a measurement of the North Star's angle in the sky.

With the ships close to one another, word would be relayed among them to collect all the ship master's measurements. When all the masters and Cronymartis agreed to what their true measurement was, it would be passed back to them to synchronize all the ships to the same reading. He would then give them his calculated angle reading for the position of the initial rendezvous point north of Egypt. If they were separated in a storm, all the ships should be able to reassemble at the predicted rendezvous point. After a few last minute instructions and questions, he dismissed them to their ships.

Some time after the midday feast, the great host of warriors began moving into position on the docks to board their assigned ships. Everything was ready for them with the sails tied to their booms in the light north northwest wind. The drum and horns were sounded, and the men began boarding the cypress long ships. It took quite some time for the warriors in all the ships to store their weapons and packs and ready themselves at the oars for the voyage.   When all the ship's oars were manned and ready, the horn was sounded to signal them to be released from there moorings.   They were pushed away from the piers until their oars could be fully lowered into the water.

The Admiral's ship was the first to leave with the warriors rowing strongly away from the docks to the west.   One ship after the other fell into line behind the lead one.   They needed to row a few hundred meters to the west to clear a small protective cape just south of Kommos.   The ships then turned south along the coastline and let the light wind fill their sails to assist them while they rowed for another fifteen kilometers. Once they cleared the great southern cape and were well out to sea, the Admiral's ship took a heading of east-southeast toward the mouth of the Nile.   The fleet formed up in their assigned sailing formation with the Admiral's ship taking the southern-most lead position.

The sight of the twelve ships in formation with their sails filled with the wind and the oarsmen rowing was a wonderful awe-inspiring sight.   The sea was relatively smooth, and the weak wind was favorable, but the fifty oars worked continually unless the wind was strong enough to carry the ships at a speed near to what the oarsmen could sustain.   The oarsmen could then rest and become passengers as the wind carried them across the sea. While the winds remained light, the fifty oars of the ships were worked constantly day and night with regular shift changes from the ship's complement of one hundred and twenty men.

Throughout the first night, the Admiral calculated they were probably making nine or ten kilometers an hour which worked out to about two hundred and twenty kilometers a day.   He took regular readings of his speed using his floating cork instrument. He estimated he had well over eight hundred kilometers to travel to their initial holding position north of the eastern most tributary of the Nile.   The Admiral knew the winds at this time of the year should be favorable for the first leg of the voyage. He estimated it would take them four or five days if everything went smoothly.

The first night after the evening meal, the Admiral and Samra met on the high stern deck and sat together relaxing accompanied by some wine. Cronymartis said, "Tell me more of these "Others", Samra. Your father told me many years ago he was studying the human mind and had possibly made an important discovery. But I've heard nothing more of it."

"I didn't believe it myself for a long time, but the truth of it has been confirmed to me many times now. At the time of my father's death even he was still somewhat skeptical about it. The "Others" are humans that are so endemically and overwhelmingly selfish they find it necessary to hide themselves and their true natures from the rest of us. Their minds reflect that of a carnivore in nature consuming its victims to satisfy its hunger. Their human victims are nothing more than food to them. That is how they view us and everyone else, as food. They view themselves and their experiences as the only true reality. To them everyone else in their experience is merely something to play with and manipulate in order to serve their desires. Their desires can be quite bizarre. Have you heard of the child killings in Knossos?"

"Yes."

"I believe the killer is one of these "Others". Evidently some of them, I don't know how many, lose control of the mask they wear tiring of constantly concealing themselves and sometimes physically express their true desires on the rest of us in terrible ways."

"How many of these "Others" do you think are among us?"

"The culling of the formation was the first chance I've had to obtain a measure of their prevalence among us. It appears they are few, but there are enough of them to do great damage. I think it may be as few as one in every hundred and as high as five or more. The fewer the better, but more studies will be needed to clarify the true number."

They sat in silence for a time on his words enjoying their wine. Cronymartis' mind stirred with the concept's implications.

"I removed them from the command because they are so different from the normal warrior and their thinking that I feared they would weaken us, and, as my father said, they would betray us when they were needed the most. Chaos follows them as part of their nature."

"There must be many more marvels in that mind of yours to enthrall me with, Samra. Let us enjoy our wine and have many more of these conversations. I have many questions for you, and I might even be able to make a contribution myself to our combined knowledge."

Samra laughed at this with the Admiral joining in. They had many long conversations while on the ship as they freely shared and consumed the knowledge of the other. Many times Telecaneos would join them to further enrich their collective insight. The Admiral learned everything Samra knew of the "Others" including how to detect them. He would use this knowledge for the rest of his life and pass it on to the future generations.

On the third day of the voyage, the winds changed to the southwest, but the rowing never ceased. The voyage went smoothly across the great sea to their initial rendezvous. As the sun rose in the east on the fifth day, Cronymartis signaled the ships with the horn to stop rowing and gather their sails to drift in the weak current to execute their pre-assigned orders. The Admiral's ship master had the lead ship separate from the fleet and row alone due south; placing a sharp-eyed lookout high on the mast sitting on the boom.

The other ships were to allow the Admiral to get far to the south but still in sight of their own lookouts. They were to follow whatever course they observed Cronymartis to take but at a distance out at sea. They were to maintain this until the Admiral reported back to them. The Admiral's ship headed south with the remainder of the fleet following about ten kilometers behind him. The Admiral knew his lookout could see twelve or thirteen kilometers ahead to the horizon. The lookout could easily make out the fleet behind him, but he could see only water in front of him in all directions.

About five hours later, land was sighted by the lookout. The Admiral had the sounding lead manned to regularly measure the depth of the water and kept moving south until he could clearly see the land himself. The spotter noticed the coast to his east was falling away to the southeast. The Admiral followed the coastline still well out to sea. It took about a half hour before he was able to recognize a landmark with certainty. He followed the coastline for a short time longer to confirm his position and abruptly called for the ship master to return to the fleet.

After returning, Cronymartis took the fleet east to a position about thirty kilometers north of the mouth of the eastern tributary. With the ships stopped and drifting in the current, they were signaled to rest and have their midday meal. After letting the men nourish and refresh themselves, he directed them to assemble in a tight 'beam-to-beam' formation with their bows facing forward toward the Admiral's ship sitting in front of them. Cronymartis addressed the ships loudly telling them they would be practicing several close quarter maneuvers that might be required for their survival in the river using the standard drum and horn signals they all knew well. The warriors were composed of many men that hadn't worked together until this voyage. They needed to synchronize their actions with practice.

Initially, the Admiral had them separate and form up into a tight 'bow-to-stern' line about fifteen meters apart. Once he observed the ships were initially well placed, the drum and horn filled the air commanding them to begin rowing straight ahead while maintaining their positions in the formation. The ship masters constantly shouted orders to the warriors at their oars to adjust their stroke; to find and keep their position in the line. Everyone was concerned about collisions with the ships being so close together. They continued rowing for several minutes until the drum and horn sounded again commanding them to immediately halt the line. You could hear the frenzy of shouting from the twelve ship masters to their men to avoid any contact of the ships. Once they settled to a halt in formation, they were ordered to row straight ahead in a line again. The process of starting and stopping the line was repeated several times until the Admiral was satisfied the ships were synchronizing sharply.

Cronymartis then had them perform a more complicated maneuver with the fleet forming a well spaced stationary 'beam-to-beam' line with their bows facing in the same direction and had them pivot on their position a quarter turn so the ship's beams faced ahead instead. The maneuver of starting, stopping, pivoting, and then moving away in formation was practiced for well over two and a half hours. The Admiral finally nodded his satisfaction to his ship master, and the drum and horn were sounded for them to rest until it was time to make their run into the tributary. Cronymartis confidently waited for the sun to reach the correct position in the afternoon sky. During this time, Telecaneos issued his final orders to the captains of the warriors.   He confirmed everyone had their assignments and all was in readiness.   Both Samra and the Admiral judged the fleet to be primed and well prepared for the mission.

About three hours before sundown, the fleet began to row steadily toward the mouth of the tributary.   The Admiral wanted to be a few kilometers from the entrance at sundown before having the ships begin and maintain a full battle stroke of the oars to race up the river as fast as they could at night to the docks of Avaris.   He knew with the cloudless skies of the Nile delta, the moon and stars would provide more than enough light for him to navigate and observe any islets or obstacles in their path.   It would be a strenuous row of about thirty five or forty kilometers up river.   He hoped to make Avaris in about three hours arriving later in the evening well before midnight.   If they were lucky, the fleet would be tied to the docks for several hours before the Egyptians or Canaanites could mount any kind of organized response.   This should give them enough time during the night to empty the contents of the treasury onto the ships and board the many evacuees for the return voyage home.

Cronymartis had sailed to the King's commercial district in Avaris many times, but he had never been required to arrive at a specific time of night at high speed up the dark river.   But it was of no concern to him.   The fleet, sitting to the north outside the mouth of the river, was far enough away from land that their chances of being detected were very small, and yet they were close enough for their fast approach to Avaris at night to maximize the surprise to any faction that wished them ill.

When the glow of the sun in the western sky was just beginning to fade over the horizon, Cronymartis judged he was in a good position with the mouth of the tributary about three kilometers away.   Samra and Telecaneos stood by him on the lead ship's bow.   He then ordered the fastest battle stroke to the warriors of all the ships with a single short blowing of the horn. The ships were arranged in a line with the Admiral's ship in the lead. They began moving very quickly into the unknown conditions of Egypt toward Avaris. They were totally committed now and could only hope for the best.

The voyage up the roughly five hundred meter wide tributary was, as Cronymartis expected, uneventful with only the occasional incredulous fishermen hurriedly rowing out of their way. Villagers along the palm tree lined river came out of their homes to view the magnificent sight of the long line of ships moving by them at high speed. Children ran along the banks laughing; trying to match the ship's speed. No Egyptian military ships or large barges were sighted to interfere with their approach or escape. If any were sighted, the Admiral would have stopped the ships briefly to attack and burn them where they sat. The first sign there had been trouble in the land was when the Admiral's lookout described a vast swath of fire damage to the crops on the lands to the west of the river.

It was harvest time for the winter crop in the Nile delta. As they continued their approach, the charred fields began showing up on the eastern side of the river also. Some time later, the lookout shouted there was nothing but destruction to the crops as far as he could see. There were no small boats on the river at that point, and very few people could be seen on the shore. The land appeared ravaged and depopulated. When the ships came within two kilometers of the city, Cronymartis slowed them to a steady medium pace to make it appear from the city walls they were making a normal approach.

As the dockyard came into view, they observed it was completely empty. There were no other ships moored to the piers at all. The signs of recent fighting were everywhere. A detailed plan for maneuvering the ships at the dockyard was worked out during the voyage. With the Admiral's ship in the lead, the first group of six ships was to make for the docks and immediately begin offloading their warriors to form up for their assignments. The other group of six would row upstream about four hundred meters to the south and throw their stone anchors overboard to maintain their position in the river. This gave them the ability to rapidly maneuver the ships into a line across the river to defend against any southern naval attack by the Egyptians. Also, they could quickly move into positions around the docks to return fire and cover a retreat by the ships moored there if the Canaanites attacked from the city.

Cronymartis thought of the Egyptian ships as big rafts designed solely to carry large numbers of warriors. Some of their ships could carry two hundred or more fully armed fighters. They were strictly river craft with no keel to speak of. They could be easily out-maneuvered and destroyed if they tried to fight the King's fleet in the open sea. But they could mount a serious attack on the river where the fleet's movements were constricted. If the Egyptians were able get their ships close enough to attack, the ship's technological advantage would be useless. They were known to organize large flotillas of warrior ships that could sustain mass attacks from the river with torch arrows and projectiles. This was a tactic they used to sack Heliopolis the previous summer.

The Admiral and Samra feared this the most even if the Canaanites turned on them. The Canaanites had very few large vessels that could be used for military purposes. They were essentially a land power whose territory ranged from Egypt in the south to the lands north of it along the coast of the eastern sea. If the Canaanites moved against them, there would be a serious fight in the city and on the dockyard. But with the suddenness of the fleet's arrival at night, it would take time for them organize an attack against twelve hundred warriors. The Canaanites and Egyptians greatly feared the King's warriors because of their reputed tremendous physical strength. If they were forced to retreat back onto their ships during a land attack, the ships could simply move out into the river out of range of their bows.

The Canaanite guards stationed on the walls saw the ships coming from the north and assumed they were friendly. The Egyptians ships always came from the south, at least, so far. Recognizing them as the King's ships, they started waving and cheering as they advanced toward the dockyard. As soon as the Admiral's ship nudged the southern-most pier, the warriors began rushing off it to begin assembling in formation awaiting Samra's orders.

Once Samra stepped onto the dock, he waited for the three hundred warriors assigned to the initial taking of the treasury to bring themselves fully to order. The remaining sixty men from the first three ships were assigned to begin securing the area around the dockyards. The second group of three ships was now tying up to the docks. Once he deemed the men were ready, he had them immediately begin to run at battle speed in formation to the treasury. It was about three hundred meters to the southeast.

Cronymartis saw to the disposition of the fleet as the other ships began offloading their warriors. According to plan, Telecaneos organized twenty small squads of six warriors each to spread out into the district. They were to alert the many officials and citizens on the King's evacuation list to prepare for their immediate departure and the transportation of their valuables and provisions. The squads were then to commandeer any wheeled wagons and oxen in the area and escort them to the treasury. After reinforcing the defensive zones around the dockyards and the corridor between the treasury and the ships, Telecaneos was to lead a group of one hundred and twenty warriors to secure the administration complex. They were to notify its officials of the evacuation and transport its important documents and valuables back to the fleet. Many teams of bowmen were stationed on rooftops at strategic locations throughout the area.

Standing by his ship, the Admiral was informed of the sighting of movement on the far side of the river. A chariot was seen racing off to the south. This concerned Cronymartis greatly. If the Egyptians were massed nearby for another attack on Avaris, there would be trouble. He commanded all the warriors to hurry as fast as they could.

The mission of the fleet's second group of six ships positioned upstream was to be prepared to respond to any attacks by the Egyptians or Canaanites. If no threat materialized after the first group had successfully taken on their evacuees and cargo, they would replace them at the dock and take on theirs in turn. The six ships already loaded would then move upstream to take up the defensive posture in the river.

With the sighting of the Egyptian chariot, Cronymartis had one of the ships from the defensive group row upstream another kilometer to a bend in the river as an advance guard. The ship's master had a lookout sitting high up on the mast's boom with his horn ready to sound the alert if any large Egyptian ships were seen coming towards them. The lookout could see well up the river for another kilometer or more from his position at the bend. Beyond that his view was obscured by the many palm trees lining the river banks.

The King's treasury guards were astonished to see so many warriors coming at them so rapidly. Some of them instinctively raised their spears and pulled at their swords but abruptly hesitated at the resounding voice of Samra.

"Stand down in the name of the King!"

Some of the guards dropped their weapons in fear of immediate death as the warriors quickly swarmed out from both sides of the formation to envelope the building. The commander of the treasury guards threw his weapons to the ground and motioned for all of his men to do the same. As he walked slowly toward Samra with his hands in the air, he shouted, "Please sir, we are loyal to the King and comply with him in all ways! We are just very surprised to see you appear so suddenly unannounced!"

"Then comply with this! Have your men stand aside from their weapons!"

"Yes sir. Yes sir. We welcome the King's warriors."

The treasury commander motioned for his men to comply. As the guards moved away from their weapons, Samra directed several of his warriors to gather them and put them in a pile some distance away. Samra called the commander to him and said, "It is the order of the King the wealth of the treasury is to return to Knossos on the fleet now sitting in the docks. We will need all the help we can get from you if you are willing and cause us no ill."

"We will do whatever you command, sir. What are our orders?"

"Oversee the speedy emptying of the treasury with my warriors and its delivery to our ships."

"Yes sir. Come with me into the treasury, and I will show you, sir."

"My name is Samraleos. If you perform this task to my satisfaction, you can call me Samra. Open the doors!"

The perimeter of the treasury building was quickly secured with the warriors poised in defensive positions. They stood anxiously waiting for the wagons and carts to arrive. The guard unlocked the large cedar doors with a bronze tool and swung them open. Only Samra and his personal guards entered the building with him. He led them into the storage rooms of the treasury. They were amazed at what they saw. There were many tons of gold and silver ingots in a variety of shapes stored on the floors and in high wooden shelves along the walls. The rooms of the treasury were filled with crates and shelves laden with gold, silver, sculptures, jewelry, and gems of all kinds.

"Command two of your guards with an escort of my men to bring the administration's accountants to the treasury immediately and return to me at once."

They were to assist in the management and documentation of the items to be removed. The oxen wagons were just starting to arrive. The first priority was to transport the raw gold to the holds of the waiting ships. The gems, golden sculptures, and jewelry were next in line to be taken with the silver and whatever else remained to be taken last.

Several wagons and carts were now waiting outside the treasury doors. Samra had the men begin loading the gold under the direction of the treasury commander. The gold could be accounted for by weight only and didn't have to be itemized to its owner. The district officials and accountants arrived with the transportation of the gold well under way. After the last gold wagon left for the ships, they started loading the crates of gems and jewelry while taking account of their ownership on papyrus scrolls. These scrolls were to be sealed by the head accountant and accompany the items on their way back to Knossos.

Samra was satisfied the process was set in motion in an orderly manner and working efficiently. After being informed by district intelligence agents the Canaanite pharaoh Khamudi had not yet issued any orders and was showing no signs of organizing or reprisal, he gathered his personal guards to walk back to the ships to obtain whatever information he could on the four couriers suspected as assassins.

The train of treasure wagons kept arriving to be emptied into the ship's holds. The Admiral's ship took on about fifteen metric tons of gold and valuables with the second ship in the line taking on a similar quantity. The Admiral's ship then took aboard several officials and their families with their baggage and provisioning for evacuation. The Admiral's ship stayed at its mooring, but when the second ship was fully loaded it was released from its pier and moved out into the middle of the river about one hundred meters downstream. Cronymartis was still on shore calmly overseeing the entire affair.

Within an hour or so, a considerable crowd of people had assembled at the docks hoping to escape from Avaris. Cronymartis commanded the warriors to control and quiet the quickly growing throng. With his men maintaining a precarious semblance of order, people on the King's list continued to be called out and taken aboard for evacuation. Once all the people on the list were aboard, others would be allowed on depending on capacity and provisioning as determined by each ship's master. The people on the dockyard could see there was obviously not enough room for everyone on the ships. There was simply far too many of them.

People began to push forward in the crowd toward the ships to gain a better position for boarding. Soon the increasingly agitated crowd was beginning to sporadically panic with fights breaking out. The Admiral sent his warriors into the mass to restore order. Two men were identified as being out of control and were summarily killed.   Their limp bleeding bodies were dragged out of the mob and thrown into the river.   This got everyone's attention, and the crowd quieted with order reigning again.   Cronymartis would tolerate no more delays.

When Samra and his guards arrived at the dockyard, it was filled with noisy tension, but the loading of evacuees seemed to be going smoothly.   As he met Cronymartis, he was informed the two men standing next to him were the masters of the ships that carried the four couriers to Avaris.   The first master reported his pair of couriers was very quiet and stayed to themselves almost obsessively.   The other master stated that one of his pair was very friendly and quite talkative.   He appeared to be the leader of the two with the other one acting as his lieutenant.

During the voyage, the ship's master arranged for certain members of the crew to befriend them and obtain whatever knowledge they could without arousing any suspicions of detection.   His crewmen gathered a good deal of information about the two of them, but much more importantly the pair was overheard in a whispered conversation on the third night of the voyage.

"Sir, it was fragmentary, but they were clearly overheard discussing the need to acquire more men in Avaris and two words stood out above all others – 'Kill Samraleos'.   The warrior that witnessed this conversation is very well known to his sergeant and swore on his family's honor what he heard was true without doubt."

"That's enough evidence for me." said the Admiral.

Samra didn't know if the four couriers he suspected of being the assassins were the only ones remaining in the plot or not.   He arranged for them to be assigned to the last two ships, the fifth and sixth, of the first group to be moored at the dock. The four couriers had been off their ships for some time now and left with another warrior also from the fifth ship. The five of them were being followed by a contingent of twenty warriors on orders from the ship masters.

Samra concluded that with this new information he had more than enough evidence to do whatever he wanted with them. The fifth ship's military captain stated the unknown warrior was a replacement for one that was seriously injured some weeks before the mission. Cronymartis informed him the warriors were ordered to detain the five for interrogation only if they made any predatory moves toward Samra or his guards. He was expecting to get a report on their conduct soon.

Samra thought the culling at the palace had probably reduced the plotter's numbers by half, and he needed to cull them further to reduce the effort in seeking the truth behind the plot. As he considered the possibilities, he thought he only needed two of the five, the talkative leader and his lieutenant, to lead him to the source of the conspiracy. Just then a warrior ran up to the ship masters and reported on the men's activities. They had gone to an official's house in the eastern sector of the district where they were being watched.

Samra said, "It's a good time to observe these assassins now everything is running well. Lead us to your warriors."

The messenger stretched his arm in the direction of the villa, and said, "This way, sir."

Samra and his guards followed him closely as he ran ahead. When they arrived, Samra motioned for everyone to gather around him.

"Men, there are two of these traitors I want to survive this night and return to Knossos. They are needed for my investigation, and they must know nothing. I want the ones the sixth ship's master described to me as the leader and his lieutenant. Does anyone know who I mean?"

One of the warriors raised his hand and said, "Yes sir, I do."

"Are you sure of this. There can be no mistakes in this."

"Sir, I am very sure but not certain. If you wish, I can return to the ships and bring the ship master to be the witness."

"We need to be absolutely sure warrior. Yes, do it quickly."

The warrior worked his way through the group and began to run to the ships as Samra spoke, "All of the others are to be killed except the official. We will take him when the time is right. The two survivors must not suspect we are responsible for the deaths of their fellows. We can blame this on Canaanite or Egyptian snipers that have infiltrated the district because of the fleet's arrival. When the ship master arrives, we will create a diversion to flush them from the villa and be identified."

Those that could reach joined fists, and Samra led them all in a muted chant of, "Success!"

The warriors disengaged with the confidence of certainty. There was power in the air, and they all could feel it. The ship master soon joined them and was informed of the plan to flush the traitors out into the open for identification in order to save two of them for further investigation. When the ship master was able to identify the two to be saved, he was to point them out to the warriors.

"Let's try to force them to leave the villa but not so fast they run and can't be identified. My personal guards need to do this first task because the traitors might be able to identify you others as warriors that sailed with them. It goes like this. Some of my personal guards will walk up to the villa and loudly knock on the door proclaiming an emergency that everyone must return to the ships immediately. Snipers have been seen in the district, and several people had already been killed. We need another group of warriors out in the yard to create noise, distraction, and plausibility. This should give the ship master enough time to describe to you the men I need saved. The ones to die will be followed by a single warrior to point them out as they walk to the ships. This is the signal for those that are to die. Now tell the others, and ready yourselves with men on the rooftops along the paths. Drag their bodies back to the villa. I think we can use them for effect. Does everyone understand?"

A quiet chorus of "Yes Sir!" filled their space.

"Be sure there are no mistakes."

Four of Samra's guards approached the doors as a group of another six men gathered on the front yard and began speaking loudly about the fake emergency of the snipers. The lead warrior began pounding on the door and shouting there was an urgent situation as the others stood behind him on the stone porch. He kept pounding until the doors finally opened. As instructed, the group on the grounds soon broke up and scattered as if to execute instructions in response to the false threat.

After a brief, but animated, discussion at the door, the warriors bowed and left as the door shut. The rouse was staged perfectly. Just a few minutes later the door again opened, and out came the warrior and four couriers scanning the grounds for any threats. They stood for a short time on the porch talking with the official in the doorway.   The ship master had more than enough time to identify them and instructed the warriors. Leaving the official inside, they walked out onto the grounds and briefly stopped and talked for a few moments.   They then split up to make their separate ways back to the ships.

The warrior separated from the other four and went off alone while the four couriers separated into the same two pairs from the fifth and sixth ships.   Silent signals were passed to the warriors that the three to be killed were on there way and their paths indicated.   As the two couriers from the fifth ship turned a corner not far from the villa, they were hit by arrows from the back; one low and one high near the throat.   Then more arrows came from the rooftops in front of them.   Without making a sound, the two fell to their death on the ground.   The warriors gathered around the two bodies with arrows protruding from them at odd angles and lifted them by the armpits to drag them back to the villa.

After turning the corner of a building, the lone warrior, without any warning, began running as fast as he possibly could; as if his life depended on it.   The warriors were startled by the speed of his approach and seeing no one following him hesitated with their bows.   The warrior passed them by unscathed.   They realized he had escaped when the man assigned to follow him came forward.

When the two dead couriers were dropped onto the ground in front of them, Samra called the men together and said, "Now we go to the villa."

Just then word came the warrior had eluded them and Samra said, "Very well, we'll give him the traitor's choice."

A chill went through all of the warriors on hearing this. They all knew what that meant.   After a few moments of disturbed silence, Samra said, "Now let us interrogate the official.   He may also be a traitor."

A short muted cheer went up, and they all turned toward the villa dragging the dead pair of couriers along with them.

Two of Samra's personal guards were left to watch the villa if the official didn't immediately leave with the others.   They glimpsed Samra and the group of warriors heading toward them and began to walk calmly up to the villa's open doorway.   They walked in to find the official with his back turned to them and talking to himself while attempting to find something in the room.

"Sir, turn around slowly, and you won't die."

Their arrows were pointing straight at him.   He turned to face them, gasped in utter shock, dropped everything from his hands, and raised them above his head in panic screaming for mercy. He was told to remove everything from his person.   Once he was searched and his hands tied behind him, they sat him on the couch facing the door to await Samra's arrival.

One of the warriors went to stand in the open doorway and called out a greeting for them to come in.   Samra had the warriors quickly drag the two arrow-pierced couriers in through the doorway and forcibly thrown forward onto the floor directly in front of the terrified wide-eyed official.   Again he gasped in shock, pushed his body back into the cushions, and began to scream hysterically his innocence begging for mercy.

Samra yelled, "Shut your mouth and gaze upon the fate of traitors."

He approached him menacingly with his large bronze dagger and said, "Now tell me truthfully everything you know, or your future will be the same." pointing his dagger to dead men on the floor.

Before beginning the official's interrogation, he turned to the warriors and told them to search everywhere for anything with scribe's writing on it, as well as any gold and valuables, and place them on the floor in the center of the room. Turning back to the official, Samra said, "Tell the truth of how you came to meet the dead men on the floor."

The official was reduced to tears and hysterically cried out, "Please sir, I have never seen them before! I was retained to assist anyone that came to me with a certain seal impression, and they showed it to me! Please sir, I have done nothing! Please! Please!"

"Who is this person that retained you and gave you this seal?"

"Sir, many months ago I was approached at a feast in Knossos by a man who asked me if I was interested in earning a good deal of extra gold. Of course, I said yes."

The man arranged a meeting at a house on the southern hill in Knossos where he gave him an excellent retainer in gold to cover a period of a year. The official was instructed to simply assist anyone that came to him with a certain seal impression. After giving him the impression in baked clay, he gave him an additional quantity of gold to cover any expenses any visitors might incur.

"Can you identify this man, and where is this seal?"

The official excitedly responded, "Sir, I can certainly identify him. I can see his face in my mind at this very moment. The seal is on the shelf above the brazier."

Samra retrieved it and asked him to describe the man to him, but his description was too vague. He asked several other questions to probe further and confirm the answers he had given before.

"Very well, you will live for now, but you're coming with us to Knossos as a prisoner for witness. Secure your wealth and valuables, and my warriors will escort you to the ships."

The warriors had torn the villa apart and dropped everything of value on the floor as instructed. Samra had the warriors collect anything with writing or seal impressions on them and put them into a sack to be kept separate from the official as evidence.

"Treat him well. Once he has secured his possessions, take him to the Admiral's ship as a prisoner for witness."

When Samra returned, the dockyard was in a state of controlled mayhem with people and cargo being frantically loaded onto the vessels. Cronymartis was standing by his ship with his guards about him. As they greeted, Samra said, "Admiral, everything seems to be complete on my end, and by my last report of a few minutes ago Khamudi's Canaanites have still not been seen or heard from in any official or military way other than an enquiry on the fleet. How are things here?"

Cronymartis smiled and said, "All is well so far with the exception of the sighting of an Egyptian chariot speeding to the south on the other side of the river. If the Egyptians come we will fight them."

The Admiral reached out his hand to Samra and said, "Come aboard now as my welcome passenger to relax and be attended to while I finish this affair."

Samra turned and waved to his guards to board the ship, but they hesitated for a second before one of them spoke up and said, "No sir, you first."

He smiled, looked him in the eyes, and started slightly shaking his head as he quietly boarded the vessel. Cronymartis felt an instant sense of recognition that Samra truly was a great "Master of the Way" much like his father. Samra was a young boy when his father first told him that Cronymartis was a great leader and "Master of the Way". Soon he would witness this for himself.

The treasury had long since been emptied and stored in the holds of the first three ships. Just as the forth ship finished loading passengers and cargo, the sentry ship stationed upriver suddenly sounded its horn in the distance. The five ships left in defensive reserve immediately took up their anchors and began moving out to their predetermined line of positions across the river. They set their many fire pots in place and were lighting them getting ready for a fight. The lookout ship stayed where it was for some time and then began to row very quickly back to the defensive line.

You could see the sentry ship's warriors lighting their firepots as they raced to return to the fleet. The whole area around the ships was lit up blanketed by the night sky. Just as the sentry ship reached the line and began to maneuver into position, the lights from the Egyptian ships came into view as they rounded the bend in the river. The lookout counted ten large ships coming at them but couldn't be sure if more were behind them. The Admiral was immediately alerted to the situation. Word was passed, and the loading of the fifth and sixth ships became much more frenzied.

The boarding of the remaining people on the list was accompanied by shouting and screams from the crowd that was threatening to turn into an unmanageable mob. One of the warriors drew his bow and shot down a man attempting to climb over people scrambling onto the ships. Two of the first four ships were already sitting in the river fully loaded. The fourth ship and the Admiral's lead ship moved out into the river to join them. The group of four ships approached the front line of six to form a line close behind them. This made a formation of two lines of ships awaiting the Egyptian attack. The two ships still at the docks were frenziedly taking on people and cargo as the battle neared. The crowd was becoming increasingly more hysterical, and order was intermittently breaking down with fewer warriors to control them.

The Egyptian ships rowed resolutely down the river in a formation of five rows of two ships abreast. The fleet was aglow with fire from the multitude of firepots on the decks of the lead ships. The Egyptians were caught unready when the chariots arrived to alert them of the King's fleet docking in Avaris. They were planning to attack the city in another seven days with a large combined river and ground attack meant to take the city once and for all. Many of their warriors had not yet arrived, and the ships were not fully provisioned with weapons and firepots.

When the alarm was sounded, many of the warriors rushed onto their ships naked with only their shield, spear, bow, and a single quiver of arrows. The Egyptian commander quickly exhausted the supplies available to him, but he decided his ten ships of almost two thousand warriors was more than a match for the King's fleet no matter the shortcomings. He positioned the ships that were best provisioned and manned with his most elite fighters to take the lead in the formation as they pushed off from their moorings up river. Realizing the critical shortage of wadding for their torch arrows, the commander ordered the warriors that managed to put on their loincloths to remove them and cut them into strips to wrap around as many arrowheads as possible.   As they approached the King's fleet, they began hurriedly lighting their torch arrows for the attack.

Cronymartis signaled the fleet with the horn to have the two lines of ships rotate a quarter of a turn, as they practiced at the rendezvous, to face their beams to the approaching Egyptians. This would maximize the firepower of the warrior's bows.   The Admiral then signaled for two warriors to fire torch arrows to test the range of fire from the deck of one of the ships on the front line.   One of them was close to being the biggest warrior in the fleet and could shoot his arrows as far as any of them. The other man was a smaller warrior that couldn't match the other's strength or range.   This gave the Admiral a good indication of when to launch their first volley of arrows for maximum effect.

When the two torch arrows landed in the river ahead of the Egyptians, its commander grew concerned.   The nearest arrow had landed only seventy-five meters in front of them, and they were still, at least, five hundred meters from the fleet.   He knew only about half of his men were equipped with composite bows. The other half were equipped with the older single-curved bows with a much shorter range.   Most of the men on the lead ships had the composite bow, but the commander knew none of them could fire one of their torch arrows anywhere near as far as he had just seen one of the King's warriors do.   He immediately sounded the drum to signal the oarsmen to greatly quicken their pace.   He thought he would have to move in fast to overcome any bow range advantage the King's fleet may have and swarm them with his greater number of warriors.

The Admiral was shouting at the ship masters of both lines and word was relayed to those that couldn't hear him.   He had all the warriors of both lines to ready themselves with torch arrows. At the sound of the horn all the warriors in the first line released their bowstrings in a huge volley of fire at the lead ships of the

Egyptians.   About five seconds later, the horn again sounded and the warriors of the second line fired their volley.

It was an amazingly wondrous and beautiful sight to first hear the great swoosh of the torch arrows leaving their bows and then see the dark night sky filled with a huge wave of fireballs from the seven hundred and twenty warriors of the first line. Then another awesome volley of fire was released from the four hundred and eighty warriors of the second line.   The warriors were ordered to begin firing at will with their standard poison arrowheads until they could be re-supplied for another volley of torch arrows.   One man from every ten warriors was designated to light the torch arrows from the firepots for the rest.   A constant deadly hail of sharp bronze and scorpion poison rained onto the Egyptians in between the volleys of the killing fireballs.

The first volley of fiery mini-javelins hammered down on the Egyptians with a tremendous impact.   Hundreds were killed or wounded instantly and fell to litter the decks.   Many of their shields were pierced outright or knocked from their hands with hot burning bits of tar splashing onto everything.   The Egyptian commander just had time to scream out for his men to gather their shields more tightly when the second volley screamed down on them with a fiery arrow piercing the back of his head killing him instantly.

A majority of the warriors on the lead Egyptian ships were now dead or wounded lying on the decks with many screaming in terrible agony.   The inner hull and decking of the ships was beginning to burn in thousands of scattered spots from the burning straw and pine tar of the bronze torches smashing down onto them.   The Egyptian oarsmen that were still able valiantly continued rowing the ships toward the Admiral's first line.   The Egyptians started throwing bodies into the river to clear the decks of the dead as a constant silent rain of poison arrows came down on them and didn't stop.

The crying and hideous screams from the wounded and dying were deafening and horrible. More men were dropping to the deck every second. Men were falling onto their oars with the mini-javelins ripping into their backs. The fires were beginning to coalesce and burn more intensely in places. Men were tripping and falling everywhere in the chaos. The oars finally stopped moving, and the lead ships began to drift out of control powered only by the current of the river. Some of the survivors started jumping into the river attempting to make for the shore. The bodies of the dead and dying littered the water around the ships.

The Egyptian fleet was now in complete pandemonium with havoc and devastation enveloping it. Then the next waves of torch arrows slashed into them. The middle rows of the fleet took the brunt of it and suffered as greatly as the lead ones had. The burning lead ships were filled with scorched bodies lying in pools of blood, but they were now within bow range of the Admiral's front line. The fires were beginning to coalesce and build into flames that began to block the vision of the men on the ships behind them. The ships to the rear were forced to stop rowing as they crashed into the sterns of the burning ones in front of them; pushing them towards the defensive lines of the fleet.

The Egyptians ships became bunched up into a mass of confusion and bedlam, but they were beginning to send off sporadic volleys of fire that began to hit the fleet. The Egyptians were courageously trying to return fire onto the fleet with some of them running wildly onto the fiery lead ships trying to avoid the flames in order to shoot off an arrow before jumping into the river. The color of the river was darkening from the great volume of blood pouring into it.

Cronymartis immediately sounded the horn ordering the oars to be manned. The remaining seventy warriors of each ship kept up a withering volley of fire on the Egyptians. When the oarsmen were ready, he had them rotate the ships a quarter turn to point their bows downstream, and, with the second line starting first, they began rowing out of range of the Egyptian fire. The Admiral signaled to the last two ships at the piers to leave immediately. They had to fight hard to brake free of their moorings amid the total mayhem of the crazed mob of thousands now on the dockyard. The ship masters ordered their warriors to fire into them to keep them from rushing onto and swamping the ships at their piers. Warriors hurried to cut the ropes holding them to the docks with their swords. As the ships desperately rowed away from the chaos on the docks, people were screaming and jumping into the river trying to swim to the ships in desperation and begging for mercy.

All of the Egyptian ships had stopped rowing by then with many jumping into the river to avoid the inferno. The last two ships in the formation were relatively undamaged and started rowing back upstream to keep their distance from the carnage ahead. The bundled group of eight ships was beginning to blaze like one great mass of flames slowly drifting downstream toward the docks. The Egyptians that made it to the eastern bank were organizing and began to fire into the mob. As people started to fall from the arrows, panic surged through them. Many people were trampled to death in the mob's maniacal attempt to escape the Egyptian arrows.

Cronymartis knew he could maneuver his ships against the Egyptians and slaughter them all at that point. But two things held him back. The foremost one was that he didn't know if there were any more ships or ground forces moving against them. Secondly, Kalpoulis had instructed Samra that the King did not want to antagonize the Egyptian pharaoh, Ahmose, any more than absolutely necessary to facilitate the renewal of good trading relations when their conflict with the Canaanite pharaoh, Khamudi, ended. The King was betting on the single-minded determination of Ahmose and the Egyptians.

There was no returning to the dock now as complete pandemonium had broken out in the frenzied multitude. Many people were still jumping into the water attempting to swim to the ships as the Egyptians started to increase their fire into the scattering horde. Cronymartis slowed the fleet to let the last two ships join them. Cronymartis coolly moved the fleet to the far side of the river to negate any possible attack from the Canaanites and formed the fleet into a single line. He didn't anticipate any aggressive response from them because they hadn't done anything to impede them so far. He thought they were probably more concerned with not antagonizing the King in order to secure their trading interests to the north in Jaffa and Byblos.

Most of the people on the docks had already left and ran back into the city away from the body strewn dockyards. Bow fire suddenly began to rain onto the Egyptians from the city, and armed warriors could be seen running toward them for a fight. The Canaanites had finally showed themselves. The Admiral and his fleet had unintentionally given them a small victory over the Egyptians. A few weeks later, word came to Knossos that all the Egyptians that made it to the eastern bank of the river and fired on the mob were slaughtered. Only the last two ships in the Egyptian formation, having rowed back to their base, survived relatively unhurt. The loss of eight ships and more than sixteen hundred warriors delayed their plan for a great combined assault on Avaris for some time.

Cronymartis sounded the horn to begin their voyage downstream. The fleet's warriors watched in fascination at the roaring fires among the Egyptian ships as they worked the oars.

There were hundreds of burnt bodies floating in the bloodied river. The Admiral knew there was nothing to impede their escape from Avaris now. The fleet had been docked in Avaris for only about seven hours. Cronymartis led them on a relaxed, steady pace downstream toward the open sea. The glow in the sky from the fires on the Egyptian ships slowly began to fade, and, after a time, the dark sky of the starry night and crescent moon reigned alone again.

Chapter 9

Return to Knossos

Cronymartis halted the fleet near the mouth of the Nile tributary before entering the open sea. He wanted his ship masters to give him their damage reports and to begin the process of transferring excess cargo and people to the six ships that served on the defensive line. He had each of the six empty ships pair off with ones that were full and lashed together to distribute the people and cargo more evenly. Cronymartis knew the only enemy they faced now was perhaps a rough and windy sea. He didn't want the ships riding any heavier in the water than necessary.

Seven warriors had been killed in the battle with another nine wounded. A few of the wounded were transferred to other ships so they could receive more individual attention from the ship master's healers. One man, whose wound was severe, remained on his ship for fear of killing him if he was moved. The ships were essentially undamaged. Their cypress hulls and decks were only slightly scorched by the Egyptian torch arrows with some minor fire damage to their provisions.

Cronymartis felt very lucky, but everyone knew it was his calm clarity of thought under pressure that had saved them from greater loss. He always regretted the lost of any of the men under his command, but he knew it could have been much worse especially if the Canaanites had turned on them at the wrong moment.

While the ships were tightly grouped preparing for the open sea, the two couriers on the sixth ship and the surviving warrior on the fifth made eye contact. They communicated with slight hand and body gestures to inquire where the other two couriers were. The warrior indicated he didn't know. The leader could only assume they were killed in the city by the snipers. They certainly had plenty of time to make it to the ships.

"There are only three of us left now. This is a complete disaster, but, at least, I and two others still live to return home."

After distributing the load of each ship's cargo as evenly as possible, they took an account of their provisioning for the passengers and crew. The passengers were instructed to bring their own provisions, but many of them had only their belongings. Some had nothing but their loincloth. Cronymartis judged he could sail the fleet for another two weeks before any rationing or privation became necessary. The Admiral ordered the ship master of the fifth ship that had the assassin warrior on it to place his ship at the end of the line when they formed up.

When the ship masters of all twelve ships signaled the Admiral they were ready, he led the fleet out of the river into the open sea with their oars. This heartened all the men. They were now completely safe from attack and on their way home with the King's Avaris treasure. Cronymartis headed north-northwest into a light northwest wind for a few hours. Once he judged they were well out into the open sea and far from any obstructing landfall, he turned the fleet northwest into the wind. The wind was too light to even consider tacking the ships with the sail.   He had them row straight into it with an unhurried steady pace in hopes of lowering his sail to catch another one of the south or southwest winds that blew in the spring.

This would fill their sails well enough to take them northwest to the eastern end of Crete in good time.   After sailing past the great cities of Zakros and Palaikastro on the eastern coast and they were well above the islands of the northeastern cape, the Admiral would then turn the ships west to head for Amnisos. As long as the winds didn't blow too hard, the fleet would make the journey in good time and in safety.

On the second day, Cronymartis halted the fleet and had them gather up in a tight formation for the burial of the fallen warriors.   The healers of the fleet prepared the bodies by cleaning them and oiling their skin before completely wrapping them in clean white linen.   One of the wounded warriors died from his injuries; making it eight men killed.   Each of the dead warriors was placed on a large decking board and reverently carried by four fully dressed warriors to the stern of the ship. Each of the ship masters gave the men solemn words on the honor of their sacrifice and blessed them to the gods before letting them slide from the boards and splash into the sea. There was a time of silence before they retook their stations and again began rowing to Crete with the sail.

Cronymartis confirmed his orders to the master of the ship carrying the assassin warrior.   The evening of the next day was cloudy and dark when the last ship in the formation began to slowly fall back to distance itself from the rest of the fleet.   The assassin was resting and drinking wine after a shift at the oar when he noticed the men around him whispering something among them.   It appeared that a message was being spread for everyone's general knowledge.   But no one bothered to whisper the message to him.   He asked the nearest man to him, "What is being passed?"

The man just nodded to him as if he didn't know when another warrior moved close and lied, "Our course has changed and a new plan is about."

He nodded in understanding and leaned back to relax and sip more wine.   The assassin was a worrier by disposition.   A feeling that something was wrong began to creep into him.

"I never would have done this if it wasn't for my greed.   It sounded so easy in the beginning, but now with the plot a failure will I ever see any gold?   I should never have done this, and I'll never do anything like this ever again.   I'll just see if there's any gold at the end of the voyage and disappear with it."

He nodded as if to agree with himself when he noticed the men around him were, one by one, standing up and slowly walking away.   His worry began to build strongly, and he became very concerned and nervous.   He was now sitting alone on the deck holding his cup of wine with fear overtaking him as he nervously looked around.

"They couldn't know I'm one of the plotters.   How could they know?   It's impossible!"

It was now obvious he had been deliberately left alone by the warriors with some of them turning toward him and reaching menacingly for their weapons.   He dropped his wine cup letting it spill on the deck as a blanket of fear gripped him.   He was trying his best to control himself, but he was panicking wildly inside.   Sweat began running down the side of his face and beading up on his skin in the cool cloudy spring evening.

He kept telling himself, "It can't be true! It can't!" when suddenly four fully armed warriors with their bows at the ready moved in front of him sitting on the deck.

Their poison arrows were sprung in their bows and pointed directly at him. In panic, he tried desperately to collect himself to face whatever was upon him. One of the warriors then loudly called out his name and angrily stated, "You're treachery is known. Stand up and move away from your weapons belt now or die where you are."

He slid away from his equipment and slowly made it to his feet. His whole body was shivering with terror consuming him. He felt paralyzed. Everyone around the scene took it as a sign of his guilt. As his body straightened up, it came upon him what they intended for his fate. He became very animated and began to vehemently protest his innocence loudly; almost screaming.

"Comrades, I have done nothing wrong. What is this treachery you speak of? I beg you! It is not true!"

The ship master and military captain were standing just behind the bowmen now. He continued begging for mercy from them and anyone else who would listen. The ship master spoke to all the warriors with, "This man is an assassin and traitor to the King for his actions witnessed by many at Avaris. Our leader Samraleos has ordered he be given the traitor's choice."

The man knew then his fate was sealed, and he was doomed. They would give him the choice to die from sharp poisoned bronze, or he could jump naked into the cold water of the open sea and take his chances. He stood paralyzed and shaking; unable to speak.

"Take off your garments now!"

He slowly did as commanded and stood naked before them. Suddenly, he fell prostrate on the deck near his weapons belt and began crying and pleading for mercy. He almost died right then and there.

"Stand up or die, traitor!"

As he retook his footing, he begged, "Please, master let me have the comfort of my bronze dagger when I jump in the water."

"No! Move to the stern for your final decision now!"

He very slowly made his way to the back of the ship. He stopped and turned to face them speechlessly pleading for mercy with his face and hands. He began to cry again and covered his face with his hands. He started to violently sob when the ship master shouted, "If you don't jump into the sea within the next few moments you will enter it as a dead man."

He was completely broken and making his decision jumped clear of the rowing oars into the sea. When his head regained the surface of the water, he started pitifully crying out for mercy.

"Please, master, I am not a traitor! Let me explain! Please! Please! I beg you!" he screamed.

There was a long tradition in dealing with the King's traitors at sea. The ship master thought, "He won't last long. The cold dark waters will quickly drain the life from him."

As the oarsmen solemnly rowed away from his cries and they faded into the noise of the oars, the ship master thought, "Now all I have to do is delay my arrival to Amnisos by a day."

He commanded the warriors to stop rowing and after calling everyone on board to his attention said, "All of you must now swear an oath not to speak of the traitor's death to anyone on our arrival in Amnisos.   If you do, you may put the lives of others in grave danger.   If anyone asks, tell them a man was lost overboard in a fight among you and that is all.   This is a King's secret!   Now raise your hands and repeat my words."

The oath was given, and the original nine members of the plot had now been reduced to two as Samra wished it.

At that moment, Synboliki was reclined on her couch casually sipping wine in the company of several guests in her villa just to the southeast of the palace.   The visitors were all members of her carefully cultivated inner political circle.   They were in various stages of inebriation and engaged in a sometimes lively conversation about Avaris.   Even Danaloi had somehow managed to show up for once.   All of them were the obsessively ambitious sons and daughters of important but aging committee members.

She had carefully selected and groomed them over the years based on the characteristics she desired.   They were tools to her, and she relied on their ruthless selfishness to do her bidding.   They confidently believed that her political ascendancy was inevitable and wanted to be on the winning side.   The most important attribute she desired in them was their capacity to be manipulated to her ends.   In a sense, she had trained them and thought of them as her puppets.

As they sat around the large oak table and in the many chairs of her gathering chamber, they were discussing the highly anticipated news of the return of the fleet.   The chattering of gossip and speculation filled the room.

"If Samraleos and Cronymartis actually succeed with this mission they will be the greatest heroes in the kingdom. They will sway the King and Queen and rule over the committees. No one will be able to say no to them!"

"If that happens, Kalpoulis and the others should be watchful of losing their positions." Synboliki didn't respond and shrugged as if it wasn't important to her at all as their conversations continued.

"It was a crazy mission in the first place. The Egyptians surely have swallowed them up like they're doing to the Canaanites. I heard thousands were slaughtered in Heliopolis last summer. I bet a few of the ships show up to report a disaster without any gold at all!"

Another one of the group stood up shakily holding onto the edge of the oak table for stability and haltingly said, "I just want some of the gold my mother gets for her share, so don't bother me with your worthless words, you idiot!"

Another guest stood up and waving her wine vessel high over her head slurred, "Cronymartis is our greatest Admiral and is the most potent "Master of the Way" in the entire kingdom. I have great confidence that all has gone well. So there!"

Waiting a few moments for emphasis and looking straight at the negative one, she haltingly said, "You will see soon, moron, when I am weighing my gold!"

Synboliki detested her guest's mention of the "Masters of the Way". She had no devotion to the truth and the techniques of the "Masters". She thought that perception was far more important than simply the facts and the truth. Perception was the only thing that was of any importance. The structured search for the truth of the "Way of Nature" was a great folly to

her.   She regularly used a subtle mixture of facts and
falsehoods to manipulate the perceptions of those around her.
The truth had no value at all except as a tool to plausibly
persuade others to her view.   It was what people believed to be
true that was critical to her; nothing else.   She thought the
"Masters of the Way" were nothing but a group of intellectual
fools wasting their time in some obscure search for the true
workings of the gods.

She missed the point of the masters and the "Way" entirely in
the name of her own narcissistic egotism.   She took the self-
centered point of view of the manipulator.   The last thing she
wanted for those she played mind games with was for them to
be actively engaged in analyzing the intentions of those games
and what was really behind them.   The victims would have far
too   much   power   in   defending   themselves   from   her
psychological manipulations.

While brilliantly intelligent, she trusted only in her feelings,
intuition, and utter selfishness.   In her egomania, she truly
believed her mind was the best in the kingdom.   She felt this
was amply demonstrated by her ability to mold and shape the
thoughts of her uncle, as well as many other important
committee members, to her ends.   She mused, "The King and
Queen are bumbling incompetents.   I should be the King or, at
the very least, the leader of one of the top committees!"

She noticed Danaloi was starting to feel his wine.   As she
looked at him, she could feel her irritation building.   This was
the first time she had seen him since the warriors left for Avaris.
She thought he had changed somehow over for the past year.
He was not nearly as useful and diligent in serving her desires.
She had witnessed Samra's culling of the warriors in the
courtyard and was certain the man killed and the other men
removed from the formation were those Danaloi had clumsily
planted in their ranks.   The only men she knew that had gotten

through Samra's trap with certainty were the four couriers recruited by Calusetne. He was much more ambitious and professional much like Danaloi used to be. She had simply requested Danaloi to provide extra manpower to help overcome Samra's personal guards if it was needed.

Frustrated, she thought, "He can't even do that properly. There's something wrong with him!"

She felt he had endangered the plot. Several times over the last several months he had failed to come when she requested his presence. She felt he was distracted and losing his edge in pursuing her interests and was becoming a liability to her when she needed him the most.

Killing Samra had become an obsession for her. She enjoyed the thought of her uncle sharing his Avaris gold with her, but it was far more critical that Samra not return alive from the mission. She thought she could deal with any threat to her uncle from Cronymartis. But it would be a disaster if both of them returned as great heroes with the gold. That would be the worse! Samraleos had to be removed from her world, and she dearly hoped he was lying dead in Egypt or feeding the fish in the sea.

She encouraged her guests to leave by saying, "Please everyone, I'm not feeling well and need to seek out my bed. It was a wonderful evening, and I'll see you tomorrow at the midday feast. Perhaps there will be word of the fleet by then."

She motioned for Danaloi to stay as she escorted her guests to the door. A couple of them were stumbling badly with the more sober ones coming to their support as they made their farewells. It was only a short walk home for most of them. After finally closing the door, she quickly turned in anger to Danaloi.

"You were sloppy and made it easy for Samra!" she quietly hissed.

Whispering he pleaded, "Don't be angry with me! Please! Yes, I recognized the warrior that was killed and the other three as my recruits, but I think one of them got through to Avaris. You didn't give me enough time! Did the four couriers get through?"

Synboliki angrily responded, "Yes, as far as I know. But you should have been better prepared! You know how important this is to me! I just hope they're able to get more men in Avaris."

"I'm sure they must have met with our official there. Are you positive the couriers got through?

"Yes, a message was received from Kommos saying they had boarded the ships. That's all I know."

"All the men Samra detained are still imprisoned in the palace. No one has been allowed to see them, so I can't be sure but that's still four and more probably five men. They'll only need to get a few more to kill him in Avaris!"

"I just hope you instructed that official well enough. We knew we would have surprise on our side, but we need some very big bodies to deal with Samra and those guards in a confrontation. Did you see the size of them? It's not like before when we had one of Karasos' personal guards working for us."

"Synboliki, there's no need to worry. None of the imprisoned men knows what I look like, and the couriers have the seal impression. The official will help them. He lusts for gold above all things.

"All I know for sure is that if five men got through they're going to need another ten to even think about dealing with Samra and those guards of his."

"They should have plenty of time to raise the men they need. The fleet will have to be docked in Avaris for, at least, two or three days. Don't worry!"

"I don't smell success."

"There's nothing more we can do. We can only hope for the best now. If Avaris is not a success, we can get him later. Besides he'll probably be killed by the Egyptians. Come, let's have some more wine."

"No, I have business to attend to and must leave."

As he gathered his things and approached the doorway, he said, "Very well, I'll go, but don't be mad at me."

She softened her look and said, "I'm not mad at you. But I want you to know I don't like it and I'm not happy."

As Danaloi walked out the door, she smiled and thought, "There was still a good chance four or five warriors could kill Samra by deception and surprise even if they weren't able to obtain additional men. It had taken only one man to kill his father. Let's just wait and see."

As he walked home, Danaloi was agitated as he always was when she vented her anger on him. He thought, "We'll know what has happened in the next few days."

Synboliki thought that with Samra hopefully out of the way nothing could stop her ambitions in the palace. Her first step in destroying him was the murder of his father, Karasos. She considered his death as her greatest achievement so far. It had eliminated a serious political threat to her uncle's position and secured the instrument of her political ambitions. At the time, it had come to her the King and Queen had asked Karasos to replace Kalpoulis on the committee. This would have significantly diminished her political influence. She could not tolerate this without a challenge and began to very subtly scheme against Karasos' well-being. She didn't care how he was dealt with as long as he was removed. She never heard that Karasos, after considering it for a time, had turned the offer down.

She examined a variety of ways of discrediting him, but nothing seemed promising. She was surprised to find him and his circle of friends impervious to her delicate machinations and discovered she had in the process engendered distaste for her in him and several others. Their reaction was disturbing and unusual for her. In time, she decided Karasos had to be killed. She felt there would be a huge added bonus to this for her. It would help to teardown and hopefully break the one she perceived as her greatest political threat, Samraleos. She knew of the great love and admiration he felt for his father.

She believed it was her best course of action, but, as usual, there could be no suspicion directed at her. As she always did, she would have her puppet Danaloi using her gold to approach those who would do her bidding. He had done this several times in the past and so far no consequences had come back upon them. They had known each other from childhood with an understanding they were different from everyone else. They gravitated towards one another in their mutual bizarre alikeness. She trusted totally in his comprehensive self-interest, and she had always rewarded him well. Over the years, Danaloi and Synboliki had developed a strong mutually self-serving relationship of predation towards anyone they perceived to be in their way. Their teamwork had rewarded them handsomely.

Synboliki viewed Danaloi as the only person who really understood her, and he felt great comfort in her company as the only anchor in the sea of mental storms that plagued him. They were occasional lovers even though they found each other physically unattractive. Danaloi had other predilections. This only happened when they felt a kind of need to feed on each other. Otherwise, their relationship was founded on their desire to be with someone else of their own kind.

One day it came to her through her informants that one of Karasos' personal guards, a man named Trabeseos, might be susceptible to corruption. He was in a state of insurmountable debt due to the neglect and mismanagement of his finances. He could never inform Karasos or any of his superiors of his problems in fear of being discredited in their eyes. Despondent and under great stress he had let it be known to a few people he thought might be able to help him raise the gold he needed of his availability for almost anything. If he couldn't acquire more gold, he would be forced to sell off what property he had left to pay off his lenders. He let it be known he was desperate.

It took Danaloi quite some time and a great deal of Synboliki's gold for Trabeseos to eventually agree to the assassination of Karasos. He never met Synboliki and her name was never mentioned. At the first hints of what they wanted him to do, he rebuked Danaloi strongly. But as time went on and the pressure of his debts mounted with gold being waved in his face, he eventually broke and agreed to their scheme with several conditions. The intersection of their interests hatched the plot into reality. He received a retainer of gold that temporarily kept the wolves from his door. They then just waited for the right time.

Unexpectedly, Kalpoulis requested Karasos' leadership for the
mission to deal with the pirate attack on the King's grain ships
at the extremely subtle and cunning suggestions of Synboliki
and her cronies.   Karasos had naturally asked Trabeseos to
accompany him on the mission as one of his trusted personal
guards.   He had always performed very well for him in the past,
and he had no reason to believe he wouldn't do the same in the
future.   He knew nothing of his financial problems.

The opportunity came when the ships were being tossed about
in the heavy seas and driving rain of a raging northerly gale.
Trabeseos accomplished his mission unseen in the great storm
by thrusting a large bronze dagger upward into his back under
the ribs into Karasos' heart.   As he started to slump to the deck,
Trabeseos briefly held him up with his dagger and, using his
own body as cover, gently pushed his dying body over the side
of the ship into the water unnoticed in the howling mayhem of
the tempest.

He had planned to kill him during any fighting they might have
with the northern Aegean pirates.   But the right moment never
came, and he thought his mission would end in failure.   The
furious north gale that overcame the ships gave him the perfect
opportunity.   The warriors were blinded by the fierce rain and
giant seas.   It was his job to be near Karasos at times like these.
Karasos told his guards to work with the ship master to help the
crew ride out the storm, but Trabeseos stayed unnoticed as close
as he could.   He felt he would only have this one opportunity,
and he took it.

When he was nearest to him and saw no one else was nearby in
the sheets of rain, he struck.   After Karasos' body splashed into
the sea, Trabeseos moved quickly to help the others in keeping
the ship afloat.   It was only after the storm subsided and the
ship became more manageable that they realized he was
missing.   The warriors were in shock with some of them openly

crying in anguish when it became apparent he was not among them. If anybody had seen anything or suspected him of the crime they said nothing.

When news of Karasos' death came to the palace, it astonished everyone into a stunned and inexplicable mourning. It seemed incredible the great warrior and "Master" Karasos could be lost overboard in a storm at sea when he had survived so many incidents of violence unscathed in the past. Synboliki showed the mourning face of a devoted admirer in the ceremonies to honor him as she looked on all the sad and tearful people around her. But underneath her mask, she was thrilled beyond description and as happy as she had ever been in her life.

She proclaimed in her thoughts, "See what I can do!" in joyous inner self-celebration.

She wanted to shout out her accomplishment to everyone and call them all worthless fools to the power of her omnipotent genius.

Samra greeted the news with an overwhelming sense of sadness and depression. His eyes shed many tears over a period of several days. But, at the time, his wife and children had lovingly helped him heal from the severe wound of his loss. From the first instant, he didn't believe the story of his father falling overboard in a storm no matter how great it may have been. He had been suspicious for some time that someone in the palace was working against them. He simply assumed with confidence his father had been murdered.

At the time, he dreamed of his father telling him to seek out the truth. When Samra regained his strength as he knew his father would have willed it, he began to quietly and intensely investigate his suspicions with all the power of the "Master" he was. It had been almost four years now, and even though he had narrowed the search to a few individuals he still had no solid proof to condemn anyone. Having a degree of evidence and mostly suspicions was just not good enough. Proof required much more. But he was determined to relentlessly pursue his investigation until the truth of his father's death was finally revealed.

It was the middle of the morning when Cronymartis arranged for the ships to dock in Amnisos' shipyard; one at a time with his ship touching the pier first. On the voyage, Samra composed a message for the civil authorities on a piece of papyrus he had taken from the official's home in Avaris. It told them two assassins were coming to Knossos from Amnisos and were being followed into the city. He told them to be ready to take up their surveillance. He tied the scroll with a strip of cloth, poured hot wax onto its knot, and, as it cooled, pressed his signet ring into it. One of his guards arranged for a runner to carry the message to the authorities well ahead of the courier's arrival on the docks. Samra and Cronymartis hugged in farewell but knew they would be seeing each other again very soon.

It turned out there was no need to rush the message to the authorities because the assassins waited in Amnisos for a few hours hoping for the missing ship to arrive. Finally, they decided to head toward the city without their absent compatriot. The leader was worried. Too many things had gone wrong for them on this mission. The two of them started walking toward the city discussing the situation. He thought, "Perhaps somehow they know of the plot. But how could it be? It just doesn't seem possible, and we are alive. If they knew surely we would be dead."

Thalion shouted up to Jena in her apartment when he noticed Samra approaching the villa with his guards. She quickly made it down the stairs and called out as she joyfully came running up to him, "Samra! Samra! We missed you!"

Jena had been getting more worried and anxious the last few days and seeing him filled her with a wave of relief. She came into his arms, and he briefly swung her around with her feet rising above the ground before setting her down and giving her a passionate kiss. The guards smiled in feeling their elation.

"Yes, I'm home, dear Jena. Did you ever doubt it?"

"No never! But that didn't keep me from worrying." she laughed as tears filled her eyes.

Thalion didn't move, but his happiness created a broad smile. His young son Antoneos was ecstatic; jumping up and down and clapping his hands. After a few moments, Samra and Jena separated, and he walked over to Thalion to give him a big hug in greeting.

"I didn't have any doubt at all." Thalion said.

They laughed, and Samra picked Antoneos up into his arms and introduced them to each of his guards.

"Men, find your comfort in my home and feast all you wish. The authorities should be here soon, so you can return to your homes."

A few moments later, he noticed an old woman slowly approaching them on the path. The guards turned to look at her as she raised her hand in greeting. She was a member of the surveillance teams stationed around Samra's villa.

As she surreptitiously flashed her seal of identity, she quietly said, "You're villa is already well guarded, Samraleos. Your guards aren't needed if you wish them to leave."

Samra nodded and turning to his guards said, "Men, you performed brilliantly as I knew you would. It was an honor to serve with you, and you're reward will be great. I sincerely thank all of you. If you don't wish to feast here, you can take your leave with nothing but my best wishes."

He then approached one of the guards with Antoneos in his arms and gave him a hug with congratulations as he did with all of them in leaving. Everyone waved to one another in farewell. Thalion grabbed Samra's gear, and they all slowly made their way upstairs to his apartment. Antoneos was jabbering all manner of questions at him in excited curiosity.

Jena said, "We were so lonely without you. Oh wait! I need to get some refreshments!"

Thalion raised his hand to stop her, as Samra handed his son back to him, and said, "Stay, Jena. I'll bring some wine and prepare the bath water. I could smell you from far down the path, Samra."

They all laughed as Thalion, with Antoneos in his arms, approached Samra, and together they both gave him another warm hug and turned to leave. Thalion marveled at the chemistry between them when he returned with the wine. He had never seen either one of them this animated and filled with happiness. He nodded to them and left to prepare the bath water.

Samra and Jena again took each other into their arms, but he gently pushed her away laughing, "Thalion's right. I smell terrible! I haven't had a bath in weeks."

Jena laughed saying, "Yes Samra, I think you do need a bath very soon."

"Then please dear give me a bath so you don't have to suffer."

She moved into his body looking up at him and said, "Is that what you really want Samra; a bath?"

They embraced and looked into each others eyes. In a low voice Samra said, "You know what I want." and they kissed.

Samra sat down on his chair near the brazier, loosened his belt, and began removing his shoes. He looked at Jena and took in her great beauty as she smiled back at him. Jena winked at him temptingly as she walked out the doorway and went downstairs to prepare for his bath.

In a short time, Thalion, with his son at his heels, had the bath's vessels replenished with hot water flowing from the shower vase. Samra assembled a pile of clothing and other items to be cleaned. Thalion bundled them and began to take them down to the laundry in the workshop when Antoneos looked up and asked, "Father, why do we have to leave? I want to stay and hear Samra's stories."

As they walked out the door, Thalion looked down at him and said, "Son, Samra and Jena want to spend some time together right now."

"But why father?"

"I'll tell you later, son."

Jena brought in a tray of wine and snacks along with some fresh shampoo, lavender soap bars, and a pile of soft hemp towels.

As she began to ready herself for his bath, Samra said, "I missed you much more than you know, Jena."

With a glowing smile, she said, "Dear, if you missed me as much as I missed you we're both going to enjoy your bath very much."

He stepped under the shower vase letting the water splash onto his head and body and said, "Come, Jena."

Still smiling, Jena let her loincloth slip to the floor and silently stepped into the bath to embrace him with soap bars in both of her hands.

Chapter 10

The Assassins

As they slowly walked on the road to their apartments, the two couriers discussed how unlucky the mission had been.

"First, it was the removal of many of us at the palace.   How could we organize anything with the fleet in Avaris for only some hours in the night?"

"They will understand the plot's failure.   We couldn't have done any more."

"I'm sure we'll hear from the missing one by tomorrow."

"You're right.   It speaks well for us we are still alive."

They both believed everything that had happened seemed very plausible and out of their control.   The leader was a suspicious person by nature, but he saw no flags waving in his mind.

"We just need to make contact and get reorganized to come up with a new better plan to kill him here in Knossos." he thought.

They coveted their reward of gold for success badly, but success had eluded them.   They both were in dire need of gold to hold them over.   It took about forty-five minutes for them to reach their respective apartment buildings in Knossos' northeastern district.

As the two couriers settled into their rooms, two of Cronymartis' personal guards carrying his seal were sent to the civil authorities to identify the traitors and their current locations.   Several casually dressed warriors followed them to their apartments on orders from the Admiral.   They were trained in surveillance, and, working separately and in small groups, they went unnoticed.

The authorities worked to quickly replace those watching so they could go to their homecomings.   The two couriers had no idea there were now ten people assigned to monitor their every movement indefinitely.   After studying the area, they made profitable arrangements with a few of the local home and apartment owners in order to commandeer strategic locations to best observe them.

Later that afternoon, Samra met with the civil authorities to discuss the child murder investigation and instruct them on dealing with the traitors.

"It's going to take them some time to reconnect with their leaders and regroup.   Their intentions will show themselves during the surveillance." he thought.

The last thing he wanted was for the conspirators to give up on the assassination plot after their failure in Avaris.   He wanted them to reconstruct their plans in an attempt to kill him in Knossos.   Ultimately, he hoped this would lead him to the source of their treachery.   Meanwhile, he would wait to see what unfolded as they were observed.

Samra needed to prepare himself for his report to Kalpoulis and the committees the next day.   During their voluminous conversations on the homeward voyage, Cronymartis and Samra concluded the plotters could not have had an official waiting to assist them in Avaris without it being anticipated for quite some time in advance. If that was true, the conspiracy must have started several months before Samra was assigned to the mission. Who else could have known with assurance he would be assigned except Kalpoulis and his inner circle?

Cronymartis knew corruption in the intelligence committee was a very serious matter and volunteered during the voyage to give a full report in private to the King and Queen on their return. He laughingly said, "I'm sure I will be granted a private audience with a fleet full of treasure being unloaded in Amnisos."

He would talk to them about Samra giving an edited version of his report to Kalpoulis and the committees to help flush the conspiracy out into the open. He would request everyone be left completely in the dark about the assassination plot and the surveillance operations now taking place in Knossos. Only a select few would know the truth. The civil authorities had been sworn to secrecy from the beginning and were told to refer anyone making any inquiries to Samraleos. Cronymartis said he would inform him of the King and Queen's response to his unprecedented request as soon as they made a decision.

Later that afternoon, the Admiral was escorted into the King's chamber. The King and Queen were there with a few other officials and guards in attendance. After greetings, the King dismissed the others from the chamber. When they were alone, the King said, "Admiral, I congratulate you on the great success of your mission. They tell me we will have to enlarge the treasury."

He chuckled looking at the Queen and turning back to Cronymartis said, "Come tell us all, Admiral. You should not inhibit your words in the presence of the Queen. She is my greatest asset and counsels me in all things so speak bluntly."

Cronymartis stepped forward saying, "Yes, majesty."

"Sir, not long after my first meeting with Samraleos in Kommos, we joined our minds and shared our knowledge in the "Way of Nature" to plan the mission for its success. I must say I believe Samraleos to be the best and, certainly, the most creative "Master" in the kingdom."

The King interrupted exclaiming, "You should have seen him working on the warriors in the palace courtyard. Now that was theatre!"

Turning to the Queen, he asked, "Didn't you think so, dear?"

Amused she responded, "It was quite a performance. I've never seen anything quite like it."

The three of them chuckled for a few moments. Cronymartis then began to give them a detailed account of the fleet's approach on the river, all the devastation he had seen, and the taking of the treasury. When he described the battle on the Nile with the Egyptians, the King became very animated and said, "If only I could have been there to see that myself. It must have been a wondrous spectacle."

He told them of the impossibility of retaking the chaotic docks after the defeat of the Egyptians, the fleet's exit from Avaris, and the voyage home. As yet, he had said nothing of the assassination plot against Samraleos. He declared many more people needed to be evacuated from Avaris, but the Egyptians were close to taking the district. All of the reports gathered from the King's intelligence agents in Avaris were meticulously described to them. He finished by giving them a casualty report.

The King commented, "It's remarkable so few were lost. I compliment you on a brilliant mission, Admiral."

"Thank you, sir. But I must speak of another important matter that has come to light. It is the primary reason for my request for an audience with you. It involves Kalpoulis and the intelligence committee."

This instantly grabbed their intense interest and they both leaned forward slightly with great curiosity and rapt attention.

"Samraleos has always held deep suspicions about the death of his father and has been investigating the matter ever since. He believed that one day his own life would be threatened by those who killed his father. He considered the Avaris mission to be, very probably, a setup to kill him."

"We have our own deep suspicions about this." said the Queen solemnly.

"This is why he culled the formation at the palace. He wanted to see if he could flush anyone that had been planted among the warriors. This would give credibility to his suspicions. He wanted to remove as many of the conspirators as possible to weaken them for the mission and for his own personal safety. His suspicions were confirmed by the warrior killed in the courtyard. That was the moment he knew the plot was real. The three other men detected confirmed a plan was at work against him. He then began weeding out warriors he considered mentally weak or unfit. He was especially looking for those his father called the "Others.""

"What are the "Others"? I've not heard this before." the Queen asked.

"Majesty, Samraleos described them to me during the voyage, but I know he could explain it much better than I."

"Please, just give me a brief description to satisfy my curiosity, Admiral."

"Many years ago, my dear friend Karasos told me he was studying the human mind and had detected something that might prove to be important. But he said very little about it explaining he needed much more confirmation to determine its validity. Samra grew up while Karasos was developing his theory of the "Others" and exposed its concepts to him early on. Basically, it states that there are some among us whose minds work like the predators in the forest and not like human beings. They look human but they're really not. The worst part of it is they prey on the real humans around them to destructively feed on their lives and spirit. They enjoy hurting others."

"That sounds like the uncle of my half sister. He's banned from our family now, but he was a monster that fooled us all for a very long time. Tell me more, Admiral." the Queen interjected.

"These "Others" wear a mask to deceive us into believing they are human. Sometimes their mask fails revealing their true nature, and they do terrible things to the innocent."

"You mean like the child killings here in Knossos?"

"Yes majesty. Samra believes the killer is an "Other" that has lost control. Only a compassionless predator could do such horrible things. How could anyone murder and mutilate a defenseless young child unless they were just an object or thing to them. The victim is just food for their hunger."

"I have seen such things myself but rarely." the King said.

"I too have seen these things over the years and have come to believe it is very probable Karasos' theory is true. I'm not sure as a "Master of the Way" how it can ultimately be proven and a solution determined, but I have incorporated this knowledge as something that could be of great value to me in the future."

"Is there a way to detect these "Others"?" the Queen asked.

"Yes, Samraleos explained to me that because their emotions are those of a predator they can be tricked into revealing their inhumanity. He has developed an interviewing technique that looks for emotional responses that real human beings normally display. If they don't, they may be an "Other". He looks to see if they are mimicking emotions and not genuinely feeling them. The smarter an "Other" is the greater their ability to imitate. There is much more to it. Samra would be able to provide you with much greater clarity on this."

The Queen immediately began to analyze the people around her she suspected of such behaviors. She thought this concept could help her greatly in eliminating those she couldn't trust.

The Queen said, "I would, in time, appreciate it if Samra could personally instruct us on these ideas. This could be most useful in our daily affairs."

"Yes dear. This new knowledge is very intriguing. We must have Samra give us a written report. Now please, Admiral, continue with your description of the assassination plot."

"Samra never thought the mission itself was threatened except possibly by weakening it with his untimely death."

The King interrupted, "I should say so!"

"I very much agree majesty. He was determined to both thwart the plot and insure the success of the mission. After he left the palace courtyard to join the march, he was approached by four men calling themselves special couriers to officials in Avaris. They possessed sealed orders from the office of Kalpoulis. Two of these men were surreptitiously overhead on the voyage by a sworn witness discussing the killing of Samra. At this point, he considered them fair game for his bronze as I did."

"Upon our arrival in Avaris, the four couriers, joined by another warrior, were followed to an official's villa. We now hold this official as a prisoner for witness under guard here in the palace. He says he knows nothing but was paid a retainer by a man he can identify here in Knossos to assist those that came to him in Avaris with a certain seal impression. He says he was merely an innocent contact that was asked to help them with any requests they may have. He states he stands ready to identify and accuse his contact under oath."

"This could be very useful. We still hold all those that were taken into custody from the formation as prisoners for further interrogation awaiting the fleet's return. We have obtained valuable facts to aid in the investigation from some of them." the King said.

"Do those detained include the "Others"?"

"Yes."

"That's wonderful news. I will be able to witness them for myself."

Cronymartis briefly mentioned the killings of the two plotters by bow fire in Avaris and the one by traitor's choice at sea. He went on to describe Samra's requests that he felt were required from authorities well above Kalpoulis.

The Queen interrupted with, "We have already considered this. Tell Samra he can do anything he wishes except kill any high officials or members of their families without our permission."

The King said, "Cronymartis, the Queen has been leading an investigation into the death of Karasos since, like Samra, the day it became known to her.   She and I both smelled a palace conspiracy from the beginning.   We knew Karasos far too well. It would have taken much more than a north gale to kill him. The mission to Avaris was hoped to provide additional facts for her investigation.   This it has done."

"Yes, and now we have much to tell you, Cronymartis!" said the Queen.

As Samra and Jena were getting ready for the evening meal, Thalion knocked on Samra's door to announce the arrival of a dignitary.   Samra moved quickly to the door with his weapons nearby to see Cronymartis standing near the foot of the stairs with his guards.   He opened the door widely and with a broad smile said, "Admiral, I didn't expect you to come personally.   I was expecting a messenger sometime tomorrow."

"A messenger would never do for the information I have for you, Samra.   Besides I wanted to see what your home life is like."

Samra chuckled lightly and said, "Please sir, come up stairs and join us."

The Admiral instructed his guards his meeting might take some time, so they should find some comfort.   Thalion overheard this, and, as the Admiral began to climb the stairs, he invited the guards to join him for some food and wine.   Two of them stayed stiffly on alert at the foot of the stairs while the other four went to share in Thalion's offer with thanks for his generosity.

Samra held the door open for the Admiral's entrance expressing, "Sir, it's a great honor to welcome you so unexpectedly into my home."

Entering the doorway, Cronymartis took in the vision of Jenaloi standing near the table. She felt her nerves starting to jangle but controlled herself and didn't allow it to show. She had heard of the great Admiral since she was a child and never imagined she would ever actually meet him. He was a little shorter than Samra with slightly wider shoulders and a heavier build. He was very impressive standing there in his official clothing with his flowing white hair and glittering eyes.

With an emerging smile and looking Jena straight in the eyes, he said, "Samra, I had no idea such wondrous beauty could be found in your home."

Jena's comfort buoyed within her with his compliment, and her nervousness evaporated. Cronymartis was well practiced at putting people at ease in his presence with simple compliments, but, in this case, he felt his comment on Jena's beauty was just barely adequate. Ignoring Samra, he moved toward her with his hand extended. She stood still and raised her hand to him in greeting. Taking her hand in his he bowed to kiss it.

With his eyes piercing hers, he said, "You must be Jena. Words will never do you justice, my dear."

Jena then did something she didn't think was possible anymore. She blushed. Samra noticed this and worked to contain a good laugh. His admiration for the Admiral grew even greater with his display on meeting Jena. He stood silently amused in the background wondering if Cronymartis would show them any more of his magic. Then he did, at least, to Jena.

The Admiral put his left hand on top of Jena's and turning toward Samra commandingly said, "Come sit, Samra. I have much of importance to tell you."

Jena had never heard anyone direct Samra with such authority before. She thought, "This is a very special day."

As they came to rest around the table, Cronymartis looked to Jena and said, "My dear, I am about to give Samra information that could possibly put your life at risk. We think we have the situation under control, but it is without certainty. Are you sure you want to hear this?"

In the past, Jena might have quietly and politely removed herself, but in the presence of the men sitting near her she felt filled with her own strength, power, and courage.

She nodded to the Admiral saying, "Speak as you wish sir."

In confirmation, Samra said, "I trust her in all things."

"My dear, I appreciate your courage, but it can sometimes be very dangerous."

He waited a few moments in silence and when Jena gave no response, he said, "Very well." gently patting her hand.

"Samra, the King and Queen have been conducting their own investigation into your father's death. They have narrowed the suspects to Kalpoulis' inner circle. They do not believe he is directly responsible but is being manipulated by others. Their prime suspect is his niece Synboliki, but there is no evidence of her guilt strong enough for the committees to approve any direct action to be taken against her."

Samra's eyes widened and lit up.

"This helps me greatly!"

"The warriors detained in the courtyard have been thoroughly interrogated. A good amount of new evidence has been revealed that led them to identify, investigate, and place under surveillance several other individuals here in the city. But these seem to be only assigned actors in the play.

All those you culled, including the "Others", are still under guard in isolation in the palace. They are ready for any additional interrogation you may wish to perform on them. The three suspected members of the plot have provided only a vague description of the man that recruited them. He was disguised. They are unable to identify him well enough to put anyone before witnesses."

"You are authorized to do anything you wish with Kalpoulis, or anybody else, with the exception of killing any high officials or their family members. The King and Queen think it wouldn't be politically expedient in the current environment. You will need their express permission for this."

Cronymartis sat quietly for a moment and said, "I hope you are happy with this."

"Yes, very happy. That is as good as I could have ever hoped for."

"There is one other thing. They believe there will be another attempt on your life here in Knossos very soon."

"There's an obsession behind this." Samra said.

There was a long silence and Cronymartis asked, "What are your thoughts?"

"Kalpoulis, Synboliki, and their associates must be put under continual surveillance."

After a short pause, he said, "I think the civil authorities are far too overburdened with the multitude of surveillances they are committed to especially with the ongoing investigation of the child killings. I will speak with Telecaneos to request a troop of one hundred volunteer warriors to expand the teams of watchers."

"I'll be taking my morning meal tomorrow with the commander. I'll tell him to recruit the men and have them assemble at the villa of a trusted friend of mine that lives fairly close. Samra, why don't you move your people into my friend's villa as a precaution? You would be very welcome, and the villa is quite large with plenty of room for all."

Samra hesitated for a moment and said, "You're right, Admiral. I think that's prudent. I accept your offer with gratitude. I didn't think there would be a problem until they reorganized themselves, but it appears there is a separate plot."

"If that's true, shouldn't we assume the villa is being watched at this moment?" Jena said.

The Admiral looked to her and shaking his head affirmatively said, "You're right, Jena."

Samra nodded his agreement, and the three of them joined freely in discussions to determine their best course of action. Jena helped both of them clarify their thoughts. She seemed to have a brilliant natural inclination for this.   She made many valuable contributions to their ideas as well; just as she normally did when she counseled Samra.   As their discussion continued, a plan of action coalesced and took life from their collective creativity.

With its details polished into refinement, the Admiral looked to Jena and asked, "My dear, do you agree?"

"Yes sir."

"Please, Jena, you don't need to refer to me as sir.   Just think of me as a friend if you think I'm worthy."

Jena smiled at him and thought, "I've heard of this great Admiral all my life.   I should be awed and intimidated by him, but he would never want that from me.   He wants my power in the sharing of his."

Their plan called for the removal of everyone from the villa with imposters replacing them.   This would be done as surreptitiously as possible.   Samra and Thalion were to march away with Cronymartis dressed as members of his personal guard.   With the attention of any observers drawn to the departure of the Admiral, Jena and Antoneos would stealthily leave from the west side of the villa that was obscured by the trees and terrain.   Two of his guards were to dress in Samra and Thalion's garments and stay in the household as imposters.

After Cronymartis' departure, the local authorities were to be immediately notified and given the task of finding a woman that appeared most like Jena to impersonate her.   Whenever a suitable candidate could be found, she was to secretly enter the villa before dawn using the same path Jena and Antoneos were to use in leaving.   Antoneos would not be replaced.   It was simply too dangerous for a young child to be exposed to the threat.   They hoped the absence of the child wouldn't give away the deception, but it couldn't be helped.

Jena carried out the first act in their plan by casually walking downstairs to inform Thalion and the four guards in the workshop of their intentions.   As she passed the two guards standing at the foot of the stairs, she whispered to them not to be surprised if things didn't appear as they should.   They quizzically looked at each other briefly and remained silent in recognition.   The guards in the workshop were enthralling Thalion and Antoneos with their stories of the Avaris mission. Antoneos sat on the floor awestruck at their tales as Thalion was refilling their cups with wine when Jena appeared.

She told them there was a plan to be carried out, and the biggest of the guards was too exchange garments with Thalion. Another one of the warriors was to remove his uniform and bundle it tightly to be taken up to Samra, so he could impersonate a guard.   Jena pointed to the one that most closely matched his size.   As they exchanged clothes, Thalion asked her about what was going to happen.   She told him all of them would be leaving soon in two groups.   First, he and Samra would leave with the Admiral as guards.   Then she and Antoneos would slip out the villa's west door and move up through the nearby stand of cypress trees to the roadway in the night.   He wasn't happy about being separated from his son, but Jena told him they would be rejoined as soon as they emerged from the trees onto the roadway.

The guard impersonating Thalion held the bundled uniform concealed under his shoulder wrap as he walked out of the workshop past the two guards and up the stairs.   The guards totally ignored their mate as he passed them.   Entering the apartment, the guard handed Samra the garments, and he began quickly changing into them.   When he appeared to be a fit member of the Admiral's guards, using his own weapons and equipment, he climbed out the apartment's west window and swiftly made his way down the side of the building using the floor ledges to enter the workshop. As Samra entered the west door and observed Thalion dressed as a guard, he jokingly said, "My friend that uniform doesn't fit you properly."

He laughed in response, "This is as big as they had, Samra. Do I look the part?"

"You'll need some adjustments, but I think you'll do fine."

"I'll try to make myself appear smaller when we march away."

Antoneos was quiet but very excited. He was hopping up and down as if they were playing some wonderful new game. As Samra and Thalion prepared for their exit from the workshop, the Admiral instructed the guard upstairs he was to stay there indefinitely until further orders, and a woman would come to them sometime in the night to impersonate Jena. They were to live in the household as if all was perfectly normal. Cronymartis told him the authorities were closely watching the villa, but they must be prepared to protect themselves at all times.

A few minutes later, Cronymartis emerged from the apartment's doorway. He waved to the guard inside and calmly walked down to join his guards at the bottom of the stairs. One of the guards called out loudly for their comrades in the workshop to join them. Samra and Thalion walked out with the other two guards and, after forming up, escorted the Admiral down the path away from the villa under the moonlight. There were several members of the authorities waiting for the Admiral well out of sight down the path. Samra, Thalion, and the Admiral's four guards immediately made their way to the northwest to meet Jena and Antoneos on the roadway as the Admiral was escorted away by the authorities.

Using the visual diversion of the Admiral's departure, Jena, wrapped in a dark cape with Antoneos in her arms, clandestinely made her way out the villa's west door and swiftly moved into the nearby stand of cypress trees.   Once she was a couple of meters inside the tree line, she was forced to stop completely.   She couldn't see anything at all in the utter darkness, but she maintained her orientation.   She set Antoneos down on the ground and took hold of his hand.   She softly whispered, "Let's stay very quiet here for a little while so my eyes can get use to the darkness."

He would have done anything she asked.   He was having a great time.   She started to make out fragments and pieces of light around her and began to very faintly see the outline of the trees ahead of her.   She started to walk ahead carefully feeling her way with Antoneos behind her to the northwest.   Several minutes later, they emerged from the trees close to the roadway. Samra and Thalion approached them from different directions. Thalion took Antoneos in his arms as Jena and Samra kissed in hushed greeting in the shadows.   The four guards of the Admiral revealed themselves from concealment and walked out onto the roadway to escort them to Cronymartis' friend's villa. They knew the way well.

The villa turned out to be the home of an influential member of the King's committee.   A woman named Mariadne.   Samra knew of her reputation but little else.   She was well known as a powerful advocate for the creation of wealth and the welfare of the people.   For many years, she had counseled the King, Queen, and members of the committees to share the wealth that was acquired by their navy and merchants as liberally as possible with all the people.

The villa was very large with well groomed, beautifully landscaped grounds.   They walked up the stone entrance way, and one of the guards knocked on its large double doors. Shortly, a servant answered and announced their arrival to those inside. Mariadne rushed to the doorway with the Admiral behind her saying, "Please. Please come in. You all are so very welcome. I am Mariadne."

Cronymartis was standing behind her as she greeted Samra's entourage at the door. Stepping forward, the Admiral introduced them, "Dear, this is Samraleos, Jenaloi, Thalion, and his son Antoneos."

She was a petite woman with fine features and large flashing eyes. Her hair was beginning to gray slightly, but she was still a very healthy energetic woman with her own special kind of beauty.

"Samra, you are as handsome as your friend is large." she said nodding to Thalion.

Samra laughed saying, "He's never been small as far as I know."

They all laughed briefly.

"Oh dear, Crony told me you wouldn't be bringing anything with you. We'll just have to do something about that."

It amused Samra greatly how she referred to the Admiral as Crony. Mariadne called her head servant to give him instructions for a few moments and said, "If you wish he can show you to your chambers. Please do as you wish. My servants are your servants. I'm sure you'll enjoy your stay here. Now come in."

Knowing their way, Cronymartis' guards quietly retired to their quarters. Mariadne led them into a lavishly furnished chamber room with marvelous frescos of the people and nature on the walls saying, "Please find your comfort.   Refreshments will be here soon.   Samraleos…"

Samra interrupted, "Please, Mariadne, call me Samra."

Looking him up and down, she said, "You didn't tell me he was so handsome, Crony.   You always leave out the good parts."

"He's taken, my dear."

"Well, it's good to dream.   Isn't it?"

Everyone laughed and any tension there may have been in the room quickly vanished.   Looking at Jena she said, "Are you the lovely one that has enticed him, my dear?   I could certainly believe that.   Do they call you Jenaloi?"

"Please, call me Jena.   What should we call you, Mariadne?"

"Dear, I am Mari to you and your friends."

Bountiful portions of food and refreshments were placed on the tables in front of them.   Antoneos jumped from his seat and started eating ravenously.   This new game made him very hungry.   Wine was poured into their vessels, and everyone began engaging in lively conversation as they enjoyed the feast before them.

Mariadne moved to sit near the Admiral and said, "Samra, Crony tells me so many good things about you.   Do you have any political ambitions?"

"Not really.   It sometimes seems like a very dirty game to me."

She laughed, "That sounds just like Crony. Yes, it is a dirty game, but it must be played for the good of the people. Crony prefers to stand aside from the leadership, but I don't think that will last for long especially after this Avaris affair. They will demand it of him, at least, for a time. They might demand the same of you."

"I'm prepared for whatever comes."

"Based on what Crony has told me, I'm sure you are. Samra, while he was still alive, I considered your father to be our most powerful "Master". Now, Crony tells me that you too are a great "Master"."

Cronymartis interrupted, "Mari is also a "Master of the Way", Samra."

He nodded to them with respect saying, "Thank you both for your kind words."

After quickly filling himself with food, Antoneos was beginning to become bored with the conversation and started to get sleepy from the long game. As he rested his head on his father's lap, Thalion said, "Mari, I think my son and I need our rest from all the excitement."

"Yes. Yes, my very large Thalion. Your lovely son needs his sleep."

She waved for a servant and instructed her to escort Thalion and Antoneos to their bed chamber.

"Thalion, if you need a bath just let them know, and you will be cared for."

"Thank you, Mari. I appreciate your kindness."

Thalion stood and took his now very sleepy son into his arms, bowed to everyone, and wished them a good night before following the servant to his chamber.

"Jena, it must be tiring for you to be surrounded by all these "Masters". Are you weary and need your bed?"

Jena smiled broadly saying, "But, Mari, Samra is training me as a "Master" too."

Mariadne clapped her hands saying, "My, isn't that wonderful. You will love being a "Master", Jena. It's changed my life greatly for the better, my dear. It alters and clarifies one's perception of the world. If you want to change the world for the greater happiness, one needs to seek out the true knowledge of the "Way" to guide their perceptions. Don't you think, dear?"

"I can see the wisdom in what you say. I think perception needs to be cleansed with something that's solid and true, or it leads to the irrational."

Mariadne stood and offered her hand to Jena saying, "Yes dear. Come talk with me in private for a bit before you retire. I've already heard so much about Samra from Crony I think I already know him. But I know nothing of you. Perhaps we could become great friends. You would like that wouldn't you?"

Jena could only nod in agreement and off they went to Mariadne's bed chamber. The two of them talked for quite awhile, drinking wine, and enjoying each others company greatly. Mari recognized Jena's keen intelligence. They both felt a strong innate connection to one another.

Samra and the Admiral had long since found their dreams before Mari and Jena finally sought out their beds. The morning sun was quickly rising over the eastern hill lighting up the bright white gypsum walls of the villa and the great palace to the south. Everyone, except Cronymartis, slept late into the morning especially Mari and Jena.

Chapter 11

The Counterplot

As arranged, the Admiral walked with his guards to the palace to have his morning meal with Telecaneos.   After they exchanged warm greetings and took their seats, the Admiral announced, "Commander, you have a new assignment.   Samra has determined the civil authorities need to be reinforced with one hundred of your warriors for surveillance duties involving the child murder investigation and the assassination conspiracy. The King and Queen believe there is an active, imminent plot to kill him here in Knossos.   There could be an attempt on his life at any time.   We have Samra and his household living in hiding for their security and have placed imposters in their stead. Samra wishes the warriors to be recruited as volunteers.   They are to be told only that they will be working on the child killings.   There should be no mention of the plot."

Telecaneos sat quietly sipping his hot herbal tea and said, "Sir, you couldn't have given me an easier assignment.   I'm sure many more than one hundred men will volunteer for that duty, and we need to do everything we can to protect Samra."

As the Admiral savored his cup of stimulating tea, Telecaneos turned to call one of his guards to him and had him bend down to whisper in his ear. Cronymartis raised his hand to interrupt them saying, "Commander, Samra is to give a report to the committees later today. We will need men to secretly secure his path to the palace."

The commander nodded in recognition and turned back to his guard to complete his orders. A few moments later, the guard stood and took two other guards with him to inform the captains of their new assignments.

Cronymartis said, "I have some of my guards informing the authorities of the many men coming to help them. Samra will be meeting with them later with his instructions after giving his report."

"Is there anything else, Admiral?

"Not for now." he said as they lifted their tea cups in a toast.

Near the end of their meal, the Admiral said, "Telecaneos, I have a very interesting day ahead of me, and I was hoping you might accompany me. I plan to talk with the official taken in Avaris and have him try to identify any of those Samra put in custody at the beginning of the mission. These include several of his "Others"."

"Are the "Others" still in custody here in the palace?"

"Yes. This will be my first opportunity to witness one of them. I hoped you might be my guide and give me instruction while I have them interviewed in my presence given your training in their characteristics and detection."

"Oh yes, Admiral! You will find them quite bizarre and very fascinating just as I did. It's one thing to be told of their characteristics, but to actually see them with your own eyes is quite another."

The Admiral listened attentively as he silently sipped his tea.

"I will be applying this knowledge to my own family soon. During the voyage, I identified an aunt of mine as a probable "Other". I will be investigating her as soon as my duties don't require me and begin educating my family about them and their effects. If it is confirmed, she will be purged from the family to starve her cruel hunger so her many victims can begin to rid themselves of the abusive behaviors she induced in them. It will be a great pleasure to accompany you, sir."

The Admiral arranged for the Avaris official to come to a designated room and sit in front of a south facing window shutter to look through a small slit to observe the men being held in the palace. This allowed him to clearly see their faces and features without letting them see him. Each man, including the "Others", was placed in front of him for identification. He recognized none of them. The Admiral said they would return to have him witness others, as they became available, and he was returned to his comfortable guarded apartment.

Escorts took them to an interrogation room where they were seated in chairs along the wall. The interrogator said if they wished, he could bring in one or two of those that displayed the most obvious "Other" behaviors. They agreed in nodding. Soon a man was escorted in, seated in front of them, and the examination began. Outwardly, the Admiral displayed nothing, but inwardly his curiosity was peaked. After a time,

Cronymartis interrupted the interrogator and took his seat. He asked the man several questions about his family and his perception of other people. When he was through questioning him, he thought, "This man told me only what he thought I wanted to hear. He has no real emotions. The only thing real to him is his own selfishness. Karasos' theory is true as Samra said, at least, for this man."

He had two more "Others" shown to him and interviewed. The last one's condition was more difficult to detect. They spent over an hour querying him. The Admiral came to know the physical expressions of the "Others" well. With the confirmation of him witnessing them, he became a true believer. They walked out into the courtyard and discussed what was to be done with this new knowledge. Their conversation lasted for quite some time as they wrestled with dealing with something so widespread and endemic. The Admiral concluded their discussion by stating, "Commander, both of us have preparations to make before Samra comes to the palace for his report."

Mariadne quietly obtained additional servants from nearby friends to arrive in the morning and help with the care and feeding of her new guests. After all of them had awakened, bathed, and dressed they were directed into the villa's central courtyard for food and drink. She had a feast prepared that satisfied everyone grandly. As Samra sat talking with Mariadne and Jena, Cronymartis arrived from the palace and approached him saying, "The time is near to go to the palace and give the committees your report, Samra. There is great excitement in the air, and they are anxiously awaiting you. Also I witnessed the "Others" being interviewed. It is doubtless and proven to me."

They immediately had all of their personal guards assembled with the Admiral and his warriors leaving a few minutes ahead of Samra. They planned to arrive at the palace separately. As Cronymartis' started to leave the villa, a flag was waved to alert six warriors to march to Samra's villa and receive his imposter for a fake march to the palace.

The imposter and his guards walked a few hundred meters from the south on the western hill's path as Samra approached on the same path from the north. They were all well out of sight of any possible observers of his villa. When the imposters completed their march near to where the path came to a tee heading due east toward the palace, they were directed by a deputy to enter a home reserved for them. They watched as Samra soon approached and turned onto the route toward the palace. The imposters were to remain there until he returned on the path from his meeting. As Samra and his guards marched back to Mariadne's villa, the imposters would march back to his villa; making everything look as normal as possible to any observers.

The imposters living in Samra's villa stayed inside as much as possible and were extremely careful not to expose themselves to observation for long. As Jena and Thalion had resorted to while Samra was away in Avaris, food and other necessities were delivered to them by arrangement with the local merchants.

With the King and Queen present and Mariadne sitting nearby, Samra began by giving a detailed chronological account of the mission to the audience. He described the culling of the warriors as a precautionary move to strengthen the force by removing any criminal, weak, or unworthy members. He introduced them to the concept of the "Others" by saying, "My intention was to select out any individuals that could be identified as what my father, Karasos, called the "Others" as unfit and a detriment to all. The Queen has requested me to give her a written report on them, and copies will be made available."

No mention relating to anything regarding the assassination plot was ever made. He characterized the voyage to and from Avaris as uneventful except for his praise of Cronymartis' mastery of navigation. The taking of the treasury and the night naval battle with the Egyptians was described in great detail. He emphasized the Admiral's brilliant maneuvering of the fleet in the river and the prowess and fierceness of the warriors. Everyone in attendance was transfixed and mesmerized. His report lasted for almost two hours, and even though he was asked many questions he gave them nothing to indicate any aspect of an assassination conspiracy.

He finished his report by saying, "All I know of the amount of treasure recovered is that it is great. You will receive a much more accurate and detailed report on it from the accountants. That is all I have for you now. Thank you for your time."

Everyone in the chamber, including the King and Queen, stood up from their seats and applauded his great achievement with a loud round of applause. The shouting of congratulations lasted for some time. He bowed to honor them and promptly turned to leave the podium. His guards quickly assembled around him, and they began their walk back to Mariadne's villa. The fake march and the incomplete intelligence report appeared to work without any mention or apparent detection. This was the way they wanted it.

As the six fake guards marched with the imposter back to Samra's household, they were observed by a man on the balcony of a home to the south higher up the west hill some fifty meters away. He had a good but distant view looking down on the south side of Samra's villa from above and to the right. He was not able to determine that it was an imposter and not Samra entering the house. Everything appeared normal to him as the guards turned and marched away. The movement of people to and from the villa during the night had gone completely undetected. He seemed well satisfied that all was as it should be and was content with no news to report.

On returning to Mariadne's villa, Samra motioned for his guards to find their comfort and went to meet the others conversing under shades in the brightly lit courtyard. Mari quickly rose from her seat to welcome him with an embrace and warm kiss on the cheek.

"Come join us on this gorgeous spring day. Did all go well?"

"Yes, very well I think."

As he turned his gaze on Jena, he noticed her hair was freshly styled, and she was wearing a new light colorful fitted dress with a glittering necklace of gold and lapis lazuli nestling in the cleavage of her breasts.

"Lovely, gifts from Mariadne?"

"Yes, everything except the necklace. It's far too valuable. She said she couldn't help herself."

"Well, of course, I couldn't help myself. I'd give her the necklace too, but it was a gift from someone very special to me. The new clothes and necklace bring out her natural beauty which brightens everyone's day. Besides she's so lovely she deserves fine things. Don't you think, Samra?"

Looking at Jena, he smiled and said, "Yes, she does."

Mariadne could see the attraction and energy between them.

"My, I should leave you two to your desires. I can feel the heat of the flames from here."

They all laughed at her comment as Cronymartis entered the courtyard saying, "Our warriors are gathering for their assignments, and the trap will soon be set. Let's just hope none of them are detected."

"Has the surveillance on Kalpoulis and Synboliki started yet?" Samra asked.

"I don't think so, but it should be starting soon. We are to receive a full report from the authorities later today here in the villa."

"Everything is as we wish and is coming together well. It's their move now."

"Does this mean you and Crony are finally available to entertain us?" Mariadne asked.

"Jena and I were having the most wonderful conversation while you where gone. We were talking about the learning of the people."

"What do you mean?" asked Samra.

"As you probably know, the long awaited stone roadway to Khania was completed last summer. Now, the entire length of the northern coastline can be traveled on a permanent stone road all the way from Khania in the west to Zakros in the east. No longer do the weavers, potters, or bronze makers in the countryside need to pull their wagons for long through the deep muddy ruts in the winter rains to trade their goods. They can use the all-weather stone roadways throughout the year instead. Where before their was little or no trade with many of the outlying areas in the west, there is now a thriving and growing supply of goods moving to and from the cities on the stone. The expense of building them was great, but the reward to the treasury will be far greater.

Even with the disruption in trade from the war in Egypt, the treasury has never contained more wealth than now. Just as the system of standard weights and measures freed the people from the barriers of trade between them, the roadways have lessened the constraints and costs of nature on their industry. Last fall and winter the road to Khania increased the flow of goods into Knossos significantly. Where trade in winter from the west used to be almost non-existent, the new road has now increased it many fold. We will probably need to expand the fleet before the end of the year in order to accommodate its volume."

"What has this to do with learning?"

"With the treasury swollen with wealth, we will be building new centers of learning in the major cities – Knossos, Phaistos, Malia, and Zakros for all the people to attend. This is to be just the start. We will have several other smaller ones built in the less populated cities and towns by the summer after next. The committee members have been so impressed with the return on the investment from the road system that now, with my continual encouragement, they have concluded that if we invested in the minds of the people we could realize an even greater reward."

"Isn't that a wonderful idea, Samra?" said Jena.

"Yes, indeed. What will be taught in these learning centers?"

"We will attempt to give instructions on a wide range of subjects including the arts and trades. It is still being considered. But the main emphasis will be on the principles and techniques of the "Way of Nature", the drawing of the sounds, and the numbers of business. We believe that the more "Masters of the Way" there are among us, the more prosperous and healthy the people and treasury will be.

You and Crony had no knowledge of it, but the wealth you brought from Avaris will help us expand and quicken our plans."

Cronymartis laughed saying, "I've heard of much of this already, but I didn't know you had managed to get your hands on some of the Avaris gold. How long have you planned this?"

"I wouldn't call it a plan but since it first came to be discussed after the fall of Heliopolis last summer."

"Don't you think it was being a bit too hopeful of you to be counting the gold so far in advance of its arrival?" the Admiral said in amusement.

"We didn't exactly allocate it, but you underestimate the confidence we in the committees have in you and Samra, Crony. Your many successes over the years have not gone unnoticed, and many of us applied great encouragement to have the son of Karasos work at your side. The thought of the two of you commanding a large fleet of warriors filled us with great assurance the Avaris gold could be accounted for."

Her smile turned into a laugh with them all joining in. Cronymartis rose with his wine in hand to stand before them and declared, "I have never helped to seize gold for a more worthy cause."

He tipped his wine cup to them and took a good sip from it as did all of them in enthusiastic agreement.

"Tell me Mari, what other things are to be taught at these centers?   Will the construction of buildings and ships be included?" Samra asked.

"Oh yes!   But filling their minds with the fundamentals must come first.   Indeed, everything about the art of making the ships from the trees will be included.   Once their minds are primed with knowledge, they will be sent to the shipyards to be instructed in their practice by the master shipwrights.   If they choose to learn the construction of the buildings that don't fall when the ground shakes, they will be instructed by the master architects.

Instruction will be provided for many other things such as the manufacture of cloth and linen, the production of oils and perfumes, the making of fine pottery, and the melting of the rocks to cast them into tools, weapons, and other useful things. We intend on focusing on the making of products for export. This is the greatest source of the treasury's wealth."

"You will create too much competition for my small perfume business, Mari." Samra joked.

"I think the quality of your perfume will stand on its own, my dear." she responded with a sarcastic smile.

"I've never heard of the idea of a kingdom investing in its people's minds.   It's quite extraordinary!" Jena said.

"Yes, it's a more aggressive way of quickening the level of knowledge among the people to hopefully begin a great expansion of ideas based on the "Way of Nature".   With this, we need a much better understanding of how the mind works and how it can be healed if it is sick or damaged.   This is why the theory of the "Others" is of great interest to me.   Any defects or impediments of the mind need to be studied and cured, if possible."

"But, my dear, if some people are irrevocably prone to destruction and chaos, they must not be allowed to attend these learning centers to take a seat from someone more worthy. They must be identified and culled like Samra did with the formation in the palace courtyard.   You must see these "Others", dear." the Admiral said.

"I'm sure it will be fascinating, Crony.   Perhaps we could do it later today."

Addressing Samra, she said, "I think your father's theory of the "Others" is a great example of the kind of things that need to be taught to the people.   Perhaps we should include it in the center's teachings as part of what should be known of the human mind."

"That would be wonderful.   The "Others" thrive on ignorance and naiveté.   The people must be informed of their true nature to shield them from their evil.   Knowledge is the only thing that can really protect them.   The religious leaders and priesthood don't want the responsibility.   This kind of knowledge has to do with the here and now in reality and has little to do with their conception of the gods.   But the priesthood does have a strong ambivalence to human evil.   It seems it would be the kind of knowledge that would need to be repeated with each year's new flock of children and many of the adults for that matter.   We don't want this knowledge to be forgotten so the people, especially the children, continue to be their unaware and gullible victims." said Samra.

Turning to Mari, the Admiral said, "You would be amazed with what I saw with the commander, Telecaneos, this morning in the palace.   We sat in on a few interviews with the "Others" detained there. It was fascinating to observe their bizarre reactions just as Samra described. The "Others" are real, my dear. It makes me wonder what foul effects they induce in the people around them and what the true cost of their evil is. There are many questions that need to be answered."

"You know, Crony, I was just thinking the Mycenaean king must be one of these "Others". He takes whatever he wants simply because he can gather the most swords to steal it. He oppresses any free expression to his will and kills anyone that openly disagrees with him. He treats his women like cattle and buys and sells people as slaves with his blade at their throats. He selfishly keeps all the wealth that comes to him except for doling out some of it to his cronies. He shares nothing with the people that give it to him in the first place. He's a barbarian pig! He must be one of these "Others". Doesn't that sound like one of them, Samra?"

"Yes, it does; very much so."

"There are so many things the children should know before they are grown. The most important of these is the "Way of Nature". There is so much that can help the people with a strong knowledge of truth and causes. It has brought us so far with our architecture and naval technologies that provide us with our prosperity. The daily lives of the people have been greatly improved with the domestic technologies like our toilets and drains that send our sewage to be washed away by the sea and our aqueducts that bring us clean water from the mountain springs everyday. The people have never been cleaner, and the oils have freed us from the pests and insects. Our perfumes make us smell wonderfully unlike the Myceneans that smell of dung like the cattle in the fields. We are healthier than any other people we know of and the wealthiest in gold. The further advancement of the "Way" gives the people the promise of an even better, more prosperous life in the future. A life all people everywhere can see as possible.

I wonder what the world would be like if everyone knew the numbers and could draw the sounds? With ideas drawn in the sounds, they need never die with the speaker to be forgotten by the distractions of conflict or the great destructions of the shaking earth. Ideas could be preserved in the drawings indefinitely. They could spread from island to island and people to people where new better ideas could be spawned from the study of the older ones. This would greatly expand the accumulation of knowledge in the "Way of Nature" and quicken the advancement of the people's happiness."

"That's a marvelous conception, but I can see difficulties in its path." Cronymartis said.

"Yes, I too see a crooked path, but, in general and in the long term, if ideas could spread much faster I think it would be possible for the world to eventually become a much more rational and healthy place. Hopefully, it would be a world where all the people could be treated fairly, and the "Others", like the Mycenaean king, would find it much more difficult to oppress us. It would be a different, much better world."

"I fear the barbarians are too many, and we are too few." the Admiral said.

Later the first day, the palace was noisy with throngs of people filling the hallways and chambers a buzz in rapt conversation. Synboliki immediately walked over to the nearest group of people questioning them about the news. They told her of the Avaris fleet's return to Amnisos and its great success; returning with a vast treasure of gold with very few casualties. The rage soared unseen within her when she realized that Samra was not only still alive but was being referred to as a great hero. This was her worst nightmare come true.

She had hoped for the success of the assassination plot in Avaris, but there was a part of her that assumed its failure. She had been gnawed by a feeling of inevitable disappointment from the moment Samra struck in the courtyard. She knew his reputation and standing in the palace would now be greatly enhanced making him a much stronger, potent political rival. Without moving an eyelash, she mentally tore his screaming body apart with her own hands. His blood splattered everywhere in her vision of venomous hatred.

"If only I could!"

She began to browse calmly from group to group hearing the news from each of them; looking for anything new or different. She heard Cronymartis was granted an audience with the King and Queen. She waited in hopes of them talking to their counselors. The counselors usually gave a brief initial report to the committees. That meant her uncle, Kalpoulis, would hear the inside news of the mission. The King and Queen had already met with their counselors earlier, and a report never came. The words that filled her ear were exactly what Samra wanted them to be. The sudden taking of the treasury and the battle with the Egyptians were great successes, but there was never any mention of assassins or a conspiracy.

"If the fleet was in Avaris for only some time in the night, the killing would have been almost impossible. If five of them got through, then, at least, one must have lived with a story to tell. I have to meet with Calusetne and Danaloi to hear of Avaris. I'll need to make other plans but this time without Danaloi." she thought.

Calusetne's family was well known in the palace. His mother was a member of one of the committees concerned mainly with local and regional matters. He was perceived as a friendly but distant person. He seemed quite secretive to some and only rarely made an appearance at the palace. Like Danaloi, Synboliki had known him since childhood, but she had seldom come into contact with him. It wasn't until their teens that she first began to play mind games with him to see if he could be of use to her.

He was quite formidable physically in a less well formed way than Danaloi, and he would probably not have faired well in a direct confrontation with him unless they used daggers. Calusetne was an extreme master at throwing the bronze dagger and, amazingly, was accurate with either hand. A secret was lost to the world if he knew it, and there was a relentless directedness to his nature. She preferred to work with Danaloi because he was much more of a puppet to her will. Calusetne was a puppet to no one. Their relationship was an intersection of their obsessive self-interests only. She wanted to impose her desires on others, and he lusted for the gold she filled his pouch with.

He had provided Synboliki's plot with the four couriers. No one knew of their relationship, and they had not been seen together in public for well over a year. They met privately several times in that period in the hatching of the plot but only at prearranged secret locations in hooded disguise. With Danaloi's continuing fall from her grace, she now thought of Calusetne as her most competent, invisible, and dangerous accomplice.

She began to consider the possibility that one or more of the Avaris assassins had been detected but allowed to come forward to expose their contacts and possibly her. She held failure in great contempt and would not allow it to fall on her again if she could.   She didn't have the slightest suspicion her villa was being watched at that very moment.

Her powerful egomaniacal mind had been thinking from the first about her alternatives if the Avaris plot failed.   She considered many other scenarios, plans, and methods to eliminate Samra but felt constrained by time.   Her current preferred choice was to have him murdered by master bowmen outside his villa or as he walked to and from the palace.   This was the reason she had Calusetne arrange for his villa to be watched.   He wasn't guarded day and night, so surely there would be opportunities.

She felt it was simply impossible for her to wait for Samra to be assigned to another mission.   Who knew when that would be?   He could do her great damage in the meantime as his power blossomed in the committees.   She knew the King and Queen had already considered removing her uncle Kalpoulis from his post years earlier.   Perhaps, given time, he would have the post for himself!   She could never tolerate that.   With time an important factor, she considered her choices.

"It must be done here in Knossos or wherever Samra can be isolated and entrapped.   But it must be done soon!"

She had long considered poisoning his food or drink and was continually studying their practicality and feasibility.   She would use her growing knowledge of poisons to help her eliminate anyone blocking her path in the future.   She was always interested in hearing of new poisons and knew the usage of many of them quite well.   The problem with poisoning Samra was he only very rarely feasted at the palace.   It seemed impossible to her to poison him in his own household.   The people around him were far too loyal and protective.   She knew of no one not frightened at the prospect of confronting his giant servant.   But there might come a time when she would be able to arrange it. She dismissed the scheme to poison him as a long term proposition. She could not wait.

The idea of him falling to the ground riddled with sharp bronze and scorpion poison appealed to her very much. She would love to watch his wounded body violently contorting in prolonged agony before finally expiring. She glowed in vengeance with images of it swimming in her mind.

"That would be so, so wonderful."

A blissful smile of hatred emerged on her face.

"Perhaps it could be arranged to appear as a simple violent robbery attempt."

Synboliki always worked diligently to divert any attention to her activities. She felt that whatever scheme she hatched must always have a strong element of deniability built into it. No blame was to ever point in her direction or to any of her close associates. She knew there would be a very intense investigation if Samra was murdered. But she felt that as long as Danaloi did what he was told and Calusetne did what he always did, then neither of them would ever be detected or identified. She was certain that given everything she had instituted in order to operate in the deepest secrecy, if they couldn't be identified then neither could she.

"I must meet with Calusetne soon to hear any news of Avaris and find out if his men are ready for the killing. If we need to recruit additional warriors so be it. Whatever the cost in gold is!" she thought.

Her family's gold could acquire any number of master warriors she desired. She abruptly remembered she had to meet with her uncle Kalpoulis to inquire if he had obtained any inside information on the mission.   She walked off to find him before returning home.   Her uncle could tell her nothing she didn't already know.   On arriving back at her villa, Synboliki sent a messenger to Danaloi requesting him to come to her.   He was late as usual.   She was not amused and thought, "The fool must be using his opium to excess or whatever else he's doing."

Danaloi was observed as he entered the villa.   They met coldly as was their practice.   She venomously told him all the bad news she heard of the Avaris mission.   Oddly, he somehow felt closer to her in moments when she expressed her anger unless it was directed at him.   The plot was a complete disaster, but everything she heard that would promote its failure seemed credible and plausible.   She did feel quite confident there was no reason to believe the plot had been compromised.   Her uncle, as head of the intelligence committee, would be one of the first to be told of anything about a plot or assassins.

"Danaloi, you need to see if you get a sign for a meeting from the warrior you think got through to Avaris tomorrow.   I need you notify me but don't meet with him for now.   I need to think about this."

"Yes, I'll take care of it beginning at first light."

"Ha!   You haven't seen first light in months.   Please just follow my instructions, and return to me with word.   Now I need you to leave me.   I have other people to meet with." she spat angrily.

"Very well, I assure you that as soon as I hear something I will return to you at once."

"Remember, don't meet with him."

"Yes.   Yes, Synboliki." he said with irritation as he walked out the doorway.

She walked into her bed chamber to retrieve a fresh white linen curtain from her cabinet and walked to her east facing window. She usually kept the shutter closed.   She started removing the existing curtain to put up a new white one.   She then widely opened the shutter to give her signal.   Already on the alert with the news of the fleet's return, Calusetne soon noticed the white curtain in her open window about two hundred meters away. He was looking out the west facing window of his bed chamber in his family's villa southeast of the palace.   The villa was just beyond the outer roadway and slightly higher on the eastern hill than the houses and apartments inside it.   He had a clear, distant view of her window signal.   He promptly changed his curtain to answer her request.

About an hour after sunset, she made her way, dressed in a hooded cape, into an area of densely packed homes and apartments separated by a maze of narrow pathways.   As usual, she used a predetermined course to her destination.   Once she entered an alley between the buildings, she started to move very quickly.   It was as if she assumed she was being watched.   She didn't believe she was being pursued, but this was the standard way she approached her contacts attempting to be absolutely sure of not being followed.   The two deputies following her lost her almost immediately.   Calusetne was sitting at the table waiting in the dimly lit room as she opened the door.   He motioned her to sit down as they exchanged greetings and began their discussion of what was to come.

The next morning Calusetne spent quite some time talking to his small number of associates at the palace about Avaris.   He tried to find out anything he could from those he knew were closest to the members of the top committees.   He listened to all the rumors and stories, but he heard nothing of any plot.

Synboliki was right. Everything seemed normal. It was just a very successful mission and nothing else. He then walked home being sure to look for his signal for a meeting.

The lead courier set off late in the afternoon on the first day of the fleet's arrival to his signal point. He had already informed his partner of his intentions. Before he left, he took a few small black river stones and put them in his pouch. Whenever he wanted to request a meeting, he was to put a black stone into a flower pot at a certain intersection in the palace district. The top of the soil in the pot was covered by crushed white gypsum stone from the quarry making the small black stone distinct. If the stone was removed within a certain amount of time, it meant he could go to a predetermined residence in the area for a meeting.

He was observed as he nonchalantly walked through the district. They did not observe him drop the stone surreptitiously into the pot. When he returned to the same area about an hour later, he saw the black stone was still in the flower pot. He left it there to see if it was retrieved before he returned tomorrow. He decided to walk home and come back the next day late in the afternoon.

The next afternoon he noticed the stone had been removed and subtly dropped another one into the flowerpot. He returned about an hour later and observed the new stone was missing. This was his signal to come to the designated location to meet his contact. In the style of Synboliki, a predetermined route was required of him to approach the secret residence. It was another neighborhood of densely packed households and apartments. The watchers had strict instructions not to reveal themselves at any time, so they could not follow him too closely. As he quickly moved down the alleys and passageways, he made four sharp turns along the way blinding his path to anyone even closely following him. The watchers lost him almost as soon as he entered the maze of alleys. He made his way to the designated door and swiftly entered the darkened room.

The room was lit with only a small oil lamp. It took several moments for his eyes to adjust to the darkness before he could clearly make out the man sitting behind the large table in front of him. As in their prior meetings, the man wore a dark hooded cape to obscure his identity. He waved for him to come forward saying, "Come sit and tell me of the mission."

As he was taking his chair, the hooded man said, "How many of you have returned?"

"Sir, I can confirm the return of only two of us."

"Only two of you have returned?"

"Yes sir. Of the nine of us in the beginning only five made it to Avaris. Two of us did not return to the ships before the fleet left the docks in Avaris. I received a report from Amnisos earlier today that a third man, one of the warriors, who I saw alive at sea after our escape is missing and has not been heard from. There fates are unknown, but there were Egyptian snipers killing many in the city."

"How could things have gone so wrong?"

He was nervous and desperate for a payment of gold and said, "But, sir, the plan was unlucky from the beginning. Being weakened from the start, we had no time to organize in Avaris. The fleet was in the docks for only several hours. It arrived late at night and left before the sunrise. We met with the official, and he agreed to help us obtain additional men, but he couldn't do anything until the next day. There was no next day. It was impossible, sir!" he said in exasperation.

"Then to have more of us missing or killed in the deadly chaos and battle was just another blow to our success. I thought the only possible course was to return to you and do my part in a new plan to kill Samraleos here in Knossos."

"We are thinking of doing just that."

"Sir, I have devised a plan that could easily kill him here in the city and provide a very strong diversion of guilt. But my partner and I are very much in need of gold to sustain ourselves after the long voyage. I hoped to receive some for our services so far and perhaps a retainer for some future venture. It would be most welcome. Whatever you feel is best, sir."

The hooded man nodded and reached for a small pouch to his left on the table. He slid the pouch over the polished tabletop to him saying, "That's very interesting, and we'll talk to you later about it. Now, here's some gold to hold the both of you over for a time."

He caught the sliding pouch and quickly felt its weight in his hand. Smiling he said, "Oh, yes sir. Thank you very much. This will do fine."

"Come back tomorrow with your stone, and I'll have more to speak to you about. I must be leaving now."

As the courier rose to stand across the table in front of him, the hooded man reached behind his head, and, in a flash of motion, threw a large bronze dagger into his abdomen. It penetrated him deeply under the ribs. He saw the bronze glint in the dim light of the oil lamp and grunted in shock as he felt the hard blow to his body. The impact pushed him back a step, and he looked down in amazement at the blade piercing him. He looked up with questioning horror in his eyes at the man that just killed him when another smaller blade struck low into his throat.   The dead man stood upright for another second and quietly collapsed in a heap on the floor.

The hooded man quickly searched his body for anything that might be incriminating.   He found nothing but two or three stones in his pouch.   He took the stones and put them in his belt pouch as a precaution along with the gold he had just given him. Being careful to not let any blood spurt onto him, he removed his daggers from the body.   The blood flowed heavily from the open wounds.   As he squatted near the body, he used the courier's loincloth to wipe his blades clean.   Dark blood was pooling on the floor.   Relieved all had gone well, he moved to the rear door.   After listening for any sounds from outside for several moments, he opened the door as silently as possible and stealthily made his way into the narrow labyrinth of passageways to disappear undetected.

Chapter 12

The Child Killer

Samra and Jena were relaxing under the shades in the courtyard enjoying a lively conversation when they noticed one of Mariadne's servants approach with the clothing he had requested earlier in the morning. Jena chuckled at the sight of the soiled garments placed on the stone table in front of them. The servant told them they were purchased from workers at a local construction site. Samra smiled saying, "They'll do fine. Thank you."

Amused, they rose from their seats at the table, gathered their attire for the day, and walked to their bed chamber to change into them. Samra wanted to examine all four of the murder sites without his guards in disguise. Jena asked if she could join him to travel as a couple. He saw no harm in it as long as they went unrecognized.

They emerged from a back entrance of the villa and soon began dusting and wiping their exposed skin with dirt to match the appearance of their clothes. They were laughing and having a lot of fun as they made suggestions to improve their disguises and began rubbing even more dirt on each another. Samra wore a woolen hat to obscure his face. Once they were satisfied with their costumes, they set off to visit the civil authorities. He needed a guide to help them inspect, as thoroughly as possible, the layouts of the murder sites. Samra had taken over the investigation only a few days before leaving for Avaris and hadn't seen the first three murder sites.

"There must be a pattern to how the killer stalked and took his victims." he thought.

He didn't believe the killer was some crazed person that was out of control throughout the process. He thought he must be coldly calculating up to the moment of gaining total control of his victim before beginning his sick frenzy of lust and violence. He was particularly interested in the evidence that the killer had never been seen or heard either approaching, during, or following any of the murders. How could he do this? He believed this was a question that had to be answered.

The receiving clerk had seen Samra only a couple of times before and did not recognize him in his disguise when they entered the administration building. Jena had never been their before. As they approached the clerk, Samra asked for the head of the district while presenting him his signet ring. The questioning clerk thought it was probably some joke, but he suspiciously took his ring down the hall to his supervisor. The clerk soon returned and asked them to follow him to the district head's office.

When they entered his office, he looked at them briefly from behind his desk. He then got up and curiously walked towards them for a closer look. Samra lifted his hat up to better show his grimy face.

"Samraleos, it is you! That is a very good disguise, indeed. I've never seen you so filthy before." he said with amusement as he handed his ring back to him.

"Please, come take your seats and comfort yourselves. I've heard so much of your Avaris adventures. Well done. It's an honor to welcome you. What can I do for you?"

"Thank you, sir. This is my associate, Jenaloi. I've come to request an escort to show us all four of the murder sites especially the first three. I haven't had a chance to examine them since taking the case."

"Yes, anything you wish."

"Please have the escort disguised to look as we do. I'm developing a theory and need to examine every site as unnoticed as possible."

He stood, went to the door, and called for his assistant. He told her she was to disguise herself to accompany Samra and his associate to show them the child murder sites. She nodded affirmatively, examined their appearance, and briefly smiled in leaving. When his assistant reappeared, she was satisfactorily garbed, but Jena decided she wasn't quite dirty enough.

"We'll need to find some dirt outside to make her look the part. Don't you think, Samra?"

Everyone laughed as the three of them turned to exit the building. Once outside, they were like kids playing in the dirt as they applied the finishing touches to her appearance. With a smile of satisfaction, Jena said, "There! You pass inspection."

About three years ago, a year before the plague, the district planning committee decided to construct an "all weather" stone roadway that allowed wagons, carts, and people to bypass the palace district when traveling north and south to ease the district's congestion.   The still standing cypress, oak, and olive trees in the area were to remain uncut as much as possible in an attempt to preserve them for the beauty of the district.   Trees could be cut down for the project only with explicit permission. This seemed to work wonderfully for all especially the killer.

The roadway to the east of the palace was shaped like a flat arc that joined to the main road running north and south.   The roadway on the west served the same purpose and ran along the top of the west hill just above Samra's villa.   The bypass roadways were quite busy during the day.   There were small park-like rest areas cut into the mainly dense cypress forest along the outside of the roadway about every one hundred and fifty meters.   Each rest area alcove had a stone bench and wooden tables with seating for the comfort of the travelers and local residents.

The roadway cut right through some of the cypress stands leaving many sections of the roadway with dense forest just a few feet on both sides of the road.   It was a beautiful walk in the daytime, but it could be very forbidding at night.   It was an extremely dark path even when the moon was full.   Travel at night was usually limited to those carrying torches.

All of the victim's bodies were found just outside the outer perimeter of the new roadway at distances ranging from ten to thirty meters.   It was always the same with the young victims lying torn and mutilated on their backs covered in blood. Samra wasn't interested in finding any new evidence specific to the crimes.   He was looking to understand how the killer physically moved in and out of position to stalk and kill his prey; unseen and unheard.

The four sites were fairly well separated from one another along the roadway, but there were similarities all of them exhibited. They were always close to a rest area alcove that could be seen from the inner buildings. They were always near an area where the trees reached close to the residences inside the circuit of the roadway. This would give him cover for his approach and escape. Surely, the bloodied killer wouldn't want to travel for any great distance in fleeing. It was far more likely he would be seen.

There was no doubt to any of the investigators, including Samra, that the same person had perpetrated all of the murders because of the character of the victim's wounds. But how could the killer attack and escape with him soaking in blood unseen from four such widely separated murder scenes? The distance between the third and fourth murders was nearly two kilometers. Samra deduced he must be using different households for each killing. Most of the residences close to the inside of the road were upscale villas, homes, and apartment buildings. Many of them were built to provide the affluent with a safe, quiet neighborhood away from the hustle and noise of the area around the palace and yet still be within easy walking distance.

The escort first took them to the northeast to the site of the second murder. After Samra examined it thoroughly, the escort then took them on a six kilometer circuit of the outer roadway visiting each murder site along the way. After they left the scene of the first murder and headed further down the road, they began to enter Samra's neighborhood. Memories of the killing were still vivid in him and began to form in his mind's eye as they walked closer. He could see Jena also tensing up as the memories gripped her. He knew the area well but still wanted to study the layout thoroughly to confirm his emerging theory of how the murders were carried out.

As they walked north on the western hill's road, they came to an opening in the forest to their right that looked down on the homes below. Samra could clearly see the southern stairway of his villa between two other homes higher up the gentle hill. As he stopped and took in the scene for a few moments, he noticed a person sitting on the balcony of the home to his left observing his villa. In the distance, he could see Jena's imposter carrying something up the stairs. He didn't think too much of it but told the escort to stay and watch. They then began to walk along the slope of the hill to study the surrounding area. After only a short time, they returned. He felt confident he understood what the killer was doing to secure his movements. All four murder sites had the same characteristics he imagined the killer most desired.

Each of them had stands of trees that filled areas between the roadway and the buildings inside it. There were also gaps and openings in the tree line that allowed the rest areas, and other sections of the roadway, to be seen from the buildings. This gave the killer the ability to observe people's travel habits and use of the rest area especially around sunset which appeared to be his favorite time to attack. He probably spent weeks observing from the comfort of a shaded balcony his most promising kills. He could dress darkly and just after sunset quickly move unseen through the trees to make his attack. He could then return through the same, or an alternate, stand of trees back to the alleyways of the buildings. This would explain him being unseen.

The only times he would be fully exposed would be when he crossed the road, when he made his attack in the rest area and carried the victim back into the trees, or when he made his way between the buildings and the nearby trees. The rest areas were cut into the forest in a way that people sitting in them were mostly blocked from view by others walking along the roadway. They could typically be seen only through gaps in the tree line from the buildings or by someone standing on the roadway near the front of the alcove.

"He must be disabling the victim quickly with a blow to the head and hurriedly taking her back into the dense forest to reduce his exposure." he thought.

When Samra and Jena returned to the escort, she told them the man on the balcony seemed inordinately curious with his villa. He had almost never taken his eyes off it even when on one was outside. He told her to have an inquiry made into who was occupying the house when she returned to her office. The escort nodded her acknowledgement, and, after thanking her for the tour, they made their way back to Mariadne's villa. He felt confident he had a solid theory about how the murders were being performed.

It seemed to him the killer must have access to more than one residence inside the roadway providing him with multiple escape routes. If a home was well situated near the road, it would be a quickly accessible place to find safety and elude detection. He thought if he was the murderer, he would want to have more than one safe place available after a kill. He must be carefully selecting his prospective murder sites and meticulously planning his kills.

Samra decided to have the property brokers in the area questioned about anyone that was especially interested in the homes or apartments lining the inside of the roadway. He returned the next day and retraced the circuit of the roadway for further study. He sought out settings where the terrain, tree stands, and residences fit what he imagined to be the best matches for the killer's criteria. He found there was someone that had been acquiring properties near the roadway for the past year. But they were being bought and not leased or rented which required more personal interaction between the parties. The brokers could only vaguely identify the purchaser as a big man. In the most recent sale, the buyer had obviously been disguised, but the seller took the gold. That was all that mattered to her.

Samra drew a map of the entire palace district on a large piece of parchment and marked all the sales of properties the brokers could provide him for the past year that matched his criteria. Once the map was complete, he marked the murder sites and studied their alignment with the roadway, trees, and residences. A pattern emerged that showed a few of the residences close to the murder sites had all the requirements he imagined the killer was looking for. He then looked for the most likely locations of any future killings. After he correlated the information for the most probable matches, he requested certain households along the roadway to be investigated and put under surveillance.

He found the best residences to have surveillance teams placed to monitor those locations and any other suspicious activity near the roadway. Twelve teams of watchers were stationed indefinitely at these residences. They were ordered to have two watchers always actively observing on the highest balcony at each surveillance location especially around sundown. Samra believed from the evidence the killer had a special affinity for sunset as the moment to pounce; just as the darkness enveloped the forest. He issued special instructions to intensify their surveillance as twilight neared. Samra hoped he had set a trap for the killer.

Several days later, as the sun weakened its hold on the day and darkness began to swiftly fill the sky, an observer looking west spotted the momentary flash of a dark human figure moving purposefully into a stand of trees about eighty meters away. Minute glints of the figure could be seen among the trees as he moved at a fast pace. The watcher instantly jumped from his seat and whispered firmly to his partner that he had just seen someone moving suspiciously toward the roadway. They both scrambled down the stairs and notified the other members of their team something unusual was seen that needed to be investigated immediately. Both of them swiftly strapped on their weapons belts and ran out the door in the direction of the sighting. As instructed, one of their team immediately ran to the nearest command center to notify the authorities. The dim light of the sun was almost completely gone.

A nearly full moon with the stars dimly assisting it soon took over from the sun to light the forest and roadway. You could see well enough in the open areas, but only the faintest light penetrated the dense stands of cypress. As quietly as possible, they ran quickly onto the roadway and came to a rest area near to where the watcher thought the figure was heading. One of them brought his hand to his mouth to insist on silence from his partner, and they stood listening for anything. After a few moments, they heard the faintest cracking of a twig to their left in the forest. They ever so quietly moved up to the edge of the trees near a bench in the rest area. One of them gave hand signals to the other for them to split up and close in from two sides on the location they thought the sound had come from. They drew their large daggers in readiness to enter the blackness of the forest.

They disappeared into the tree line and crept ahead very slowly. It was extremely difficult to see anything in the almost utter blackness, but the moon allowed for the faintest detection of what was around them as their eyes adjusted. Both of them suddenly heard another rustle of movement, and they moved toward it more deliberately from their positions. The watcher to the left came to the edge of a small open area among the trees and could barely make out the outline of a figure wrapped in a hooded cape crouching over a small body lying on the ground. Just as the watcher started to attack, the dark form turned in a flash of movement and threw a dagger deep into his chest. With a loud yelp, he fell to the ground squarely onto the dagger's handle; driving it deeper into him. He lay silent and unmoving.

The other watcher was just able to see his partner hit the ground and started to run at the killer but stumbled over the small body and lost his footing. The watcher lunged at the killer with his dagger in falling. The killer was jumping to his feet and turning as the dagger struck him through his cape in a glancing blow to his ribs below the armpit. He yelped sharply in pain as the blade cut and tore jaggedly into his flesh. The killer recoiled from the searing sting as the watcher fell to the ground and quickly started to scramble back to his feet. The killer lashed out with another dagger and stabbed the watcher high into his back. The watcher screamed loudly at the blow and dropped to the ground seriously wounded and defenseless.

The killer moved to finish him with another dagger blow but froze quickly scanning the forest around him in fear. He swiftly turned to make his way into the trees to the west; parallel with the roadway. Realizing he had escaped immediate death, the wounded man started yelling as loudly as he could for help and to warn the others.

After he traveled about a hundred and fifty meters, he turned to the north toward the roadway attempting to make it to his other safe house in the neighborhood. He reached the edge of the forest overlooking the path and stealthily peered down it in both directions. He saw no one but could hear the man yelling and the sound of people quickly coming to his aid. He regretted not killing the man. Suddenly, from somewhere nearby, the air was pierced by the sound of a loud horn and then another one some distance away.

He felt panic grip him as he got his bearings on the roadway. He turned back into the forest and moved west another thirty meters, and after, again, looking to see if anyone could be seen, he swiftly ran across the road into a stand of trees that would take him into a residential area. His safe house was close by. If he could just make it there unseen, he would go undetected. His wound was bleeding badly and filled him with worry.

Heading north through the stand of trees, he began to see more and more glimpses of the moonlight. He came to the tree line near the walls of a home and spied his surroundings. Seeing no one, he darted into the nearest passageway and made his way toward the house. He had scouted the area thoroughly and knew it very well. He abruptly stopped on hearing the scurrying of footsteps close by. If they came down his passageway, he would probably be discovered and captured.

He gulped in fear and stood utterly still as the footsteps passed him by. Strangely, the fear exhilarated him as he eluded detection. He stealthily moved forward and peeked around a corner to see the entrance of his safe house. Two armed men were standing in front of it. It didn't look like they were on guard. They appeared to be just waiting. He decided to stay put for a short time to see if they moved off. Two more armed men came to join them and then another. They talked briefly and took off in different directions, but one of them stayed near the home.

He began to make his way to the home's back entrance when he suddenly heard movement behind him in the passageway. It was much too dangerous for him to stay where he was. He knew of another place he could make his way to, but it was, at least, five hundred meters away, and the loss of blood from his wound was beginning to weaken him. Blood drenched the side of his body inside his cape. He felt he had no choice. His best chance now was to return to his own villa in the direction of the palace. It was only about two hundred meters to the north, and he knew of a good secretive route to it.

Once he was well away from the safe house, he began to attempt to make himself look normal. Keeping pressure on his wound, he began to walk as if he was just out for a sojourn in the moonlight of the early evening. He started to nervously giggle to himself in the rush of almost being caught. He felt giddy in self-admiration for his escape, but the pain from his wound was flaring. He pressed his hand to it more firmly to reduce the bleeding. The pain was excruciating, and he desperately tried not to scream out. He began to feel dizzy and started to worry he might pass out from the loss of blood. If he fell unconscious in some passageway, he would be doomed. In a growing panic, he willed himself to make it to his villa.

Coming close, he stopped and surveyed his approach to it from the side of a building. He saw no one, and everything appeared to be quite normal. He stayed there for several moments straightening his garments and wiping the blood showing on his leg with his cape. Shaded from the moonlight by several trees, he walked to the villa's side door. Once inside, he rushed to make his way upstairs to his living chamber.

He briskly walked into his bath throwing his cape and garments in the corner on the floor with his good arm. Naked, he drenched himself with water from the basins letting the blood wash down the drain. Toweling himself dry, he applied honey to the wound, and wrapped linen around his chest to stem the bleeding. He put on a dark robe that would hide any blood stains from his wound. He then used wet towels to wipe up the drops of blood on the floor from his path in the chamber and the stairway leading to it. After throwing the towels into the pile of garments in his bath, he sat in front of his bronze mirror and, staring at his reflection, began combing his hair.

He smiled in amusement in the mirror over his narrow escape from death. If it wasn't for his dizziness and the pain of his wound, he would have been enjoying himself greatly. He then realized he needed someone to help him sew up the jagged gash under his armpit. It was impossible for him to do it. His hands just wouldn't reach. Feeling his servant's knowledge of the dagger wound would endanger him, he could think of only one person he trusted enough to help him.

Holding his bandaged side, he moved to his chambers. He wrote a short message on a small piece of parchment and sealed it with his signet ring. Bracing himself, he stood and walked shakily to the window shutter by the door. Opening it, he called for a servant to come to him. Leaving the message on the small table by the door, he walked over to sit and collect himself into a semblance of normalcy on the couch. When the servant arrived, he calmly told her to personally deliver the message on the table to Synboliki and leave them in privacy when she arrived. The servant nodded in understanding and left immediately at a quick pace. She noticed nothing out of the ordinary.

"I'll get through this yet. The truth will never surface!" he thought as his weakness and pain muted his desire to celebrate.

Arriving at Synboliki's, she told the answering servant she was to personally deliver a message from her master. He recognized the servant girl and allowed her to enter the villa to stand by the door as he moved off to alert his mistress. She was eating dinner with friends when he made the announcement. She was not happy with the interruption but pleasantly excused herself from her guests and went to retrieve it. After rudely swiping the message in irritation from the servant girl's hand, she turned to read it in privacy.

"Return to your villa. I'll be along soon."

Returning to her guests, she told them she needed to leave for just a short time and to continue to enjoy their food and drink. She went to her bed chambers to get a shoulder wrap. As she was about to leave, she abruptly stopped with an instant sense of remembrance and turned to approach her night table. She opened a hidden side drawer and lifted a small brightly decorated faïence vial with a cork stopper from it. Putting it close to her slightly grinning face, she looked intently at it for a few moments before promptly putting it into her leather belt pouch and turning to leave.

It was just a short walk. On arriving at the villa, she was escorted up the stairs to the door of his living quarters. The servant girl stepped aside to let her enter the room and closed the door to leave them in privacy. As she came toward him with a quizzical look, he painfully waved her closer and whispered, "I'm cut badly and need your help."

"What have you done now, Danaloi?"

He opened his robe to show her the linen bandage. Blood had seeped through the bandage in a dark blotch.

"Please, I need your help to sew the wound."

She hadn't heard the horns and didn't have any suspicion he might be in any kind of real trouble.

"How did this happen? Who did this to you?"

"I was involved in a fight over a personal matter."

"Why don't you want your servants to know anything?"

"It's something I don't want publicly known.   Please, I need your help and discretion.   Please, Synboliki, help me!"

"Your private life is an invitation to things like this."

"I'll give you plenty of time to degrade me later."

She chuckled and said, "Come take off your robe and get into the bath so I can see this."

He was weak and raised his hand to her for assistance.   She helped him into the bath and began removing the wrapping from his chest.

"Oh, that's ugly!   It looks like someone was trying to tear you open.   I'll get some water and clean it."

She retrieved a water vase with some cloth and tried to get him to lift his arm but he couldn't.   He slowly got down on his hands and knees and, using his good arm, leaned forward to let his other one hang limply beneath him revealing the wound. Standing over him, she poured water on it and carefully pulled the loose skin and flesh open to thoroughly clean the wound. He wanted to hysterically scream out, but the consequences muted him.   He grimaced in great agony, and his body shook violently from the searing pain.

"Prepare some opium for me.   Please!" he quietly spat out in misery.

"I'll need a sewing kit first."

His contorted face nodded the direction to her as he grunted, "The cabinet over there."

She returned with some honey and began to sew the wound. The pain was almost more than he could bear, but he remained fairly still down on the floor of the bath as she worked on him. When she finished, she smeared a thick coating of honey it. He agonizingly straightened up and got to his feet. She wrapped clean linen around his chest to cover the sewn gash and secured the bandage with pins.

She helped him put on a fresh robe, and he began to comb his hair. As she slowly assisted him to sit on the couch, he appeared well enough on the outside.

"Now where's your opium? I'll make you some tea for the pain."

He pointed to a cupboard in the hall. Amused, she thought, "There will never be a better opportunity than this."

Opening the window shutter, she called out for the servant to bring her some hot water for tea. It soon arrived and she began to prepare the dried poppy heads by chopping them into very fine pieces. She put them into a vessel and poured the hot water into it. After adding a small quantity of vinegar to increase its acidity slightly, she let the mixture steep for a few minutes and then filtered it through a fine cloth producing a brown liquid in the large drinking cup. Its taste was intensely bitter.

"You do want honey in it don't you?" she asked from behind the partition wall.

"Yes, please."

As she was adding the honey, she thought, "This is it! This is the perfect time." and pulled the poison vial from her pouch with a mischievous grin.

Her plan was to kill him with the poison and lay him on the couch to clean up any indications of it.   Victims typically bled from the mouth.   He was already severely wounded and drinking opium.   Who could know how much opium he consumed after she left?   While leaving, she would simply tell the servants he wanted to be left alone.   This was what he normally did.   No one could seriously accuse her of any wrongdoing.

The poison was a special preparation of plant roots.   It was very powerful and fast acting.   She had planned on doing this for several weeks now, if the opportunity arose, and felt her best chance was now.   She was resolved that if the plot against Samra failed, she could well afford to rid herself of Danaloi's incriminating knowledge of her activities.   She poured a good amount of the poison into the tea and thought, "He will never be able to taste anything in a drink like this."

When she was satisfied she had added more than enough, she thought, "That will surely kill him." and stirred more honey into the mixture.

After carefully re-corking the faïence vial, she returned it to her pouch and brought the large cup of opium tea out into the chamber to him with a warm smile.   He stiffly, but anxiously, took the cup with his good hand and, at once, began to sip as deeply as he could on the hot brew.   It warmed and refreshed him.

"Oh, thank you.   I don't know what I would have done without you."

"It was nothing, any time."

She wanted to laugh at the fool but just displayed a slight smirk. She was enjoying herself greatly.

The opium would normally begin to take effect within about a half an hour, but the poison was meant to overcome him in less than six or seven minutes. He was lifting his cup for another sip when unexpectedly there was a knock at the door. His servant announced an important messenger had arrived for him. He set his tea cup down and straightened himself in his seat to look as fit and healthy as he could.

Once he was satisfied with his appearance, and Synboliki had taken a seat next to him on the couch, he called out, "Yes. Come in."

The servant girl opened the door and stepped back out of the way onto the landing. A large casually dressed man with a menacing bronze dagger ready in his hand coolly walked into the chamber. He silently moved to his right away from the door. Danaloi and Synboliki were stunned and speechless in shock and fright. A second large man entered the room with his dagger drawn and took a position on the other side of the door.

Brazenly, Danaloi called out, "What's going on?! Who are you?! How dare you enter my home?"

A third, even bigger, man walked in to stand by his compatriot to the right. None of the men said a word. After a few moments of utter silence, then, to their amazement, Samraleos walked in to confront them with his big bronze blade glittering in the lamp light. They were totally astonished and speechless for a time at the sight of him standing threateningly in front of them.

"What are you doing here, Samraleos?!" Danaloi stridently asked with a mixture of rage and fear.

"A deputy was murdered in the area, and someone was seen entering your villa." Samra softly said.

Feeling the pain from his wound and realizing he wasn't going to be immediately killed, Danaloi reached for his cooling tea and gulped down a good bit of it. After momentarily glancing up at Samra in utter disgust, he drank down the last of it.

"There's a blood trail leading from the crime scene to your villa. Do you know anything about that?"

At first, Synboliki was stung with shock and paralyzed in fear she might be killed. But now she began to panic realizing that if Samra didn't leave very soon, Danaloi was going to die right in front of him. In silent horror and growing dread, she thought, "What can I say? I must think of something."

"Of course, I don't! I know nothing of this. Now leave me before the authorities are summoned!" he yelled.

Samra chuckled softly and said, "You were seen making your way from the crime scene and followed here. The young girl, whose throat you injured, is well and indicates she regained consciousness enough to identify her attacker. Also, the deputy you stabbed, who still lives, is willing to be brought here now to witness your face. Should we do that?"

There were several tense moments of silence with no response at all from Danaloi.

"Yes, I should have known he was the killer! How could I have been so stupid, and he's already taken the poison!" she thought showing only her cool mask. Her mind embraced panic and danced from one thought to another as she tried desperately to focus her mind in search of a way to deal with the situation.

Danaloi ignored Samra's question and excitedly yelled, "There must be some mistake!   "Leave my home now!   My father will have your head!"

"We know you are the child killer, Danaloi." Samra said firmly.

Abruptly, Danaloi simultaneously felt a wave of dizziness as his stomach began to cramp painfully.   He leaned back into the couch feeling and looking nauseous.   His face paled noticeably before them.

"Our witness said he stabbed the killer in the ribs.   Stand up and prove you are innocent by showing us you are not wounded."

"I'll show you nothing!   Now leave me!" he shouted with the last three words being slightly blunted and slurred.

"Open your robe, or we'll open it for you." demanded Samra. He waved the warriors in toward him.

"Wait!" Danaloi said.

He briefly tried to stand up but fell heavily back into the couch. He moaned in pain as he began to convulse and cramp very hard.

"I...I don't feel well." he said.

"This isn't the opium.   What's wrong with me?" he thought.

He turned to look into the cold dead eyes of Synboliki staring at him and instantly realized with certainty she had poisoned him. Her expression was unchanging. She was like a statue before him. She wasn't going to show anything to Samra and the warriors. She hated him for having her come here and put in this situation.

With great difficulty and exasperation, Danaloi pushed himself away from her on the couch and lifted his good arm to point to her while struggling to speak out. Blood began running from his mouth. His abdomen was a mass of overwhelming pain as tears came to his eyes.

"She's the one! She's the one!" he stated with determination.

Shivering and convulsing, he turned to Samra and weakly slurred, "Karasos! She did it!"

His arm fell limply into his lap as he slumped back into the couch and passed into unconsciousness near his death. Samra commanded the warrior to his right to secure Synboliki. He did so and removed the empty vial of poison from her pouch sniffing the contents.

"It's poison."

He took a strap from his kit, tied her hands behind her, and held her by the arm in front of Samra. Staring at her with his anger building, he calmly said, "Sounded like a confession to me. What do you think?"

He looked at the warriors each in turn, and they all nodded in agreement. One of the warriors opened Danaloi's robe, and they saw the linen bandage wrapped around his chest.

"He's the child killer without doubt. I wonder what else he is?" he said looking straight into Synboliki's remorseless eyes. She didn't blink.

"Take her into custody for the murder of Danaloi, and put her under guard in the palace. We need to secure and search their villas."

Later that evening, the official from Avaris was escorted to Danaloi's home to see if he could identify him as his contact in Knossos. His body was laid out on the couch waiting for the authorities to dispense with it. Before he arrived, the villa was searched, and several cylinder seals were found. Impressions were made from all of them for the official to witness. The official identified Danaloi almost immediately as his contact. He also identified one of the seal impressions as the one given him.

With the independent confirmation of the official, Samra believed he had enough evidence to prove that not only was Danaloi the child killer, but he was, at least, one of the members of the plot to murder him. He expected only to capture the child killer, but now with Synboliki in custody he might be able to determine the truth behind the killing of his father.

"It was fortunate she was there at the moment of his capture, but even if she wasn't the trail would have soon led to her." he thought.

He began to feel a warm joy knowing the children of the district would be able to feel safe again from the monster that plagued them for so long. Well, at least, not until the next monster came upon them. Hopefully that would be very far in the future.

"What are we to do with these beasts?"

He thought he would deal with it later and needed to focus on Synboliki. He wondered if the dying confession of a child murderer would be enough to have her accused or would her connections and uncle Kalpoulis be able to save her. She was undoubtedly the killer of Danaloi, but could he prove anything else. He worried he needed more evidence to confirm her guilt to the committees. He hoped something could be found in her villa to incriminate her. But how could he find out who his father's killer was if she couldn't be forced to speak?

"If I could just gather enough political support, I might be able to have her seriously interrogated." he thought.

He needed a few very important questions answered. Who was the killer of his father? It couldn't have been Danaloi. He wasn't on the ship. Were there any other active plots in Knossos, and who else was involved? If she could be forced to talk, all could be known. He felt he was very close to the truth with these new revelations. But he believed the political power of her uncle and the falsehoods they would invent to defend her could thwart him.

Samra, Jena, Mariadne, and Cronymartis spent the evening at the villa talking about how wonderful it was the children could, once again, play without fear in the district and the implications of the new evidence regarding the death of his father. They had no way of knowing, but word of Danaloi's death and Synboliki's arrest spread swiftly throughout the palace district that evening. There were several meetings requested by the King and Queen with many members of the committees. The Queen was instrumental in the guiding of policy on this matter.

"Let's see what tomorrow brings." Samra thought as he snuggled next to Jena in bed and went to sleep.

Chapter 13

Synboliki's Truth

The next day, Samra arrived in the palace to find Kalpoulis engaged in a heated argument with the head of the civil authorities in the hall.   As he approached, Kalpoulis glanced toward him and demandingly said, "Samra, what's happening here?!   I'm told you have my niece in custody for murder. This is ridiculous!   Explain yourself!"

"Yes, its true sir, but now, if you'll excuse me, I have an appointment." Samra stated coolly as he moved off down the hall.

Kalpoulis was aghast, enraged, and shouted angrily "You work for me!   Come back here now!"

Samra ignored him and walked on to his meeting.   After being announced, he entered the royal chamber and was warmly greeted by the King and Queen.   Cronymartis and Mariadne had arrived earlier and were in attendance with several other influential politicians.   The King raised his hand to speak saying, "First you bring us the Avaris gold, and now, so soon, you bring us the child killer.   It's a truly amazing achievement, Samraleos.   One your father would be very proud of, indeed. Please give us your thoughts regarding the new evidence implicating Synboliki in your father's death.   She is now saying that just before you arrived she discovered what he had done and killed him for it."

"She didn't mention it last night.   Sir, I believe Synboliki is the leader behind both my father's death and the assassination plot against me.   I know the evidence is weak for her involvement in my father's death with only the word of a child killer to condemn her.   But if she is released from custody without being seriously interrogated, the truth might never be known."

With an incendiary flash of anger in her eyes, the Queen responded, "It would be a travesty to let the snake free from the noose of the truth!   I have been thinking about something that should get the truth out of her, but it would let her live in exile. Do you think the truth is worth letting her live, Samra?"

"Yes majesty, if her crimes are finally ended, and it leads us to my father's murderer."

"It has come to me that Synboliki has an acute abhorrence of pain, no matter how slight, and does exceptional things to avoid it.   We could use this to aid us in convincing her that the truth is her only path.   Mariadne in her gracious compassion has told me of a story about justice being administered to a murderous criminal in Palaikastro a few years ago.   This person, like Danaloi, was known to mutilate his defenseless victims.   They stripped him of his garments and stabbed him with a dagger in the joints of his arms and legs to weaken and disable them.   His hands and feet were joined behind him and tightly bound with rope. He was then thrown into a pen filled with well-fed hogs. It was said it took a long time for the screams to end."

After a pause, she looked at the King with a slight smile and said, "Of course, we would never do such a thing."

The King quickly interjected, "We could make an exception in her case, dear."

Still smiling, the Queen said, "If she believed this was her fate, beyond any doubt, if she didn't tell us the truth, I think she would comply especially if she was allowed to live. Do you agree, Samra?"

Samra chuckled slightly and said, "Yes, majesty."

A feeling of warmth grew within him, and he knew the truth was near. He had all the political support he needed. The Queen told him the intelligence committee would no longer be led by Kalpoulis. Cronymartis would temporarily take over the leadership and move to rid it of any cronyism or corruption that had blossomed under his reign. Kalpoulis would be informed of this after they dealt with Synboliki and extracted the truth from her. This would be very soon.

Kalpoulis had desperately been trying to get an audience with the King or Queen in order to have his niece released into his custody without success. He wasn't used to being told no. Synboliki was summoned to the King's chamber for interrogation; escorted by two guards with her hands bound behind her. She was rigidly instructed to say nothing to anyone before beginning her interrogation. As she passed Kalpoulis in the hallway, he called out, "What has happened!?"

He was exasperated and incredulous that she could be in her present state. She shook her head at him and attempted to adamantly demonstrate her innocence using her facial expressions.   Her mask became illuminated with a show of helpless unknowing wonderment as they pushed her along.   On entering the King's chamber, the leather straps binding her wrists were removed, and she was placed in a chair in front of the King and Queen among the onlookers.

"Does it feel good to have your hands free, dear?" the Queen soothingly asked.

She submissively said, "Yes, majesty.   But I am innocent my Queen. I was …"

The Queen lifted her hand stopping her from speaking any further and said, "Be quiet and listen for once.   We know much more than you think we do, my dear.   You have been under investigation since the day we learned of the death of Karasos."

Synboliki tried to stand up and interrupt the Queen in protest, but one of the warriors stepped forward to grab her shoulder, squeezed it hard, and slammed her back down into the chair. She flinched and cried out from the intense sting of his fingers. She hated pain above all things.   No other person had ever done anything like this to her since she was a child.   She winched and grimaced in her struggle to deal with the sharp throbbing ache.

"Listen carefully, my dear.   There is only one way you can still live.   You must tell us everything you know truthfully.   If you tell us just one lie, your life is forfeit.   Give us only the truth or you die in great torment and agony.   It's as simple as that, dear."

The Queen let the point be emphasized.   The silence in the room was total.   Synboliki just assumed she could talk her way out of the situation she found herself in as she had done so many times before. She now began to realize she was in some very real trouble.

"We want to hear you give absolutely truthful testimony regarding your schemes against Samra and the death of his father, Karasos. Also we have a great deal of information on your other sinister activities in Knossos and wish to know completely about these."

Synboliki sat silently in astonishment at the Queen's statement. She thought, "It's impossible to tell the truth. They will surely kill me if I give them the truth even if they say I will live. But if they've been investigating me for all this time, how much do they really know? How can I be sure of what they know and what they don't?"

She became filled with worry and doubt but still thought she had options. As her mind raced to create more brilliant rationalizations and plausible lies to cover the truth of her involvement, the Queen menacingly said, "Arrangements have been made, and you will soon be shown your fate if our investigations reveal even one falsehood from your lips. Remember dear, all it takes is just one lie."

"Yes majesty. But please, majesty! I ..."

The Queen waved to the guard and gave him a prearranged signal. The warrior walked in front of her and slapped her solidly on the left side of the face. Her head and hair violently whipped as she yelped loudly from the blow. Mortification and humiliation flooded her as the warrior stood before her shaking his finger in her face in warning.

The Queen calmly said, "The next one will be much harder, my dear. I suggest you remain silent until you are asked to speak."

At her words, the warrior stepped to his left and retook his position at attention.   She had never been treated like this before in her life and was appalled and horrified beyond her wide-eyed expression of shock.   The evening before, the Queen and Mariadne agreed the only effective way to extract the truth from her was to terrorize her mentally with humiliation and fear mixed with a good dose of physical abuse and the infliction of, what she hated most, pain.   They wanted Synboliki to be constantly kept off balance and intimidated; always wondering what horrible thing was going to happen to her next.

The Queen and Mariadne had even choreographed certain actions they wanted the guards to perform during her "breaking down" process.   Earlier, much to their amazement, the Queen herself in the presence of Mariadne had personally given detailed instructions to them before the interrogation.   She wanted them to be harsh with her but not so rough as to seriously injure her.   That would delay her testimony and give her deceitful, evil mind time to think.

"Take her away and show her the fate that awaits her for one single lie.   One little lie is all it takes, my dear!   Do you understand!?" the Queen angrily shouted.

Synboliki was so traumatized she didn't respond in any way. She was in a kind of dulled acquiescence of whatever was to come as fear began to cloud her mind.   Her hands were again bound tightly behind her with leather straps.   The guards turned and pushed her stumbling toward the closed chamber doors. The two guards took each of her arms, and when she was close the guards slammed her forcefully into the thick cedar doors.

She screamed as her face and body slammed into the thick cedar.   As the guards stepped out of the way, she bounced off the door violently.   With her arms flailing, she fell backwards onto the floor.   She landed on her side and rolled onto her stomach; dazed and nearly unconscious. Her nose was bleeding profusely, and there was a small streak of blood running from her forehead. After a few moments, she started to groan and roll slightly from side to side on the floor. One of the warriors looked questioningly back at the Queen for her approval. She answered his silent question with a smile as she nodded affirmatively her satisfaction.

The two warriors grabbed her by the armpits and tried lifting her to her feet, but her feet didn't seem to be working yet. They shrugged and pulled her semi-conscious body out a side entrance from the chamber with her head hanging and feet dragging on the floor.

The Queen laughed and, smiling at Mariadne, said, "These warriors seem to enjoy their orders."

Mariadne chuckled, nodding in amusement, and leaned in close to the Queen's ear saying, "Her arrogant abuse has left a wide trail, my dear."

"She never imagined a day like this would ever come to her. Let's see if our plan gets her to speak only the truth when she returns."

"I have great confidence this will work very well. She has no courage at all, and I think we can rely on the warriors to perform their assignments with precision and enthusiasm."

Shortly after being dragged from the chamber down a lightly traveled hallway to leave the palace, she lifted her head slightly to take in her surroundings and started stumbling to regain her footing. Once the warriors were satisfied she was able to walk on her own, they immediately began marching her at a fast battle pace. It was very difficult for her to keep up. If she slowed, they would roughly push her ahead. A few times, they jabbed her with the butts of their daggers to encourage her with the pain. They took the stone road north to Amnisos and turned east on a dirt road leading to a small hog farm about two kilometers from the palace. Earlier in the day, the farm's owner was notified they were coming and made preparations for their arrival.

Three employees came out to greet them as the odd-looking trio approached. When the warriors stopped to talk to them, Synboliki abruptly sagged into an exhausted faint hanging from their hands. The woman in charge pointed to a wet muddy empty pen that a large group of hogs had recently been removed from. The warriors pulled her to her feet and pushed her towards the pen's wooden fence. There were many hogs in an adjoining pen engaged in a cacophony of snorting and grunting. She immediately started gagging as the powerful stench coming from the thick layer of wet mud, feces, and urine filled her bloodied nostrils.

As she shook her head in protest trying to imagine what they were going to do to her, they forced her down on her belly on the ground next to the fence with her wrists still bound behind her. One warrior took her by the shoulders, and the other one grabbed her feet. They started to swing her back and forth. On the third swing, they threw her high in the air above the pen. She tried to kick her legs to change her orientation, but her face landed solidly with a loud splat into the thick putrid mixture of the pen.

It was a soft landing and she was not injured, but her senses were assaulted as never before by the filth enveloping her. For a moment, she panicked and thought she might drown in the deep fool mix. She quickly rolled her body to lift her face from the muck; spitting clumps of it from her mouth. Turning her head, she gagged, and violently vomited several times. After she stopped vomiting, she started coughing and sputtering.

When she started breathing normally again, she sat straight up in quiet astonishment at what had just happened to her.   With hog feces dripping from her face, she shook her head fiercely to better clear her eyes and turned to glare furiously at the warriors.

"Get out now!" a warrior commanded.

Her rage and contempt soared as she slowly worked herself to her knees and made it to her feet in the slippery muck.   As she stood before them in the pen, the two warriors and nearby farm employees couldn't help from laughing at the sight of her. Synboliki, the narcissistic egomaniac, appeared to be a pathetic spectacle of humiliation as the filth dripped from her.

"I'll have them all killed for this." she thought.

The warriors observed her venomous hatred and, glancing at each other, started laughing heartily in amusement.   One of them waved for her to get out and mockingly commanded, "Hurry up, great lady!"

She slowly slogged her way through the slick manure toward the fence.   The laughter was beginning to die down as she finally reached it.   She looked up at the guards amid their snickering as if to plead with them to help her in getting over it. Amused, they both stepped back to let her manage the task on her own.   They had no intention of touching her.   Her exasperation and frustration had never been more pronounced than at that moment.   She was dizzy with anger and wanted to scream at the top of her lungs.   She held back in fear of the warrior's reaction.   While attempting to step over the wooden rails, she slipped and lost her footing.   She toppled over the fence onto the much harder dry ground outside the pen; landing on her shoulder.   A searing thunderbolt shot through her.   She screamed piteously and began crying from the pain, but she wasn't seriously hurt.

"Get up you filthy monster!" a warrior barked contemptuously.

Her inflamed anger faded into an overwhelming sense of resignation. The fear of what was next overtook her. Eventually, she regained her footing just as one of the employees opened the gate to the adjoining pen, and the hogs were prodded into the pen she had just left. The woman in charge, on instructions from the warriors, joined them and said, "These hogs are very hungry and haven't eaten for some time. They will fight each other for their food and eat very fast. But if the hogs are well fed they can take much longer."

The warriors were handed rags to keep their hands clean, and they forcefully held her in place to face the hogs. Two workers arrived carrying a large side of meat and threw it into the middle of the pit. The carcass hit a couple of the hogs on their backs making them squeal loudly before splashing into the mud. The grunting hogs attacked the meat with a mad, ravenous frenzy of hunger.

A warrior spoke threateningly "This is your fate if you tell just one lie, murderer!"

Synboliki was far more than just frightened now. She was near to a state of shivering catatonic panic. While she desperately held onto her mask, she couldn't help but widen her eyes in horror at the sight. She inwardly gasped at the thought of being thrown into the pen as a piece of meat to be devoured alive.

"This kind of death would be a hideous torturous one, indeed!"

She was overtaken by another huge wave of panic, and her mask failed her. She dropped her face to block the sight from her eyes and held back a scream of terror. She felt faint and slipped from the warrior's grip crumbling to the ground on her side looking away from the pit shaking in dread.

No more tears came to her as she lay there, but she appeared broken and shattered to the bone. The warriors observed this and felt they had accomplished the Queen's instructions to her approval. As she lay on the ground whimpering, one of the farm workers appeared with a large pitcher of water and dumped it onto her head and shoulders to wash some of the filth from her. She flinched wildly from the drenching as one of the warriors loudly barked in her ear, "Stand up!"

Blubbering, she slowly rose to her feet and was prodded ahead to follow a worker to the employee's bathing area. Standing near a drain, two more pitchers of water were splashed onto the front and back of her. No one touched her as more of the muck slipped down into the drain. More pitchers followed which removed most of the filth from her. This slightly relieved her agony, but the throbbing in her shoulder forced her to grimace constantly. The image of the hogs tearing at the meat in the pen was seared permanently into her mind.

"Now that you've seen your fate for just one lie we can return to the palace. Remember just one lie!" one of the warriors said.

The warriors were instructed to emphasize the concept of "just one lie" to embed it thoroughly in her mind; leaving her in no doubt of its consequences. They pointed her in the direction back to the palace and let her take the lead. Suddenly, she cried out as she was jabbed harshly in the back with the butt of a dagger to get her to move faster. They returned the way they came; at the same fast battle pace. The warrior's swift stride forced her to almost run along in front of them to maintain the pace. She couldn't keep up and was painfully prodded with the daggers many times; marking the journey with her screams.

As they neared the palace, she was almost delirious and becoming hysterical from the multiple searing lightning bolts of pain in her back. She was badly bruised from the many stinging blows of the daggers. Her face was covered in a sheet of tears and mucous. She was heavily winded; sucking in all the air she could. She smelled terribly. Her mind was shattered and numb from the many stabs of blinding pain enveloping her. She was totally broken and would do anything to save herself. She just wanted to have the horrible pain leave her and live another day.

She stared numbly at the palace escorts awaiting their arrival when one of the warriors abruptly yelled, "Halt!"

She was exhausted and stumbled in attempting to stop. With no hands to support her, she fell yet again onto the ground in front of them. To the escorts she appeared to be a pathetic caricature of a wrecked human being. As she slowly regained her footing, blood started pouring from her nose again. The palace escorts stepped away from her and pointed out the direction they wanted her to go. No one assisted her. She weakly made her way past them as they guided her down the hall to a nearby bath.

The straps binding her numb wrists were finally removed. She was quickly stripped and washed with soap and shampoo by three servants. She started to babble something when she screamed hideously as one of the bathers firmly rubbed her injured shoulder. They ignored her and continued to clean her like an animal for sale. She was given only a simple loincloth and shoulder wrap to wear. The Queen ordered them to bathe her because no one in the chamber wanted to endure the stench of her during her interrogation.

The warriors returned to usher her into a hallway just outside the King's chamber to sit waiting to be called. Her body was covered in bruises from her many falls and the terrible jabbing of the dagger butts on the march. Her swollen face and nose felt numb and her back and shoulder throbbed horribly. Her injuries wracked her continually with pain. It totally consumed her, and she dropped her face into her hands in self-pity. She sat there in muted terror; shivering and shaking in fear of what awaited her. Finally, through the agony, her tormented mind began to work again.

"If the King and Queen authorized what was just done to me, my uncle and his political cronies are powerless and scurrying to find their own safety. I'm alone!"

A feeling of utter helplessness and isolation raced through her. For the first time in her memory, there was no one she could use or manipulate to her aid. Her destiny was sealed, and doom surrounded her world of pain. She would do anything to avoid the fate that awaited her. She worried about what they really knew of her activities from their investigations and felt she couldn't be sure of anything. It dawned on her that the only way not to be caught in a single lie and avoid her hideous fate was to simply tell the truth.

"It's the only way!" she thought in desperation.

Synboliki resolved herself to do something she normally only rarely did. She was going to tell them the unfettered truth as best she could. She only told the truth if it suited her interests. Today, it suited her interests to live and not be eaten alive by the hogs.

As another great wave of pain washed over her, and her delirium returned, she kept repeating the same thought, "Just one lie. Just one lie...."

Her name abruptly rang out loudly in the hall, "Synboliki!"

The slightest movement caused her tremendous agony. As if in answer to her summons, she screamed out inhumanly as the warriors grabbed her by the arms to lift her. They ignored her completely and quickly marched her through the doorway into the King's chamber. She was groaning, winching, and babbling with bloody mucous running from her nose as the fierce pain kept crashing through her. After she entered the chamber, she was seated on a plain oak chair with the warriors taking their position slightly behind and at each side of her.

The King, Queen, and everyone else present when she began her nightmare journey to the hog farm were still there. They were looking intently at somebody they could only barely identify. She appeared to be a totally different person. The stark difference in the audience's before and after image of Synboliki was shocking to all of them. The swelling of her nose, cheek, and forehead added to the hard grimace on her face distorted her features enough to make her almost completely unrecognizable. They all knew it was her on close examination, but the striking contrast amazed them.

The Synboliki of before was sitting up regally with her shoulders back in a posture of arrogance and exaggerated importance. She spoke with respect but with an underlying air of confidence like that of a self-anointed genius assuming her superiority. The woman in front of them now was stiff and shivering in her chair with bloody snot running from her nose. She was, at least for the moment, no longer the proud arrogant Synboliki musing down on her inferior underlings. After briefly surveying her audience shaking in fear, she hung her head staring at her bruised hands and arms. For the first time in her life, she was broken, humbled, and compliant.

Devoid of sympathy, the Queen commanded, "Look at us! Show your face!"

She snapped her head upright. As if constantly waiting for the next scream, her face was grimacing and very pale. She had a large bruise around a small tear in the skin on her forehead from being thrown into the chamber doors by the warriors. The wound no longer bled, but liquid slowly oozed from it. Her nose had stopped pouring blood during her bath but still dripped red mucous. Her face was relatively clean, but it was quite swollen and distorted especially her left cheek. In the silence of the stunned audience, a small table was placed in front of her and she was roughly told, "Keep your hands on the table at all times!"

As she fearfully looked on, a warrior brought in another chair and placed it directly in front of her about three meters away. There were two scribes in the room to her left to record information revealed during the proceedings on parchment. Samra moved to sit in the chair as everyone eagerly waited for the questioning to begin and, hopefully, the truth to be known.

"Tell us of all the plots you are currently actively involved in. I don't want to know about all the manipulative political games you play until later. Everyone here knows of a long list of those. I want to know of your schemes to physically hurt others for now."

She struggled to compose herself when she realized he had finished speaking and haltingly said, "There is only one."

There was a collective chuckle in the room at her use of the word 'only'.

"Tell us everything starting with the names of everyone involved."

"Calusetne and Danaloi are the only two. I know little of their recruits."

Some of the witnesses were overcome by silent shock at the mention of Calusetne. His mother was a well known member of one of the regional committees. From behind her, Cronymartis quietly cracked open the door and whispered an order for his arrest to a warrior just outside.

"The plan was to kill you in Avaris with nine warriors. Five of them were recruited by Danaloi and four more by Calusetne. They were told to kill you at their first opportunity. But the main plan was to ambush you and your guards with poison bow fire and then move in to finish you with bronze. If possible, they were to hide the bodies and encourage people to believe you had been captured or murdered. When the fleet left to return to Knossos without you, there would be nothing to lead any suspicion to us."

She dropped her head with a soft whimpering chuckle and thought, "This is some horrible nightmare come true. How could things have gone so wrong? Here I am sitting in front of Samraleos and telling him how I intended to have him killed."

She slightly shook her head in disbelief as her nose dripped dark mucous onto her hands.

"Why did you want me killed?"

"You were a threat to me."

"Did you have anything to do with my father's death?"

"Yes."

"Tell me the names."

"Danaloi was able to bribe one of your father's personal guards. His name is Trabeseos."

Another wave of shock swept through the spectators. Several in the chamber had known and liked Trabeseos.

"Why did you have my father killed and want to kill me?"

"Both of you were threats. Anybody that threatened my uncle's position was a threat to me."

"How was my father a threat to your uncle?"

"It came to me Karasos was to replace my uncle on the committee."

"He turned the post down, you idiot!" the Queen angrily yelled.

She quickly glanced up at the Queen and meekly lowered her head again. Everyone in the room felt odd and uneasy at the way she calmly and emotionlessly talked about killing people. Her victims were nothing but things. They were just obstacles for her to do away with as she pleased. But she was singing the truth like the birds in spring for all she was worth, and for that everyone in the chamber was happy.

"How was I a threat to you?"

"You are too strong with your star on the rise and take the light away from me. Politically, you were in my way."

"Was your uncle Kalpoulis involved in your schemes?"

"No, he is far too easy to manipulate and stupid to be trusted."

"So you didn't do any of this for your uncle?"

"No, it was all for me. I don't care anything for my uncle. He's just somebody I use to get what I want as everyone is."

He asked her what she knew of Trabeseos' whereabouts. She stated she heard he had gone north to the Kolonna trading district on Aegina but couldn't be sure where he was now. Samra knew he had left Knossos several months after his father's death to live somewhere in the Cyclades. A team of investigators was already being hastily organized to arrest Calusetne and to find and return his father's murderer to Knossos for judgment and punishment.

Samra changed the interrogation to one of the workings of her mind saying, "Your family, as I understand it, is composed of your Uncle Kalpoulis and your younger brother and sister. Does your family include anyone else?"

She looked at him quizzically and said, "No."

"Do you enjoy abusing the members of your family?"

"Yes." she calmly answered.

"Are their any members of your family you do not enjoy abusing?"

"No."

"Do you prey on their minds and lives?"

"Yes, I need it. They are nothing to me. I am the only one that's truly real. I am far superior to them in every way.

They're just things that take up space around me. I play with their minds to get them to do what I want."

"Do you feel you are wearing a mask to deceive them to do this?"

"Yes, all the time."

"Why do you fear not wearing a mask?"

"I can't show my true intentions to those I play with, or the game would end. I must be subtle. If I did something obvious to them like wounding them with a dagger, there would probably be someone like you that would seek retribution on me. The consequences are much too great as you can see."

There was a general uproar of laughter in the room by everyone except Synboliki. Once they had settled down, Samra returned to his questions.

"What do you do to abuse your siblings, and what is the result of your abuse?"

"I instill frustration, chaos, and anger in them by exploiting the trust they feel for me as a member of the family. I subtlety paint a picture of the ugliness and selfishness of everyone around them, except for me of course. This makes them obsessively self-centered, angry, and abusive incapacitating their ability to have healthy relationships with other non-abusive people. I destroy their self-confidence to debilitate and cripple their ability to achieve anything good in their lives. My intent is to create new abusers from those I abuse so their abusiveness will fill the lives of the people around them. The innocent victims of the abuse become the new abusers, and it passes on from person to person. My legacy is perpetuated forever."

"Was Danaloi like you?"

"Yes, he understood me as I understood him. We were the same in many ways, but he was weak. He wasn't as comfortable in his skin as I. He couldn't control the beast inside. There was something wrong with him."

Again, laughter broke out in the room.

"How many other people have you met that are like you?"

"I'm not certain but probably six or seven others besides Danaloi."

He told her to identify these people to the scribes. They were to be investigated and, if they were determined to be one of the "Others" like Synboliki, studied for the damage they had done.

The interrogation continued until Samra was satisfied he had all the big questions answered and exposed the true nature of an "Other" to everyone in the room. He stood up from his chair and said, "I'm through with her for now. Would anyone else like to ask questions of her?"

He walked over to the scribes and inquired into how well the recording had gone. She was thoroughly questioned by most of those in the chamber regarding the assassination plots. Many of their queries addressed her nature as one of the "Others". By the time they were through, everyone in the room believed his father's theory of the "Others" was something real and beyond doubt. Synboliki was removed to a detention cell in the palace by the warriors and placed under guard indefinitely. When she left, everyone immediately gathered in intense conversation about what they had just witnessed.

Mariadne asked, "Samra, do you think she is truly one of the "Others" of your father?"

"Yes.   Her behaviors meet all the theory's criteria.   I think I understand what they are and how they operate.   When I'm through investigating her and several other people I have in mind, I'll compose a report to describe the theory and have the palace scribes make copies for you."

"She's not really human is she?   My pet monkey has more compassion and empathy than she does." said the Queen.

"She has no conscience at all!" said Mariadne.

Over the next few days, Samra and several others interrogated Synboliki with an intensity that weakened and drained her as she healed from her injuries.   When he was satisfied nothing of any significance was left in her, he began interviewing the people closest to both her and Danaloi to determine if any of them were "Others" and to search for anything else he could learn.

Synboliki's younger brother and sister were illuminating examples of the effects of her abuse, but they were not "Others" according to the theory.   They were real human beings she had poisoned and breathed evil into.   They strongly showed the effects of their abuse like anger, insecurity, self-obsession, deceitfulness, manipulativeness, and a distorted, overly cynical view of humanity.   But they were able to cry real tears and feel true compassion and sympathy for other people.   In their mind's eye, they could easily place themselves in the shoes of someone else.   They expressed regret and remorse for the bad things they had done.   None of them were "Others", but their lives and outlooks were brutalized and crippled.   Once his interviews were complete, he set about completing his report on the "Others" to the Queen.

Chapter 14

The Others

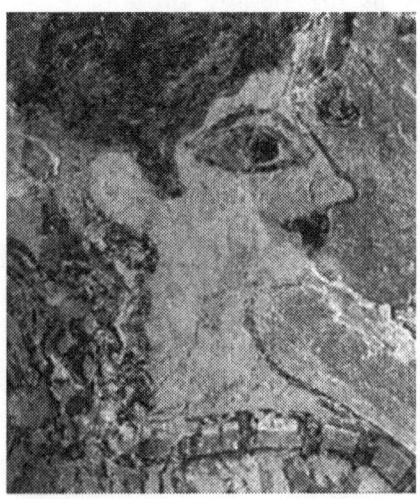

Majesty,

First of all, I must qualify this report on the phenomenon of the "Others" as preliminary in nature. My father's theory of this disorder of the mind requires an organized effort to more fully understand it. But the existence and character of the "Others" is undeniable. I can describe how they express their predatory behaviors, but I can only deduce their prevalence and the magnitude of their destructive influence. The cause of this aberration is far beyond my understanding.

At the time of his death, my father, Karasos, had come to view his concept of the "Others" as a very probable but still unproven explanation of certain human behaviors he had observed over the years. He did not necessarily believe the "Others" were truly among us. He was actively searching for more evidence and confirmation to either prove or disprove its validity.

For many years, I was curious but never really believed it to be true. But I did use my father's interviewing techniques and his study of body movements to help me detect deception and mental weakness in the people around me. It seemed too incredible that there were actually "Others" living among us. I thought such behaviors could more reasonably be explained by disease or injury. I was wrong.

Since I first began to examine people for signs of the "Others", I have observed several individuals that have fully met the criteria. I have come into contact with many more people that have exhibited, in varying degrees, their characteristics and behaviors. When I was asked to investigate the child murders, I suspected an "Other" might be involved. As a result of my recent investigations, I have finally and irrevocably come to believe their existence is real beyond any doubt.

The bizarre behaviors of Danaloi and Synboliki are ample evidence that, at least, they do exist. With only the information gathered from the culling of the formation, there prevalence among the people can be estimated to be from one to five in every hundred.   I will now attempt to describe, in a summarized form, my latest conception of the theory of the "Others" to the best of my ability. I still find it incredible and disturbing, but the overwhelming evidence dictates the following conclusions.

The "Others"

Their greatest deception is that they look just like the rest of us. It's a universal assumption that if you look human you must be human. Not all beings that appear human are human. The "Others" are distinct from real humans in that they are utterly devoid of conscience. No uninformed, real human being would ever imagine their truly inhuman, evil nature.   With the camouflage of their human appearance and a mask of sincerity, they operate among us unrecognized in clear sight.

They are predators that prey on their own kind.   People normally find some reasonable balance between the extremes of total selflessness and total selfishness.   The opposite of the purest priestess they know only total selfishness.   The people around them are nothing but objects of potential food to be consumed by their hunger.   Just as the lion in nature uses stealthy techniques to stalk and kill a calf from the herd, the "Others" use a delicate toxic web of deceit and manipulation to consume their human prey.   As the lion is nourished by its victim's flesh, the "Others" feed on their victim's suffering. The food of the "Others" is human agony and misery.   They seem to find it quite delicious!   Deceitfully masking their true nature, they prey on the psyche of the innocent.   They rarely lose control, but when they do they can commit hideous offenses to human flesh and bone including the ritual mutilation and cannibalism of Danaloi.

Their comprehensive egomania is so delusional that they regard themselves as the central focus of all things.   It's literally all about them, and consequently they have absolutely no sympathy for the feelings and sufferings of others.   With no conscience to restrain them, they can perform the most destructive, hideous acts of selfishness imaginable without even the slightest feelings of remorse, shame, or guilt.   Underneath their façade, they are capable of anything.   The hunger they feel for what they want seems to be their only real concern and the driving force of their lives.

The "Others" have weaknesses that make them detectable. They have difficulty imitating the emotional responses and feelings of real human beings.   Their facial expressions when confronted with statements like "Your mother has been found badly beaten and raped." are muted and flat.   Their emotional verbal responses are hesitant and delayed as if they are struggling to find the correct words. When their answers do come, they are like their facial expressions - shallow and blunted. Many times during their struggle for the words their hand and foot movements quicken and become more noticable.

With a need for stimulation, they live in the moment and are inclined to boredom, frustration, and impulsiveness. They have a predisposition for sexual promiscuity and tend not to have enduring relationships except with those that tolerate and enable them. They desire to live parasitically on the backs of others. They accept absolutely no responsibility for their actions and renege on their sworn commitments whenever it is convenient or self-serving. They tend to exude the disingenuous charm of someone coolly waiting to tell their next lie and have a desire to deceive or fool others into self-destructive acts. The more intelligent they are; the more dangerous they can be. They can refine their mask so realistically that they are extremely difficult to detect and neutralize.

Their Methods

With credibility as its foundation, their ultimate technique is the cultivation of their victim's trust. As long as it is within the bounds of plausibility, they will do anything to sway the perceptions of their victims to their favor. They use and abuse everything that is good in humanity by exploiting our compassion and empathy for others to direct it deceitfully and selfishly onto themselves. They will make displays of apparent unselfishness to lure their victims deeper into their toxic web of trust.

If anyone takes a stand against them to protect their victims, they will prey on their weaknesses to erode and destroy their credibility. These heroes need to be strong in the face of their foul winds. They will invent any number of plausible rationalizations and lies and even stage or manipulate events to destroy them in the eyes of their victims.   They will attempt to form alliances with their victims by inciting the aberrant behaviors they induced in them to turn against these heroes.   If the heroes are unsuccessful and the victims are lost to their seduction, they are vulnerable to any form of deceit and betrayal.

They hide their true nature by imitating the behaviors of other humans using the mask of an actor.   This is a performance they have to maintain at all times in the presence of real humans in order not to reveal their inner-self.   If the truth of their inhumanity was known, they would be ostracized, shunned, and lose access to their prey.   The loss of food for the generation of degradation and chaos would be a terrible blow to their desires.

Some of the "Others" find maintaining their act of deceit very difficult, and they can sometimes lose control to the monster inside.   They can commit insane, ghastly acts like those of the child killer, Danaloi.   In effect, he was a flawed, defective "Other" that couldn't control his inner evil.   For every "Other" like Danaloi, there may be a hundred or more non-criminal ones that are able to control themselves and go unnoticed.

The non-criminal "Others" act out their destructiveness in less obvious ways like the mental and emotional abuse Synboliki perpetrated on her younger brother and sister.   They come in all shades of active and passive.   Many of them are more complacent and attempt to live comfortably behind a rigid façade of mimicked 'real human' behaviors to control their disorder; not fully comprehending they are any different from anyone else.   But they inevitably exude their insidious underlying nature on the innocent humans around them.   They drench them in the poison of their "Other" behaviors just as effectively as the more active ones.

The Victims

Any prolonged contact with an "Other" can be damaging especially to young children. Their victims, even though they are real humans, can display many of the behaviors of the "Others" as a byproduct of their abuse. The psychological and emotional damage can manifest itself as anger, rage, selfishness, impulsiveness, insecurity, mental rigidity, deceitfulness, manipulativeness, irrational abusiveness, and an easy acceptance of the "Others" dark view of humanity.

The more subtle and long lasting the damage is, the more the victim's aberrance seems normal. These behaviors can be profound if the victim is born and grows up in the family of an "Other". They will think that's just the way things are or that's the way he or she is, and the abuse lives on unrecognized and unchecked. The abused innocents then become the new "Non-Other" abusers and create new victims and more aberrance in their wake.

These disturbed behaviors spread out from their source and are passed down from parent to child, relative to relative, and generation to generation in one form or the other until they are finally ended by the attainment of knowledge and treatment. While abusive families tend to produce dysfunctional, abusive children, non-abusive families tend to produce healthy, non-abusive children. Non-abusive children are much more likely to live balanced, fulfilling, happy lives. The heroes that work against the abuse need to be unyielding and resolute in their knowledge and compassionate toward the victims. But if the induced malignant behaviors of the victims are ever to dissipate and fade away, they must never be enabled or rewarded. The "Others" deserve no compassion or empathy at all. They are the true foundation and life blood of all the evil among us.

Social Consequences

Almost nothing is known about the social consequences of the presence of the "Others", but it can be assumed to be very negative. A major study would be required to determine their true incidence in the population and how destructive they really are to humanity. The harmful consequences to society of having them in positions of political, economic, or civil authority are frightening. Their capacity for inducing destructive chaos would be greatly magnified. Synboliki's egomaniacal desire was to attain as influential of a decision-making position in the committees as she could. The overall impact of this malignancy must be very significant.

Hypothesizing, if we were to assume that something like one in twenty is an "Other", or one so deeply poisoned they are almost indistinguishable, and perhaps another four times that many have some degree of induced aberrant behaviors, it is very probable the "Others" are the underlying cause of much of the endemic crime and violence among us.

There will be many innocent people physically maimed and murdered and mentally tormented and traumatized by the "Others" and the poisonous behaviors of their innocent victims. The lives of many family members will be filled with anger, irrationally, and self-destructiveness. Danaloi's, utterly cold-blooded, sadistic disposition for calculated predatory violence, and Synboliki's sneering, murderous contempt for the rights and lives of others and the abuse of her brother and sister are vividly representative of what we are dealing with.

Causes & Therapy

The cause of the "Others" is unknown and can only be guessed at. Some possible causes could be the inheritance of the disorder from their parents, physical injury, or disease. I know

of no treatment for the condition of the "Others". But many of
their victims can be helped with the knowledge of how they
were abused and their desire to rid themselves of the poison.
Since the victims are typically real human beings, they are
innately capable of becoming better, more understanding, and
compassionate people for themselves, their children, and
everyone else in their lives. My father, Karasos, told me that
many years ago he witnessed the, at least partial, correction of
these destructive behaviors in many members of a family he
suspected of suffering from the abuse of a possible "Other".
He said it took time, but the victims were greatly strengthened
by the power they felt from their understanding of the "what's
and why's" of the abuse they had been subjected to. Their
power was in their knowledge.

Self Defense

It is the responsibility of every real human being to educate
themselves and their loved ones to achieve an effective defense
against the "Others". If their victims were alert and
knowledgeable instead of typically being oblivious and naïve,
their insidious effects would be greatly reduced and subdued.
The ultimate solution for the health of the victims is the removal
of the "Others" from access to their lives. Once a victim
becomes aware of their true inhumanity, they should lock the
"Other" out of their lives permanently with no regrets. It is
only then the victim can begin to fully purge themselves of their
induced toxic behaviors.

Recommendations

I think the best immediate course of action would be to begin a
secret investigation within the committees and administration to
remove any "Others" that can be found. This will give us a
better indication of their incidence in the population and help
secure the government from corruption and abuse. There is a

critical reason for secrecy. If word were to get out about the characteristics we were looking for, they would adapt their mask to counter our knowledge. They are more easily detected and thwarted when they are unknowing and off-balance. A school to instruct a special group of investigators trained in the ways of the "Others" would need to be setup. We could use Synboliki and those in custody to demonstrate their true nature in the flesh. Once the purge is complete, every new potential entry into the service of the King could be investigated for signs of the "Others".

It would be useful to consider changing the criminal laws to account for their special status as carriers of evil to better protect the people. If they are caught in criminal activity, they should be given no mercy and the hardest sentence possible. As for the non-criminal "Others", the only way I can think of to counter their contagion is to educate the people, especially the young, in their existence, characteristics, and methods. If this process is to be successful, it will need to be a sustained, recurring process of public education or the concept of the "Others" will fall through the cracks, and they will continue to benefit from their existence being cloaked in ignorance.

After receiving Samra's letter, the Queen and the King's committee immediately began to organize a special commission to study the new knowledge of the "Others" and provide alternate courses of action for their consideration. The commission included Samraleos, Cronymartis, Mariadne, and several other trusted leaders and "Masters of the Way".

The first action they took on initially convening was to ban Kalpoulis from the government and force him into retirement to his family estates without a pension. Cronymartis temporarily took the position to initiate a thorough investigation into any possible corruption within the committee and to oversee its reorganization. Mariadne was selected to permanently head the

King's committee to direct the same process and lead it with her wisdom to promote her policies for the growth of wealth and its equitable distribution for the betterment of all the people.

From the beginning, the commission members disagreed about what was to be done with the "Others". Two of the things they did find easy to agree on was the purging of the entire government and military of all "Others" and the harsh treatment of those committing crimes. Criminal "Others" were, depending on the severity of the crime, either executed, condemned to long terms of forced labor in the stone quarries, or exiled to their almost certain death among the barbarians in the far west.

From the beginning, there was broad disagreement on what was to be done with the majority of "Others" that committed no crimes. They did agree to include instruction on the knowledge of them in the new learning centers and encourage the priests and priestesses to incorporate it in their admonitions on evil. Some on the commission wanted to be quite proactive and forcibly remove those they found from the population to put them in exile. They selected a small town to attempt a pilot program using this policy to gauge its effects. Too many of the families howled with indignation at the taking of their relatives when no crime was committed. They estimated there was probably something like five thousand "Others" in Knossos alone. This idea was soon dropped as impractical.

In the end, they decided the "Others" that committed no crimes could only be dealt with by educating the people, disqualifying them from service to the King, and instituting new laws to protect the innocent, especially the children, from their physical and mental abuse. The "Others" detained in the palace from the culling of the formation were eventually released after being thoroughly studied for months. They were not involved in

Synboliki's plot and had committed no crime, but they were removed from the legion of warriors.

Mariadne retained the services of several of the best "Masters of the Way" to study the "Others" to see if a cure could be found for their disorder and to give her more clarity on the government's policy toward them.   The study went on for several years before the "Masters" declared that no cure could be found and was dropped.

Initially, Samra concentrated on building a team of about one hundred "Other" investigators.   After certifying their qualifications to the King and Queen, they were immediately assigned to detect, in total secrecy, any "Others" in the committees and administration.   When the "Masters" arrived, he did the same with them and, once they were certified, directed them to train their own groups of investigators.   There were safeguards instituted in the process to prevent abuse. Multiple independent investigators were required to agree that an individual was actually an "Other" before any action could be taken against them.   The purge of the "Others" and the reorganization of the King's service took well over a year to complete, but the end result was a great success for the people.

The abuse laws prompted by the "Others" immediately began to bring people to the attention of the authorities with justice handed out to many.   The combination of the continued wealth from trade brought in by the king's ships, the completion of the main road system, the reorganization of the government, the new learning centers, and the abuse laws created, after only a few years, an environment of greater happiness and prosperity that had never been seen before.   Continual progress came to be naively expected by the people like the rains in winter.

Cronymartis' greatest wish was to retire to his family estate in Agia Triadha, just west of Phaistos, as soon as he could.

Eventually, he left Knossos for home some ten months later. He was satisfied his work in the committees was, even more than his many military victories, his most important contribution to the people.

Before Cronymartis left to join his family in the south, he attended the ritual joining of Samraleos and Jenaloi in the palace. It was a grand affair with the Queen herself assisting in the ceremony. Several hundred people were in attendance including many important dignitaries. Throughout the day, the palace was alive with feasting and vibrated with the music of the lyre, flute, and drum. The festival continued until late into the evening with synchronized dancing and a wonderful display of the dance of the bulls in the courtyard.

Samra had no political aspirations. He had a personal distaste for it. His interests were in his research in "Nature's Way" and creating wealth from his family business dealings. Ultimately, he desired to move to Khania, about one hundred kilometers to the west, and live on his family's estate with Jena near his son and his family. Samra stayed on in Knossos for another few years, and then he and Jena finally moved west for a new life there. They went on to live very happily and eventually have four beautiful healthy children together.

Thalion and Antoneos stayed on in Knossos and established their own perfume and body oil business from the wealth he had earned while in Samra's employment. He became the exclusive distributor for Samra's Iris and Chamomile products from Khania.

Chapter 15

The Assassin's Escape

After hearing of Synboliki's arrest that evening from a messenger sent to his mother, Calusetne knew he must leave immediately and make his escape from Knossos. If it turned out she was detained in error and everything was as before, he could always return. But if she was arrested and strongly pressured, he knew she would eventually expose him. He had to leave now for his safety. He put together a traveling pack and sent for a donkey to make his getaway in the night. He quietly took all the gold he could from the villa, and after telling his mother he would be back soon, he headed north on the roadway to Katsamba on the coast to find a boat to leave the island.

It was late at night when he arrived, but he managed to find a decent room and a stall for his donkey. He slept very little that first night worrying about what might happen to him. He knew if he was accused and an authorization for his arrest was issued, they would never stop trying to find him. If they did find him, he could be legally killed on sight or doomed to execution.

He pondered his alternatives. He wanted to be far enough away to avoid arrest but close enough to hear the news from Knossos. If an authorization hadn't been issued he wanted to know it, so he could return to the comfort of his family's villa. The thought of living among foreigners and barbarians was abhorrent to him. If he really was in trouble, he felt his best chance was to get lost in the large populations of Tiryns and Mycenae on the mainland, but he considered the Myceneans to be a primitive and filthy people with bizarre backward ways. He thought Troy to the north would be a more comfortable but less safe place to run. But, for now, he decided he would make for Thera, about a hundred kilometers to the north, as a pivot point in his journey. He thought it was the perfect place to make a decision to return or run.

At dawn, he abandoned his donkey and walked out onto the docks looking for a boat to discreetly take him north. He was vague about exactly where he wanted to go to. Word soon spread that a man with gold was looking for a boat to take him to one of the islands in the Cyclades. He wanted to go to the booming, heavily populated islands of Thera. He had visited the islands two years earlier and knew the layout fairly well. He wanted to do whatever he could to divert any notice to his arrival. He thought it best if he secretly arrived on the southern coast near Akrotiri. From there, he could walk the five kilometers north to take the ferry to the southern end of the inner island. He felt this would minimize any attention to his appearance in the main port city.

Two fishermen eventually offered to take him to the Cyclades if the price was right. But they insisted on knowing where they were going, and he must show them his gold, or the deal was off. He had the look of running from something that concerned them. The men made sure they were well armed for the trip. After making an effort to secure their secrecy, he told them he wanted to go to Akrotiri on Thera. He had them vow to tell no one of his destination.   The fishermen complained if they left now they would arrive well into the night and tried to delay him to take a night voyage for an arrival the next day.

He would have none of it.   He wanted to leave immediately and offered them a little more gold to induce them.   He fed them a story about a family emergency that required his immediate attention, but he wanted it to be a surprise.   The men were seduced by the sight of his gold.   They had the boat provisioned in a short time as they prepared it for the trip. While quickly gathering food and drink from his home with Calusetne standing in the doorway, one of the fishermen whispered to his girlfriend he was going to Akrotiri and would return tomorrow with a tidy sum of gold in his pouch.

A medium wind was coming from the west that would give them a relatively easy sail to the north.   It was a typical fishing boat; a little less than ten meters long with a large square sail. They had made the voyage many times in the past.   The trip was uneventful with Calusetne sitting in the bow most of the time.   He was armed with his many daggers.   There was one in his pack, one strapped to his back under his cape, and another two daggers sheathed on his weapons belt.   The night fell darkly on them as they neared Akrotiri.   It was partly cloudy with a half moon.   The clouds regularly drifted in front of it to block its light.   When the faint lights of Akrotiri on the coast were finally sighted, he told them to head west of the town to drop him off on an isolated beach.   The fishermen knew the area well and pointed out a path to Akrotiri for him as they sailed the boat up onto a narrow sandy beach lined with sheer rocky walls.

As the boat slid onto the beach, Calusetne jumped from the bow.   He was followed by one of the fishermen while his partner tended to the boat.   As the boat was pulled further up onto the beach to better secure it, Calusetne reached for his gold pouch to pay them. Smiling gently and thanking the man for the trip, in a flash, he stuck one of his belt daggers into the man's abdomen and twisted the blade. The fisherman yelped loudly in pain startling his friend tending the boat. As he fell to his death in the sand, Calusetne, with lightning speed, reached behind his head for his large throwing blade and threw it into the other man's abdomen. It sank deeply into him with a thud. He briefly wavered before his eyes rolled up into his head, and he fell onto the shoreline with his face in the water.

Calusetne dragged his first victim toward the boat and, being careful not to get blood on him, lifted the body into it. Rolling the other fisherman over onto his back on the beach, he pulled the shiny dagger from his flesh and rinsed both of his bloody blades in the water. He calmly wiped them dry with the bottom of his cape and returned the big knives to their sheaths. He picked the body up and physically threw it into the boat to join his friend.

After pushing the boat out into the water a short way, he shoved it as hard as he could back out into the sea. He thought the wind would slowly take it away from the island with no one the wiser. Killing the men was not something he enjoyed. He was not an "Other". It was simply something he felt he had to do for his self-preservation. As he stood watching it for a few quiet moments in the dark, the boat slowly drifted out into the water with its sail loosely fluttering in the wind. He then decisively turned toward the path to make his way beyond Akrotiri to seek the road leading to the ferry town that would take him to the port city of Thera.

He could get lodging for the night there while he waited for the ferry in the morning. His basic plan was, after getting a good night's sleep, to go to the inner island and become as anonymous as possible in the large port city. All the news from Knossos would be readily available to him with commercial ships arriving from Crete almost every day at this time of the year. Once in the city, he would rent an apartment with a high balcony overlooking the harbor to find his comfort and monitor the activity of the ships.

Shortly after beginning his walk and cresting a hill, the lights of the big city's fires and oil lamps came into view. It was a grand sight at night. After arriving in the ferry town, Calusetne soon found a comfortable room and began to settle in and relax. He was very tired having slept little the night before. He took a hot bath and, after eating and drinking his fill, found his bed. He felt he had covered his tracks very well and slept wonderfully.

After Synboliki exposed him as a conspirator in the king's chamber, a detachment of palace guards was immediately sent to his family's villa to arrest him. They questioned his distressed mother and everyone else in the household while thoroughly searching it. They learned he was last seen leaving the evening before with a packed donkey heading north on the roadway and had not returned.

Messengers were rushed to the authorities in the ports and fishing villages on the coast where he was initially seen heading. They also sent express runners out on the main roads to Khania, Phaistos, and Malia to determine if he had taken any of those routes out of town and to alert the authorities. Three or four hours later that afternoon, information came to them that a man had hired a fishing boat to go north into the Cyclades and had left his donkey unattended. After being found and questioned, the worried fisherman's girlfriend said she was told they were heading for Akrotiri.

The authorities immediately made arrangements to send two fast ships loaded with a full complement of warriors, officials, and investigators. Included among them were a few people that could identify Calusetne on sight. The first ship left its pier in Amnisos about an hour before sundown and, without delay, took off for a fast nighttime run to Akrotiri. It was much smaller than the huge long ships being only about twenty meters in length. But it was built for speed with a narrow beam and had thirty oars with a large sail. It carried only human cargo and was very lightly provisioned. The King's ships were within a day's sailing of supplies almost whatever their heading in this region of the Aegean.

The first of the King's ships made excellent time and tied to the docks in Akrotiri a couple of hours before dawn. Several people were dropped off to wake the authorities from their beds and alert them Calusetne was wanted for conspiracy to murder Samraleos. A comprehensive search of the area was promptly initiated in the dark of night. At this point, they knew nothing of him killing the courier or the two fishermen. The ship soon left Akrotiri and rowed about six kilometers to the west along the coast until it reached the opening in Thera's outer encircling island, and they could see the lights of the city inside it. The ship master headed straight to the military dockyards on the north side of the city's harbor. After they moored to the pier, the ship was hurriedly off loaded as the first faint light of dawn lit the eastern sky.

The second of the King's ships left Amnisos about two hours after the first. It bypassed Akrotiri entirely and headed directly to the port city on the inner island. As they tied to the military docks about a half hour after the sunrise, the first ship was being prepared to leave with a hastily gathered crew to take it on the short voyage back to the docks in Akrotiri. Within thirty minutes, the second ship was released from its mooring and took the same course. They wanted the arrival of the King's ships to be as unnoticed as possible.

The authorities in the military district were soon alerted and told how badly the King and Queen wanted Calusetne for his involvement in the assassination plot against Samraleos. Messengers were organized and hurriedly sent out to notify the civil authorities of the entire city to be on the lookout, but they were instructed not to apprehend him. They wanted to first determine if he had any criminal associates on the islands. They were given a detailed description of his features and distinguishing particulars accompanied with a drawing on parchment of his face. The people that could identify him were made available at various locations throughout the city.

The first groups of deputies were sent to investigate any recent night dockings in the commercial docks with some of them sent to monitor the southern approaches to the city from Akrotiri. Watchers were strategically stationed throughout the city but mainly in the areas with lodging houses and apartment complexes. They were to look for anyone new on the island. Once the civil authorities had the investigation well under way, the warriors and others that made the night voyage to Thera were assigned to quarters to let them sleep.

Calusetne woke with the dawn and began preparing himself to take the southern ferry to the inner island. He felt very confident he was in no danger. The only way he could be in any trouble was if Synboliki had named him. If she did, she would be implicating herself and would die for it. He knew how mentally creative and fearless she could be and felt assured she could withstand any normal questioning for, at least, a number of days. He was wrong in assuming she would be interrogated normally.

He was sleeping soundly when a woman and two men walked into the ferry town before dawn. They were investigators from the first ship that had been dropped off in Akrotiri. They took the most likely path he would have taken to enter the port city from the south.   They had no way to know if he was there or not.   They were ordered to simply identify and take up surveillance on him if he was found.   They sat in the grass slightly up the slope of a hill under a small grove of olive trees overlooking the ferry to wait for the sunrise and see what came.

Calusetne opened his window shutter and took in the light of the dawn to see the emerging bustle of people waiting for the ferrymen to arrive.   The investigators merged discreetly into the crowd.   They were told he was very dangerous and known to be a master with the dagger.   They just wanted to hopefully identify anyone that matched his description on the ferry dock and follow him.   They thought it would take some time before the authorities on the inner island were fully alerted and knew they would be on their own if he was sighted.

The ferry's stone dock with wooden piers moored two large multi-keeled flat boats.   They were twenty five meters long and eighteen meters wide with thick cypress decking and outboard seating structures for the rowers.   The structures provided space for ten rowers on each side of the boat.   Wooden rails separated the rowers from the passengers and carts.   The ferry was the main access point in the south for all wheeled and foot traffic between the islands.

Calusetne was almost immediately spotted as a possible suspect by the investigators as he approached the docks.   He matched the general description, dressed expensively, and carried a new heavily laden travel pack on his back.   The rowers began assembling on board the ferries and setting their oars.   The wagons and carts started rolling into position and were secured on the decks.   When this was complete, the people were then allowed to crowd onto the decks.   All three of the investigators walked onto the same boat as Calusetne having seen no one else matching his description.   He didn't have the slightest suspicion he was detected and being watched.   His ferry traversed the short distance over the waterway in just a few minutes.   As he walked onto the inner island, he noticed there was a good deal of new construction since he had last been in the area.   There were several new buildings in the vicinity of the ferry docks and along the roadway leading into the city.

Thera was basically two separate islands composed of a roughly circular inner one that was, almost completely, enclosed by an outer island that ringed around it.   The mostly flat plain of the inner island ranged from six to eight kilometers wide.   The outer ringing island was fourteen kilometers from east to west and eighteen kilometers from north to south.   The closest they came to touching each other was about four or five hundred meters.   There was a single three kilometer opening in the southwest of the outer island that allowed access to its interior from the open sea.   The two islands were the remnants of an ancient marine volcanic caldera.   Any ships anchored inside the outer island were protected from all the winds and rough seas beyond it.   It was the finest natural harbor in the whole of the Aegean.

Thera was the largest Minoan commercial trading and manufacturing center outside of Knossos on Crete.   The dockyards and warehouses of the port city of over forty thousand people were located on the western side of the fifty square kilometer inner island.   The huge palace complex was about two and a half kilometers to the east of the port near the center of the island.   It stood proudly above the town on a low wide human-sculpted promontory that dominated the fertile plains of the island.

Thera was an important naval base for dealing with the persistent problem of piracy especially in the northern seas.   It was strategically located in the south central Aegean within easy sailing distance of the Myceneans in the west, the Hittites in the east, and the Trojans and Thracians in the north with a

direct connection to Knossos in the south.   Much of the trade in
the entire area, especially from the north, was shipped there for
distribution to Knossos and far beyond.   Products from Thera
found there way to the Egyptians and Kushites in the south, and
the Canaanites, Hittites, and Assyrians in the east.

There were several towns and villages on the islands.   The
largest of these was the port city of Thera on the inner island.
The biggest town on the outer island was Therasia in the
northwest.   There was a causeway and bridge joining it to the
inner island.   Therasia was about twice the size of Akrotiri in
the south.   Everyone else on the outer island had to take a short
boat or ferry ride to access the inner one.

With only about one hundred and sixty square kilometers of
land, the two islands couldn't possibly support the population of
over one hundred and twenty thousand people living there.
They were sustained by the influx of goods coming into its
ports.   Large quantities of barley and wheat from the Thracian
grain shipments were stored in huge warehouses for year round
processing and consumption.

The climate was generally dry with almost no rain in the long
hot summers, but the mild winters could be quite wet.   The flat
roofs of the buildings were slightly sloped to let the winter rains
flow into terracotta drain pipes that filled their water cisterns for
storage.   The harvesting of water was mandatory for every
masonry structure on the islands.   In times of drought, water
was imported like so many other things.

Wood for the numerous construction projects was mostly
imported to save the sparse amounts of timber left on the island.
The islands would have been totally denuded of trees long ago
if the administration hadn't stepped in and sharply regulated it
mainly for aesthetic reasons.

The Therans practiced a very high level of animal husbandry, and animal stock was imported in great quantities for food. The sheep, goats, pigs, and cattle were all domesticated and stabled or fenced outside the towns. Sheep and pigs were the staple meat diet of the people along with some cattle, but goats and deer were also consumed. The goats and cows provided the people with milk. Dried animal dung was used, as much as possible, to help fuel their braziers, kilns, and smelters. Much of their clothing was spun and weaved from wool, and their shoes were made from leather.

The animal's skins, sinews, and bones were used as raw materials for an extraordinary number of things. Shell, bone, horn, and teeth were used to make tools, weapons, art objects, etc. Horn and sinews were used in making their bows, and oxhide covered their shields. Boar's tusks covered their helmets, and leather was used in their body armor.

Thera was the leading manufacturing center of textile products in the Aegean. There were several factories employing thousands of workers setup expressly to weave the sails of ships, clothing, and many other finished woolen and hemp products. Many of the villas and homes on the islands had their own weaving looms. Ships loaded with bales of wool filled the harbor to feed the factories. There was a significant sector of the workforce devoted to the production of fine jewelry and pottery for export. The profits of trade and production filled the treasury with gold. The people's standard of living was very high especially compared to the barbarian Myceneans in the west.

Calusetne had never visited Thera in the springtime before. It looked even more beautiful than he remembered from his previous visits. His eyes were always drawn to the extraordinary red, black, yellow, and white layered rock pinnacles and sheer precipices of the walls of the outer island ringing the large plain of the inner one. The fertile fields of the islands were green expanses of mostly open pasture land. The grass and evergreen scrubs were dotted with patches of mainly oak trees mixed with groves of olive trees, junipers, and vineyards. Moving among them were large flocks of sheep and goats with smaller herds of cattle. Wild goats and deer lived in the hills of the outer island.

As he walked into the city, the roadway split into three routes. The western road ran along the dockyards. The central road took people into the center of the city, and the eastern route led to the road to the palace complex. The western road was already very busy with several carts and wagons heading to and from the southern ferry. He decided to take the central roadway into the city.

He thought he would find a lodging house on the north end of the city near the military dockyards to monitor the movement of ships there. This would provide him his best chance to determine if the authorities had come to Thera to arrest him. He would still be close to the commercial shipyards to find a boat to escape, if necessary, and he would also have the option of taking the causeway to Therasia to make an escape. He needed to find a suitable lodging house that would give him a good high view of the movements of the ships in the harbor especially the military ones. If anyone was going to seek him out, it would be from there.

Calusetne found a tall apartment building near the docks that gave him an excellent view of the harbor from a fourth story balcony. His pack was quite heavy, and he was glad to relieve himself of it as he settled into his room. He didn't want to leave his gold unguarded until he was completely satisfied he was safe from the authorities. That first day, he arranged for his meals and other necessities to be delivered to him while he sat out on the balcony observing the activity in the harbor.

Calusetne could see all of the military harbor facilities and most of the commercial port from his location.

The commercial dockyards were huge and constantly bustling with activity. He made a mental map of the military ships in the harbor and waited to observe any new arrivals that might threaten him. He obtained his view of the harbor too late to see the two ships sent to apprehend him. He started to relax more and more as the day went on with no new military arrivals. He began to think he was probably off the hook from Synboliki's arrest and thought her uncle Kalpoulis must have pulled some political strings to get her released.

The authorities were committed to holding off on Calusetne's arrest until they could determine if he was alone or not. They would continue to observe his actions for a few more days before deciding on the best time to take him. The next day with his confidence assured, he made his way to the palace complex to deposit his heavy pack of gold in the treasury. Once his gold was assayed and weighed, he rolled his cylinder seal into a clay tablet to indicate the deposit and was given a parchment record of the transaction with the treasury's seal on it. Relieved to only have to guard the gold in his belt pouch, he returned to the area of his lodging and began to survey its eateries and amusements for a two week stay before returning to Knossos.

On his return, he found what looked to be a good place to get a meal near the docks. He ordered some sliced mutton on flat bread with vegetables. He thought his waitress was quite attractive and said, "I haven't been in town for a couple of years. Where can somebody have a good time around here?"

She smiled and said, "There are plenty of drinking taverns with girls for hire. You won't have any trouble finding them. Just walk along the dock road. But you can have these and much more with enough gold." as she cupped her hands under her breasts and bounced them near his face.

With a mischievous smile, she pinched her nipples and stretching her breasts slightly said, "Want to play?"

"Yes, indeed, I want to play. Perhaps we could meet later this evening so you could show me around?" he said with a smile as he patted his pouch of gold.

"Sounds like fun. If you come here for your meal at sunset, we can start from there."

She turned and lifted her loincloth to show him her smooth buttocks. He moved to touch her, but she quickly stepped away and dropped her garment back into place. As she slowly walked away from him, she looked back with a smile and said, "That's for later."

She repeatedly flirted with him throughout his meal, and he gleefully thought he would have to return to Thera for pleasure much more in the future. Pleased things were going well, he returned to his lodging to have a good bath and continue observing the shipping in the harbor.

When he walked away, a woman came forward to speak to his waitress. The waitress had worked with the authorities in the past as an informant and was asked to do the same with Calusetne. With a reward of gold, she immediately agreed and was given instructions to elicit any information she could about his associates, if any, on Thera. She was told to be careful because he could possibly be very dangerous.

She laughed saying, "Who isn't dangerous around here?"

"There will be others near you at all times, but we want to determine if he has friends.

"If he has, I will surely find out." she said with a confident smirk.

The woman from the authorities asked her where she planned to take him if he came to meet her later.   They wanted to plant people in the drinking halls ahead of time to minimize the possibility of their detection.   She made it clear to her that they were just watching him for now.   Once all the arrangements were made, they maintained their surveillance and waited for the evening to come.

With still no new military ships in the harbor, he left to mingle with the people to hear any news he could gather.   He had conversations with many people that second day but heard nothing of the two ships that entered the military harbor briefly at dawn on his first day in Thera.   Even if he had heard of their docking, he wouldn't have been concerned.   He would never have thought it was possible that they could come after him so quickly.

During the afternoon, he purchased a new loincloth, shoulder wrap, and shoes.   He also bought a light body harness to hold two of his daggers, one on each side of his body under his arms, hidden by his shoulder wrap.   He preferred not to wear his uncomfortable back dagger harness and left it in his apartment. With the two daggers in his weapons belt, four weapons were now available to him if any trouble loomed.   He had been practicing with his bronze daggers from a very early age and had long ago mastered their use with both hands as his growing list of victims demonstrated.

He came for his evening meal to meet the waitress and was impressed to see her hair newly styled.   She smelled wonderfully of perfume. They were served by others as she sat with him describing what she had planned for their evening together. He was looking forward to discovering the nightlife in Thera anew from his prior visits. He had never taken in the amusements in this part of the town before. Throughout the evening, they had a wonderful time moving from one entertainment hall to the other. All of them had stout wine, beer, music, and dancing girls much to his liking.

Three nights later, Calusetne and another woman he had recently met walked out laughing in conversation from the doorway of a tavern on the waterfront close to his lodging. The pair took a few steps onto the stone before she abruptly stopped for a moment. Searching her pouch, the woman looked up at him quizzically. She told him she had forgotten something and would be right back. As he stood on the paving watching her reenter the hall, he noticed two men almost immediately move to fill the open doorway with their bodies as she passed and begin staring at him menacingly.

He curiously scrutinized them and, in an instant of recognition, turned his head to look up and down the road. He was horrified to see two men coming out of the nearby alley to confront him with drawn daggers. Hearing footsteps behind him, he turned to see another pair of men with daggers moving out into the road to block his path. His only open direction of escape was to run and jump into the water of the harbor, but he didn't know how to swim. Suddenly, he started running at full speed straight at the closest pair of men to his north as he grabbed his two body daggers. Without hesitation, he threw them at the men. He was in full flight as both men were struck and fell to the stone. One was hit low in his abdomen near his crotch. The other one was hit just under the ribs. Both men screamed loudly and crumpled to the stone as he ran past them.

He now had a clear line of flight to the north and, in panic, ran for his life toward the causeway to Therasia. Abruptly, he heard a loud horn blare out nearby and then another and another. He was being heatedly chased by the four surviving deputies. They were slightly out of dagger range, but they were slowly closing in on him. He had just made his way onto the causeway when he saw several men running towards him from the other side. In terror, he suddenly stopped in his tracks and made a move to jump off the causeway into the shallow water below.

At that instant, there were three daggers flying in the air towards him from behind. The first one missed his head by mere centimeters. He saw the large blade glint past his face. An instant later, the second one struck him hard in his right side. Almost simultaneously, the third one sank deeply into his thigh just under his buttocks. He staggered for a moment as his leg collapsed under him. He fell off the side of the causeway into the shallow water and mud beside it. The deputies quickly jumped in after him and rushed to get his head out of the water just in case he was still alive and able to talk. As they lifted his face above the surface of the water, his eyes briefly surveyed them as a mixture of blood and water gushed from his mouth. His eyes then rolled back in his head showing only the whites, and he fell limp in their arms.

Calusetne never regained consciousness and died soon after they dragged him onto the shore. The deputies removed the daggers piercing him with blood pouring heavily from his body. After letting his blood soak into the soil until the flow had ebbed, they dragged his body onto the stone to deliver it to the nearby military authorities building just east of the dockyard. The next day, one of the King's ships headed back to Knossos carrying Calusetne's body. The other ship headed for Kolonna on the island of Aegina to follow up on information they had gathered about Trabeseos; the murderer of Samra's father, Karasos.

In the fall of the next year, a ship entered the harbor of Miletus on the eastern mainland. It appeared to be a typical trading vessel and aroused no attention. A woman awaiting their arrival walked up to greet them as Samraleos and his guards, dressed as oarsmen, offloaded. One of his guards had a brief conversation with her. Once she had confirmed their identities, she turned to escort them to a lodging house south of the town. On coming close, the woman motioned for them to wait for her signal. Just as she reached the open doorway, she stopped and nodded her head slightly to someone inside. She then backed away from it to surreptitiously wave Samra and his guards forward. The woman walked toward them as they approached and said, "He's sitting with his back to the door talking with one of our agents."

Samra calmly walked into the room with his guards close behind him. As he approached the table, the agent talking to Trabeseos saw him and abruptly got up and walked away. As Trabeseos curiously watched the man walk off in the middle of their conversation, Samra came from behind him and sat down in the seat to face him. He said nothing as Trabeseos turned to look into the eyes. Trabeseos dropped his head, shaking it softly, and began to quietly chuckle. With a smile, he slowly looked to his side and behind him to see the guards ready to kill him if he made the wrong move. As he looked back at his murder victim's son, Samra smiled saying, "Hello Trabeseos; beautiful day."

Trabeseos then smiled broadly and again lowered and shook his head softly chuckling. After a few moments, he raised his head and looking at Samra quizzically said, "What took you so long?"

He began to eerily laugh and cry at the same time. A blade was placed on the back of his neck. Samra rose from his chair and said, "Rise slowly and drop your belt, Trabeseos, if you wish to see another moment."

He was now sobbing with tears falling onto the tabletop. He slowly rose and unfastened his belt letting it fall to the floor. One of the guards put a dagger to his throat as two of the others grabbed his arms. They tightly bound his hands behind him with a leather strap and led him back to the ship for the return voyage to Knossos.

He was drenched in guilt and freely admitted it during his interrogation. Judgment was swift, and he was given his choice of death. Without delay, he made his decision and was given a cup of poison which he swallowed deeply. Two bowmen were standing close by to see if he refused to drink the potion. They were instructed to seriously wound him only. They wanted to let the poison on their arrowheads, and not the bronze, kill him. He had seen the horrible effects of the scorpion poison before. Trabeseos soon began to cramp up, and his head fell forward to bounce on the table in front of him with blood running from his mouth.

Chapter 16

The Death of Synboliki

Synboliki was sentenced to a lifetime of house arrest in her family's small villa on the hill east of the port of Amnisos. Her uncle Kalpoulis and a few others were allowed to visit her, but if she was ever seen leaving the grounds of the estate the hogs would feast on her. Kalpoulis came to view her as a pariah that had caused his downfall and contemptuously refused to visit her while he was forced to pay for her upkeep. Her younger brother and sister had received treatment from the "Masters of the Way" assigned to analyze and heal the abuse inflicted on them by her. Once they understood what she had done to them, they were determined to rid themselves of the venom they had been injected with. They were grateful that they never had to endure her abuse and torment ever again.

Synboliki was miserable and loathed her life of boredom, devoid of victims, in the villa. But, at least, she was still alive. She hated life on the coast with its howling winds and spray from the sea. She felt very isolated except for the presence of her two servants. Her servants were instructed to talk to her only when necessary, and they were to report any abuse she perpetrated on them to the authorities. The consequences restrained her natural tendencies. But occasionally one or two her 'friends' would visit her especially if they needed to borrow some of her allowance of gold. She drifted into fatalism and simply waited for her death. She began to over-indulge her appetite for opium, and her health began to deteriorate.

Some years later, the thunderous cacophony of roaring ear-splitting booms and explosions from Thera saturated the sky around Synboliki's villa. Since the beginning of the eruption, she had usually stayed in her bedroom chamber with the doors and windows tightly shut, but she was drawn to the amazing sight of it. She covered her ears with thick folded pads of cloth held in place by a strip tied around her head. The volcano had been erupting massively for the last four or five days giving her very little sleep. The ground rolled and shook regularly from the many small to medium earthquakes. The sea was confused and filled with floating whitish pumice stones thrown out by the volcano and looked more like land that sea. The sky was clear with the west winds blowing steadily to the east in the early summer and no ash fell on Crete's northern coast. Her villa was about one hundred meters above sea level on the southeastern hill of Amnisos. She had a perfect view of the Theran volcano's looming, gigantic eruption column that towered into the sky over forty five kilometers high.

The massive writhing white, grey, and black column with its dark sky of ash fall moving downwind to the east was an awe-inspiring colossal sight to behold. From her vantage point, it seemed to grow out of the surface of a small island about ten kilometers to the north of her villa. The column was filled with the brilliant incandescent flashes of lightning bolts crackling on its surface accompanied by more softly muted bursts of light from deeper within it. Synboliki knew Thera was something like one hundred and ten kilometers away, and she felt certain nothing that distant could possibly harm her in Amnisos.

And yet, the ominous dark column and bellowing ash cloud that blotted out the sky to the north seemed so huge and so very, very close. She had to crane her neck to look up at the top of it and was becoming alarmed at the loud thunderous booms that seemed to be getting louder and occurring more frequently. The waves were irregular and chaotic. Some of the waves were huge and intermittently crashed onto Amnisos' beach below her. Quite a few people had evacuated the port city to move inland in fear for their safety.

A few months earlier, Thera began to erupt and sent a column of ash high into the sky, but it was nothing like the current massive cataclysm. The winds were coming from the north and rained a thin layer of fine yellowish orange-brown ash unto Synboliki's villa. Some relatively strong earthquakes and many smaller ones were felt at the time, but the damage was mild, and the ash fall was soon cleaned up by her servants. The volcano then went completely to sleep and rested peacefully for months. The ash was washed from sight and memory by the winter rains that came soon after. Everything seemed normal and serene again as life went on as before. There had been several small earthquakes in the area since the initial eruption but nothing of any concern. Synboliki was used to the rolling and shaking of the earth and had experienced many small to moderate quakes since childhood.

She was sitting in her lounge chair on her balcony with her ears covered watching the fascinating sight of the volcano when she noticed a wavering and then a slumping of the column into the sea. Later, she noticed that the shoreline was receding out to sea; slowly at first and then much faster. A few people that had been watching the eruption high on the beach began running out onto the newly dry land of the receding shoreline to pick up fish that had become stranded among the pumice stones. She then noticed the horizon of the sea begin to grow taller and taller as far as she could see.   At first she was confused at what it could be but soon realized that a gigantic wave was racing at a fantastic speed towards them.   She watched in amazement as the sea grew and grew in height and soon overcame those few that had been enticed by the fish flopping madly in the sand.

It grew to a height of sixty meters and moved with a suddenness that astonished her.   She had never seen anything like it.   She couldn't believe it was possible for such a huge wave to exist. It quickly crashed into the port facilities and swallowed the entire city destroying everything in its path.   Huge ships were lifted high into the air and tossed inland to crash onto people and structures.   Everything was shattered and destroyed by the power of the water.   Once the wave spent itself and began to recede, it took much of it's destruction with it back out to sea. The surface of the water around Amnisos was littered with all manner of debris.   It looked like a like a floating garbage site filled with thousands of dead and dying people mixed with the wreckage of the town.

The town was unrecognizable.   It seemed no one in the city below had any chance at all of survival.   She could see a few people holding onto broken pieces of wood and waving their arms as they were carried out to sea by the huge receding wave. It had all happened so swiftly it seemed like a dream to her.

"Thank the gods I 'm high on the hill."

Her fascination with the scene in front of her was broken by the shrieking and screaming of her servants that had run outside to see what had happened.   They were the lucky ones to have survived, but many of their family members that lived below in the town must have perished.   Synboliki couldn't care less about the people, but the sight was captivating and entertaining to her.   Relatively soon, the sea settled back into a chaotic normalcy, but it was filled with destruction and death. The great port city of Amnisos was gone!

Synboliki smirked and thought, "Well, at least, I'm safe."

About four hours later, a titanic pyroclastic surge of super-heated dry steam and gas exploded under tremendous pressure from a huge base vent in the Theran volcano. Out squirted an enormous eleven hundred degree centigrade gas bloom traveling in excess of the speed of sound at over thirteen hundred kilometers per hour headed south for central and eastern Crete. It reached the northern coast of Crete in about five minutes and the southern coast one and a half minutes later with a temperature of six to seven hundred degrees centigrade.

It was just after sunset, and Synboliki was watching the activity of the volcano drinking wine on the balcony when she noticed something strange. The very bottom of the column was immersed in a line of utter darkness, and it seemed to be slowly growing taller blotting out more and more of the light from the base of the eruption. She started looking very closely at this mysterious phenomenon and became alarmed.

"Is it another wave?"

After only a couple of minutes, the layer of darkness on the horizon grew to almost a sixth of the way up the column. She thought something terrible was coming. Fear gripped her and she hurriedly rose from her lounge chair carrying her wine and entered her bed chamber to close the door tightly behind her. She rushed to close the two small window shutters on the north side of the room; making sure they were securely latched and did the same with the other windows. She felt relieved she was safe inside and everything was tightly secured. She began to relax and moved toward her table by the brazier to light another oil lamp.

She was frightened and felt something terrible was heading toward her as she looked toward the north windows with apprehension.   A few moments later, the window shutters instantly exploded into the room; flying past her and smashing into the south interior wall.   She was almost simultaneously thrown a short distance into the wall by the tremendous force of the wind as she felt an incredible heat engulf her.   She sagged to the floor as the amazing hot wind swirled in the room.   She just had an instant to open her mouth in shock and take in a short breath.   It was the last breath she ever took.   The inside of her lungs were scorched beyond repair.

Her hair, skin, and clothes were instantaneously set afire.   All of the skin on her body began to peel away leaving the unbelievable, all-consuming heat to cook the flesh underneath.   Synboliki's body began to curl up like bacon in a hot pan.   All of the wooden beams, furniture, and draperies in the villa were instantly set ablaze and burning intensely.   Synboliki's bed chamber was a mass of fire as the fantastic wind continued to howl into it.   Her disgustingly filthy life as an "Other" was over but so were those of everyone that came into contact with Thera's incredible pyroclastic surge of super-heated dry steam, volcanic gas, and dust.

The supersonic wind began to drop off, but the gas bloom's ferocious heat took several more minutes to cool and dissipate in the steady west wind.   By now, everything that it had touched throughout all of central and eastern Crete was furiously ablaze.   Almost everyone was scorched alive and lay dead cooking in the heat just like Synboliki.   All of the cities, towns, villages, and farmsteads were all on fire.   The great forests of cypress and oak were burning with a vengeance as every square centimeter of their surface areas was set afire instantaneously.   The incredible blanket of fires continued to burn until everything was thoroughly consumed.   Perhaps over a million people had been roasted alive within a minute and a half of each other. It was an instant holocaust of much of the Minoan civilization.

About thirty minutes later in its final throes of eruption, Thera cataclysmically exploded into the sky with an ear-shattering series of thunderous booms. With the fires raging on the land like a blanket of hell, the biggest of all the tsunamis struck the northern coast of Crete. It was over one hundred meters tall and extinguished all of the fires near the coast. It finally spent itself as it washed up near to the burning palace of the dead King and Queen. With the fires out on the coastline, the landscape below the palace was unrecognizable with charred destruction, wreckage, pumice stones, and death as far as the eye could see. The huge tsunami washed tens of thousands of roasted humans and animals into the sea to mix with the previous masses of floating destruction from the first tsunami. The fires still raged on the land to the south untouched by the immense tsunami.

Knossos, Amnisos, Phaistos, Agia Triadha, Kommos, Malia, Gournia, and Zakros were all incinerated by the colossal pyroclastic gas bloom. Only a few people that were in tightly sealed rooms not damaged by the super hurricane force winds or fires survived the phenomenal blast of heat. Samra, Jena, and their four children survived unscathed in Khania far to the west as well as his son's family. But his daughter in Phaistos and Cronymartis in Agia Triadha were all dead from the heat. The bodies of the King and Queen lay scorched and blackened on the floor of the palace in Knossos. Almost everything living was roasted alive! It was an all-enveloping, devastating holocaust!

The winds were still blowing to the east as the fantastic gas bloom dissipated and minimized the spreading of the fires to the untouched lands in the west. The western survivors that witnessed the wall of flames were terrified with many of them mindlessly running for their lives. Most thought it was the end of the world. They believed the gods were reaping a terrible vengeance and would strike the rest of them down at any instant. Once the survivors first began walking into the scorched areas, they were horrified and awestruck at the unimaginable magnitude of the destruction.

Even before the flames had died and with the smoke of the ruins still heavy in the air, there were some that saw this as an opportunity to loot the gold from the burnt palaces and villas of the wealthy. Once the first few returned with their bounty, it set off a veritable gold rush to the east. The civil authorities in western Crete tried their best to take command as soon as they could, but the looting was wide spread and rampant for weeks.

The day after hearing the news of the disaster in Khania, Samra and his son began traveling on the stone roadway to Knossos. They took three donkeys and a large four wheeled wagon with them. He didn't believe the stories he heard of the devastation and thought they must be wildly exaggerated. Samra intended on inviting Thalion and Antoneos to come live on his estates if their home had been damaged too severely. He thought the steam distillery equipment that he recently loaned to Thalion might have survived undamaged.

A few days later as they approached Knossos, they came to the edge of the destruction zone. A rainstorm had quenched any remaining smoldering embers and left a vivid jagged dividing line running north and south in the hills west of Tylisos contrasting the lush fertile, green of early summer in the west and the burned, charred death in the east. Coming to a high point in the road overlooking the hilly plain of Knossos below, Samra and his son first witnessed the true scale and vastness of the utter destruction before them. Both of them gasped in astonishment at the sight. It was as if some gigantic angry god had first burned everything, and then the sea had swallowed it; scraping everything to the ground in a layered, chaotic, twisted mass. As they got closer to Tylisos, they began to be overcome by the stench of the rotting corpses from the expanse of dead humans and animals lying everywhere around them. Samra abruptly stopped and looked out at the wasteland before him for several minutes. Tears came to his eyes as he turned to his son and said, "No one could have survived this. It's over here. Let's go home, son."

Epilogue

The Minoans were a highly rational, humane civilization that believed they had mastered reality with their intellects and the power of their universal tool of Science that they called the "Way of Nature". They used its objectivity and reason to mold and shape nature to their wishes. It had vastly improved the quality of life for all their people and showed many other less advanced peoples how it could be done. Their sophisticated culture borrowed whatever they found of value and quality from all the peoples within reach of their ships and fashioned them to their own tastes.

They were millennia ahead of their time in social development by practicing the equality of the sexes, distaining slavery, and distributing the wealth of the kingdom to its people. Their social, political, economic, technological, artistic, and architectural achievements set a new, much higher standard for all the peoples of the Aegean. They showed what a reasonably fair, well-organized society was capable of to all the peoples of the Mediterranean especially those of the Aegean. They desired to conquer no one but searched for partners to trade with in order to create wealth.

Now not only Thera, their great international maritime trading hub, was utterly destroyed, but all of the major population centers on Crete were gone as well. The survivors in western Crete that walked into the vast destruction zone all asked themselves the same question, "Why have we been punished so severely?"

"We must have offended the Gods with our arrogance."

They thought the Gods had disapproved of their actions and cruelly crushed them for their misguided ways.   The monumental pyroclastic gas surge from the Theran volcano had not only destroyed most of their civilization physically, but it ripped the soul, spirit, and confidence from those that survived it.   The Minoan's naive concept of perpetual progress was shattered in the fires forever. They thought they had conquered nature, but it had turned on them with a vengeance and brought them to their knees.